Love in Manitoba

Love in Manitoba

E.A. Wharton Gill

WILDSIDE PRESS

Originally published in 1911.

Published by Wildside Press.
Visit us online at wildsidepress.com.

CHAPTER I

Otter Lake lay in the warm and rosy glories of a Manitoba sunset in the middle of August. The spruce-covered slopes of its western shore were already in the shadow, and a soft grey line of mist was blurring the narrow strip of shingly beach that separated the waters of the lake from the sombre masses of the thick bush beyond. Half a mile across the lake the sunlight lingered in soft fading shades of pink and opal on the shoaling waters of the shore, lingered in warmer tones upon a little clearing of two or three acres of ripening corn; lingered on the bright red shingles of the roof and whitened walls of a little log house, lingered most gently and regretfully of all upon a quiet figure leaning against the flag pole by the wicket-gate of the little garden patch, between the house and the lake shore.

A quiet figure, yet it had not the quietness that goes with the decline of mental and bodily vigour, but rather the quiet repose of one accustomed to finding himself equal to the emergencies and uncertainties of life; for Christian Nielson in his sixty odd years, had never turned his face from a storm or his back on a duty. Still, storm of ocean and passion of heart had left their deep impress on form and face, in the years before he brought the wreckage of his life's happiness to the quiet haven of the little shieling by the lake shore. At twenty he was the lightest-hearted sailor boy in the Danish navy, with the merriest laugh and the liveliest foot to the scraping of the fiddle in the fo'csle, and the first at the yardarm to furl the flapping and bellying sail in a squall of wind. At thirty he left the service and settled down in his native place, buying a share in a fishing schooner and making his home with his widowed mother.

Five years later a fierce Atlantic gale drove the little schooner for shelter and repairs into a far north Norwegian fjord—and there he met and loved and won Olga Gudbranson—blue-eyed and golden-haired, quick of temper and warm of heart, a true daughter of the north. Fearless and undaunted by the perils of the sea, fearless and unashamed of the perils of love, she read down to the depths of Christian's simple nature and, finding there no shallows of fickleness or shoals of deceit, she gave herself to his keeping without a doubt or fear. Their wedding in the little stone church on the hill was followed by three days of simple feasting and dancing by the fisher folk of the little village, and then they sailed away to the south.

Then followed the happiest years of Christian's life—no boat was so fortunate as his in all the little fleet that put out from Funen port, no welcome so true and glad as when Olga and little Ludwig waited his homecoming on the little pier. It was within ten days of the fourth return of his wedding day, when Christian sailed on what was to be the last trip of the season. The shadows of evening were falling when Christian stepped ashore on his return, on the eve of the very day itself—a throng of women and men were standing at the pier head, but there were no loud and cheery words of greeting, no eager questions as to the luck of the fishing, or when Rasmus' or Peter's or Mads' boat would be in, no greeting, but a shuffling of feet of the men and a stifled sob of the women, as the group fell back and left two figures apart—the old Herr Pastor and Christian's mother. The swift intuition of love told Christian the worst; yet he asked of his mother: "Is all well with the boy?" and of the pastor: "Is all well with the wife?"

"All is well with the boy, Christian, my son." "All is well with his mother, for she is with God," and the Herr Pastor bared his head.

Walking with uncertain steps as in a dream Christian made his way to his home—passed through the little living-room—raised with careful stillness the latch of the room beyond. That vision of his departed happiness was never far from the mirror of Christian's soul, in the long years to come —as he steered the course of his little schooner under the starlit heavens, as he paced the deck of the mighty steamer that bore him to the great solitudes of the west, as he watched that summer evening, the sun smiling behind the spruce-clad hills, beyond the Otter Lake. Clear to-night, as on that fatal night twenty years ago—the wood fire on the hearth casting a flickering light on the tear-stained face of little Ludwig, sleeping in his little cot, and a little table standing by the white covered bed, and there in deeper, calmer, purer rest than sleep—Olga. One hand rested upon the white coverlet, the hand that bore the wedding ring, the token of their love, the other clasping to her stilled heart the tiny angel baby that had come as her messenger and herald to the peace of heaven.

The last glow of golden light faded from the western sky, deeper and more sombre shadows gathered in the ravines of the spruce-clad slopes, the chill breath of the evening breeze shivered along the surface of the lake and rustled among the reeds. "There shall be no night there," said Christian softly to himself, as he turned from the wicket-gate and walked slowly to the house door and entered.

Without was the solitude of the west, within all spoke of the homeland and the sea. The smooth hewed logs of the walls were spotless white, here hung in a quaint frame of Christian's carving, a print of King Christian IX., there a faded photograph of Olga in her bridal dress, here under the king a model of Christian's first ship, the *Zealand*, there beneath his bride, daintily fashioned and true to the least detail of sail and rigging, a facsimile of the schooner in which he brought his Olga home; tables, chairs, and cupboard, all of the plainest and homeliest fashion, made in the long leisure hours of the winter evenings when Christian first took up his homestead in the bush. One end of the room was curtained off by two large moose skins hung from the low ceiling, behind which, built ship-fashion against the wall, were two berths that served as beds for the father and son.

First lighting the lamp that hung from the rafter, Christian set about preparing the evening meal—a bright fire was soon burning in the stove, the table neatly spread with a rough but cleanly cloth, cold pork, butter, and bannock were brought in from the little stone dairy behind the house, sliced potatoes were frying in the "spider" on the stove and mingling their odour with the pungent fragrance of the new made coffee. A click of the wicket-gate, a quick step on the garden path, and the door opened and Ludwig entered, followed by a big Danish hound.

"Home again, Ludwig; home again, good dog, and supper ready for you both, and both ready, I warrant, for your supper," said Christian, as he placed the large dish of smoking potatoes on the table and poured out two large cups of coffee, while Ludwig hung his gun above the door, placed in the corner the heavy bag he had carried over his shoulder, and seated himself opposite his father.

No wonder the past never dimmed in the memory of Christian, with Ludwig passing from childhood to youth, and from youth to manhood—ever with him in the lonely life of the homestead by the lake, the same tall and supple form, answering in every motion to the quick and impulsive nature within, the same clear and open blue eyes, reflecting every feeling of the heart as readily as the surface of the Otter Lake, azured to the blue sky of a May morning, or darkened to gloom under the pall of a later summer thundercloud. To-night the blue eyes were troubled, and a sharp reproof sent Trofast trailing to his mat in the corner when he ventured to put a reminding paw on his master's knee. Pushing back his almost untasted food, and with a muttered word of feeding the oxen, Ludwig rose from the table and went out into the darkness.

"We shall know all about it by and by, good dog," said Christian as he coaxed Trofast to his supper. "We shall know all about it by and by, and whatever the good God sends we must make the best of, for the while."

Half an hour later, when Ludwig re-entered, the supper things were all put away and Christian was seated by the table, reading and smoking his long-stemmed wooden pipe.

"Well, Ludwig, what did you hear to-day at the store? Have any of the neighbours started their harvesting yet?"

7

"I don't think I heard any news, father," said Ludwig slowly; "but," and he hesitated, "but I met Gus Anderson—he is making up a gang to go harvesting on the Portage Plains. He wanted a man to go with him to work his second team and to stay with him till the end of the thrashing in the fall."

"Is it for the sake of the wages, Ludwig?" asked Christian.

"It was at the first, father," said Ludwig. "I'd been thinking if we had a team of horses I could draw all the cord-wood we cut last winter to town, and in the spring I could work on the new railway, and perhaps by next fall we could make the house a little larger and—it's very quiet and lonely here for you, father, when I'm away so much."

"True, my boy, it is very quiet, but not lonely," and his eye rested on the faded picture above the little schooner; "and what answer did you give to Herr Anderson?"

"I told him I would be at his place by noon to-morrow if I were going; but that is not all, father. I came home by the winter trail that passes by the Swansons' homestead, and I went in to tell Ole I should not be able to help him in the harvest this year if I went south."

"Well, Ludwig," said his father, "that need not trouble you; Ole and I can manage well enough their crop and for our few acres here."

"Oh yes, father, it's not that, I didn't see Ole. Amanda was in the garden, and I told her why I wanted to get the horses and to make the house a little larger and what company you two would be to each other while I was away on the railway or in the woods."

"And what did Amanda say to you?" asked Christian.

"Why, she laughed at me and said that your books would be better company for you than a giddy girl, who would be chattering all day, and not one word would she say but to tease me about forgetting her and finding a sweetheart among the Canadian girls on the Plains, and she is going away herself."

"Amanda going away?" asked Christian.

"Yes, father, Herr Hardie's wife is not very strong and she has four little children, and he is to come for Amanda to-morrow, and she is to work there till the 'freeze up.'"

"And you, my poor boy?" asked his father gently.

"Oh, I must go away and work and work. I could never stay here in the quiet woods, thinking of her at Herr Hardie's, and all the young English fellows that go to the English Church on Sunday and then spend the afternoons at Herr Hardie's—jesting and laughing and making love to the little Swedish girl for amusement—if one of them dared to have a light thought of her," and Ludwig's blue eyes flashed at the image of his own imagination; "if one of them dared."

"Patience, my son, patience; be not angry with the fancies of your hasty passion. Amanda, for all her light-hearted raillery, is a true-hearted girl, and all true hearts are in the good God's keeping."

"But you would not have me stay, father?"

"No, my boy, go and do not despair because the little wild bird of the woods does not come to your first calling. Ole and I can well manage to harvest our little crop, and perhaps once or twice I may take a day from our work and go and see little Amanda and send you word to keep your heart from fretting, till you are home again in the little log house."

"Well, father, things never seem so bad when I talk them over with you," said Ludwig; "but when I left Amanda all the plans that I have been dreaming over so long seemed to be wrecked, and I was angry with every one—with Gus for offering me work, with Herr Hardie for taking Amanda from her own people, and with myself for caring whether she found an English lover or not."

"Thank the good God, my son," said Christian solemnly, "that your anger passed without hurt to any one."

"I'm afraid it has hurt some one already," said Ludwig, laughing, "but it was not very serious. I came across that half-grown boy of the old Indian, who has his 'teepee' up the Lake—Black Hawk—he had a half-starved dog tied up to a tree and was amusing himself shooting at it with a bow and arrow. The wretched creature was yelping and howling, so I set it free and broke the young rascal's bow, and gave him a couple of cuts over the back with the pieces. It served him right; but I expect he got part of my ill-temper with myself."

"It were better not to have laid a hand on him, Ludwig," said Christian. "Perhaps he deserved it, but the lad is but a heathen and they have long memories, my son, of an injury."

"Oh, I don't think we need trouble about him," said Ludwig lightly. "I expect he often gets much harder blows from old 'Black Hawk'; and now, father, I think we had better 'turn in,' for I have to be up early in the morning to get my things ready for my trip south."

Soon the lamp was put out and father and son were sleeping the deep sleep of those whose days are spent in toil in the open air, and darkness and silence reigned in the little log house by the lake.

CHAPTER II

Herr Hardie's homestead was the first farm outside the Scandinavian settlement of Danes, Norwegians, and Swedes, which was officially called New Scandinavia, but was generally known as "Sweden" among the English settlers to the south of it. Not only was it the nearest farm to the Scandinavian settlement, but the main road out through the timber land of "Sweden" passed along "Herr" Hardie's fence, and his house stood back only a hundred yards or so from the road. The road itself went southward through the "English" settlement to the little town of Minnedosa, twelve miles away, where the English and Scandinavian settlers alike bought their supplies of food and clothing and found a market for the produce of their farms.

Herr Hardie himself was a great favourite and highly respected among the Norse folk, for not only was there a warm welcome and ready help for belated settlers returning home if overtaken by the winter storm, but Herr Hardie always treated them with a certain simple courtesy that won for him a very real respect. Not that he stood at all on his own dignity; among his own people, even to Dave, the "chore" boy, he was Jim, and to have been greeted as "Mr." Hardie by one of his English-speaking neighbours would have made him feel as if he were being kept at an unfriendly distance.

On the morning on which Ludwig left home, Jim Hardie and Dave were up by sunrise and while Dave went to the stables to feed the horses Jim lit the fire, put on the kettle and the water for the porridge, and tidied up the house with the deftness of one who had "bached" in the old days before wife and children came to the farm. Then with a cheery call at the foot of the stairs, "Wake up, mother; wake up, children," Jim took up the pails and went to the milking.

Passing through the little poplar bluff at the back of the house Jim went first to the stables to bid Dave brush down Molly, the old mare, and to put the harness on her, and then he went to the corral, where the cows were beginning to stir round restlessly, anxious to get the milking over and to be let out to the pasture. The milking of the eight cows and straining and putting the milk away in the bright clean pans, in the little stone dairy, took some time, but it was finished at last, the corral bars were let down, and the cows filed out and down the lane to the pasture, while Jim and Dave returned to the house.

The children, two boys of nine and seven and a little girl of four, were already seated at the table and eating their porridge, while Mrs. Hardie with a baby on one arm, was frying some bacon and potatoes on the stove, for a more substantial breakfast for their father. There was a striking contrast between Mrs. Hardie and her husband. Jim, though some years older than his wife and with every year of his life marked in the grey hair and beard and in the deep lines in his forehead and eyes, yet spoke in each alert movement of limb and in every cheery word of an invincible optimism. Looking into his face one would never dream that life had been easy to him, or that he had ever been free from care or anxiety, or that victory had been gained without conflict of soul and will, yet indubitably the victory was assured. Did sorrow come to a neighbour's home or sudden calamity through hail or frost overtake his crop, that neighbour always felt, not only consolation, but a fresh incentive to face the troubles of life after he had heard the first quiet words of Jim's steady voice and felt the close grip of his ready hand.

Mrs. Hardie was not a discontented woman, but she always gave one the impression of being a little sorry for herself. She had been a pretty light-hearted girl when Jim brought her as a bride to the homestead, but the monotony of a farm life—with its washing days, scrubbing days, baking days, its butter-making days—week following week, with little break or new interest from the outer world, these need more than an unresisting acquiescence in existence. If the silver lining were not yet in sight Jim was fully persuaded that it was there, and would wait cheerfully for its appearance, but Mrs. Hardie would only accept it doubtfully when it was already an assured reality, dulling the brightness of its coming with forebodings of its early departure.

This morning Jim was in the highest of spirits, carrying on a spasmodic conversation with every one in turn in the intervals of a very hearty breakfast.

"Well, mother, you had better take it easy to-day and leave the hard work for the 'hired girl' to help you," said Jim. "You and Nellie can just loaf round with the baby, and Frank will help Dave with the chores, and Ted can go with me to 'Sweden.' "

"I don't know how I can take it easy, Jim, when this is churning day," answered Mrs. Hardie.

"Oh, leave the churning, mother, I will do that after I come home, and Amanda can make up the butter in the morning."

"Amanda make the butter!—I expect I shall have to teach her before she can make butter or do very much else."

"Bless your heart, mother," said Jim, "Amanda has been doing half the work of the house for the last three or four years at home."

"May be," said Mrs. Hardie doubtfully, "but we'd better not trust to it. Dave will turn the churn for me, and we can manage to do it somehow."

"Then can I go with you and Ted, father?" asked the eldest boy.

"Not to-day, sonnie; if mother and Dave do the churning, you will have to take care of Nellie and the baby, but I shall want a good boy to go to town with me next week; and if there's one round, why, I'll take him," said Jim, and Frank brightened up as if he knew where the boy might be found.

"And Nellie and I will bring the cows home and gather the eggs," said Frank.

"Of course, you will meet us at the lane gate, and we'll give Nellie a little ride home. Now come along, Ted, we must be starting," said Jim, rising from the table and exchanging his working jacket for his town coat.

Old Mollie was soon hitched up to the buckboard and, with kisses to mother and the baby, Jim and little Ted started off.

It was a great day for little Ted; not only a day's holiday from school, a thing desirable to every real boy on general principles, but his father all to himself, and he allowed to drive Molly. And then there were questions to be asked—and surely there never was any one like "father" to answer questions, and to tell wonderful little stories about every bird that flew across the trail and every flower that glistened in the morning dew by the wayside.

For the first mile or two there were quite large fields of grain on either side of the road; but soon came big bluffs of white poplar, with only a few acres of corn land around little log houses among the trees, and then came the spruce and tamarac woods. Now the way would be steep and winding along the side of the deep ravine, now they would be jolting slowly over the rough corduroy road that crossed a shallow slough. Every now and again little side trails, roughly cut through the woods, would branch off from the main road, leading to some settler's home in the deeper woods, and Jim seemed to know them all and the strange sounding names of the "Swedes" who lived in them.

At last they themselves turned into one of these narrow tracks, only just wide enough for the wheels of the buckboard among the stumps, and with the spreading wings of the big spruce, meeting over their heads. It was all so dark and silent that little Ted was beginning to think of some of his father's winter stories of bears and wolves that did not approve of little boys who did not want to go to school, when a sharp turn in their path brought them out into the bright sunshine again, into a sunny opening with the road leading through a little field of golden oats with the blue lake beyond, and a log house with a garden facing the lake shore.

"There, Ted, there is Otter Lake," said Jim, "where I come fishing in the winter time, and there is Mr. Nielson's house where I stayed when I was out hunting last fall and shot the big moose, and there is Christian himself in the garden. Come, Molly," and with a shake of the lines and a flick of the whip they were soon at the wicket-gate.

A deep bark from Trofast, who had been lying in the sun by the house door, and who now came walking down the garden path, made Christian look up from his work.

"Goot morn, Mr. Nielson," called out Jim cheerfully, with what he imagined was a truly Scandinavian twist to his English, out of compliment to Christian's nationality.

Christian's quiet face brightened when he recognized his visitor, and he came quickly to the wicket-gate.

"Welcome, Herr Hardie, welcome, and to you also, little boy. Come into the house and I will put the horse in the stable, and you will stay for dinner."

"Not to-day, Mr. Nielson," replied Jim, "for I have to go on to Ole Swanson's. Amanda is to come up to our place to help the wife for a month or two and they will be looking out for me."

"I hope that the good wife is better," said Christian. "Ludwig told me yesterday that she was not strong, and that Amanda was going down to you for a time."

"Oh yes, of course, Ludwig would know all about it," laughed Jim; "I expect we shall have Ludwig coming down to see how we get on with our harvest. Where is the boy this morning? I was wondering if I could get him down for a week or two later on, when we are doing the threshing, like we did last fall?"

"Not this year, Herr Hardie. Ludwig has hired with Gus Anderson to go to the Portage Plains with Gus's second team till 'freeze up.'"

"Well, well, that's too bad; I'd been thinking——" but Jim did not complete his sentence. "The wife and I will be very glad if you can come up for a day or two yourself, Mr. Nielson; you'll be lonesome here with your boy away—get a ride with one of the neighbours some Saturday, and Dave can bring you back when you're ready."

"Thank you, Herr Hardie. Yes, I will come down and see you and Amanda—her mother will be glad to hear of her—she's such a bright, happy girl, that the house will be very quiet without her."

"Well, be sure and come, Mr. Nielson, and stay as long as you can, and now we must be going," said Jim, getting into the buckboard and picking up the reins. "So long, Mr. Nielson, so long! Come, Mollie," and they drove off, round the corner of the garden, past the little house and the stable-yard, and into a well-worn trail through the woods again.

CHAPTER III

Half an hour's driving brought them to another clearing and to Ole Swanson's house. A larger, higher house than Christian's, with quaint dormer windows in the roof, and a wide veranda round three sides of the house and a big lean-to kitchen at the back, for Ole had a family of growing boys and girls to shelter and provide for. Here was the same neatly fenced garden as at Christian's, but on either side of the garden path from the gate to the front door were beds of old-fashioned flowers, stocks and pinks and pansies, with clusters of sweet-smelling mignonette, and the veranda was almost closed in with a luxuriant growth of wild hops, hanging in festoons from post to post and making a green frame round the little door.

Jim drove round the garden to the farmyard at the back, and here they found Ole himself, just putting his oxen in the stable for their noonday rest.

"Just in time for dinner, Herr Hardie, and the wife is waiting for us. Here, August, put Herr Hardie's horse in the stable and give it some hay," said Ole, shaking hands with Jim and leading the way to the house. "You'll have had a long drive and be hungry."

"Pretty well for that, Mr. Swanson, pretty well for that, and how are all 'the care'?"

"All well, Herr Hardie, but busy these days, what with the haying to finish and the oats ready to cut, and the cows to look after—plenty work—plenty work."

"That's the way with us all," said Jim; "but we've had a good spell of weather to do it in, and your crops are looking fine here in the colony."

"Not too bad," said Ole, "if it lasts; but you never can tell," which truly represented Ole's slow-thinking, rather-doubting philosophy of life.

Ole was a big, rather stooping man of some fifty-five years, fair haired and blue eyed; he had spent nearly twenty years in slowly clearing the timber from the land around his house, and now was a very prosperous settler, with twenty or thirty acres of crop, a goodly band of cattle, and always a large pile of cord-wood to draw to Minnedosa in the winter. After most of his neighbours bought horses, Ole still drove oxen—their steady, stolid plodding, according naturally with his own character. He had been a small man in the old Sweden, half peasant, half tenant farmer, paying the rent of a few scant acres with his own labour, here, in the new "Sweden," he was a

14

man of some importance, with his hundred and sixty acres of homestead, his big band of cattle, and the largest crop in the settlement.

When the settlement was formed into a municipality, Ole was chosen for the first "Reeve," and the rival candidates for the parliamentary constituency, of which "Sweden" formed a part, always looked on Ole's influence as being quite an important factor in securing the Swedish vote for the Manitoba or Dominion legislatures. Not that Ole ever talked much on political questions, or was over-ready to express very fixed ideas—indeed there were not wanting those who said that he had no ideas on such matters at all, and that his habitual, "I'll think it over," meant till he had been schooled by Mrs. Swanson, and who averred that her good will was what counted most on election day. If that were so, she was surely a wise woman, for, in public at least, she always referred all matters to Ole for decision, and prefaced her commands to the children with an invariable, "as your father says."

She it was who stood at the open door and welcomed Jim and little Ted and ushered them into the "living-room," where the dinner was already on the table.

"Sit down, Mr. Hardie; sit down, 'father.' Amanda and I had dinner with the boys, who have to take the butter to the store," said Mrs. Swanson, as she busied herself to pass the vegetables and to pour out the coffee.

It was always a matter of surprise to Jim to hear Mrs. Swanson speak English. Most of the men and children in Sweden could talk English with a certain readiness, though with a limited vocabulary—the men, the rough-and-ready colloquial English of the Canadian farmers for whom many of them worked in the harvest field and in the threshing gang. The children were taught by English-speaking teachers in the three or four public day schools in the colony, but it was very rare for the older Scandinavian women to know more than a few words of English, relating to the farmyard or house work. But Mrs. Swanson spoke English as Jim said, "like a school marm," with a certain correctness of grammar and of accent that made him feel very conscious of his own deficiencies. If Jim was surprised at the elegance of Mrs. Swanson's English he would have been still more surprised had he known the ambitions that lay behind it, ambitions that, gendered by chance circumstances, had grown in depth and intensity till they had become the ruling power in her scheme of life.

When the little log schoolhouse was built, four or five years before, the trustees had engaged as their first teacher a bright English girl, Evelyn Raye, who had left an "Old Country" rectory to tempt fortune in the west, and careful Ole suggested to his fellow trustees that, as his house was the nearest to the school, the "school marm" should board with him—not unmindful of the weekly three dollars that Miss Raye was to pay for the privilege. A mutual liking sprang up between Amanda and her teacher—to Miss Raye, Amanda's impulsive disposition and quickness to learn were a welcome change after the rather unresponsive and stolid character of many of the children, and for Amanda she became an ideal to be worshipped and copied from afar.

As she watched the two together in the garden on summer evenings, or over their books in the long hours when she sat knitting by the stove on a winter night, Mrs. Swanson began to see visions of a different future for Amanda, than the hard work and drudgery of a homestead in the bush. Her own past life of monotonous toil from early morn till she lay down weary at night—of feeding the cattle and milking the cows when Ole was away, the churning, the washing, the making and mending of children's clothes— it all became hateful to her; not for herself but as a possible future for Amanda. Vague discontent led to repulsion, and from repulsion sprang a deepening resolution that Amanda should be saved from a repetition of her own hard lot in life.

Behind Mrs. Swanson's broad, smooth forehead and deep-set grey eyes, lay a strength of purpose equal to much more than the deciding how Ole should vote at an election, or what price he should set on a yoke of oxen to be sold to a neighbour. She set herself to learn English—not the broken English with which Ole was quite satisfied—but English as Miss Raye spoke it, and often, when the children were away at school and her husband chopping cord-wood in the bush, she would sit down by the hour and con over the lessons which Amanda had been studying with Miss Raye the night before. By degrees English took the place of Norse in the every-day conversation of the family at meal times and work—a change which gave Ole a sense of discomfort, though he submitted, on his wife's assurance that it would help the children with their schooling.

At the end of four years Miss Raye was called home to England by the death of her father, and the school was closed for lack of a teacher. Amanda was now seventeen, and in her father's opinion had education enough for any farmer's daughter—it was time she was helping her mother and taking her share in the work of the house. Mrs. Swanson submitted for the time, but when Jim Hardie came with his request to her that Amanda should go to them for a few months to help his wife, she promised readily to talk it over with "father," and "father's" respect for "Herr Hardie" as a prosperous farmer, and the eight dollars a month, won the day with him.

It was not the début for Amanda that she had imagined for her when she sat listening to Miss Raye reading aloud stories of beautiful English homes, and of lovely girls of low degree being wooed by handsome young men of lofty birth and proud possession, but at least it would take Amanda away from the rough life in the woods, and Mrs. Swanson had heard that there were rich young Englishmen, learning farming for amusement, and much given to hunting and the like among the English settlers of the south.

Then there was another danger to Amanda in the woods—the danger lest the boy and girl cameraderie of Amanda and Ludwig Christian might ripen to a deeper passion, and here Mrs. Swanson was conscious of a twofold danger that might be too powerful for even her steadfast will. One lay in the deep-seated, silent power of Ole's love for his own people, for in his own heart Ole held that, while all this English speaking and these English ways were well enough as a matter of helping in material well being, yet in the matter of blood—Norse to Norse. The other rock lay in Amanda herself; bright and lovable as she was, readily yielding in the little crosses of home life, warm-hearted, if sometimes wilfully fond of teasing those she loved best—yet did her mother suspect that, if occasion came that touched her deeper nature, Amanda might be found as resolute and firm of purpose as herself.

Dinner over, Jim and Ole went to look at the crop and the young stock, while one of the younger boys carried off Ted to see a young wolf that was being brought up in captivity in the barn. Ole had misgivings as to the effect of a slight touch of autumn frost a night or two before, and wanted Jim's opinion as to whether it had touched the oats—from the oats back to the barnyard to complete a leisurely deal for a yoke of steers which had begun when Jim was last in the colony. When the bargain was concluded and the inspection of the pigs and calves completed it was well on in the afternoon and time for making a start for home; so, leaving August to hitch up Molly, Ole and Jim returned to the house for the inevitable coffee, without which no Scandinavian allows a guest to depart.

A small home-made box and one or two parcels were standing at the door as they entered, and by the time Jim and little Ted had drunk their coffee and eaten their cake Amanda herself appeared, ready for the journey. Jim had known her since she was a little child and had given her the pet name of the "Rose of Sweden" long ago, but never had he been struck by her beauty as this afternoon—by her beauty, and by the fact that she was no longer a child, but on the very threshold of womanhood. At other times when he had seen her, she had usually worn the short print frocks in which she went to school, the grey home-knit stockings and stout boots, the neat handkerchief on her head, pinned beneath the chin, and the little square shawl over her shoulders—the peasant dress of the old land reproduced in all its national features in the settler's daughter of the new. Yet her dress today was quite simple, though the pale blue of her blouse and skirt had not the starchy stiffness of the prints, the trim neatness of the shoes was very different from the stout laced boots in which she had been wont to go to school, or to tramp through the bush after the cows, and the square shawl

17

on the shoulders and the handkerchief on her head had been replaced by a light fluffy scarf and a sailor hat.

Mrs. Swanson's ambitions for Amanda were not satisfied with giving her an English tongue and accent—her observant eyes had stored away every detail of Evelyn Raye's ladylike dress and Amanda's metamorphosis was the result. It is true she had had her difficulties—Amanda herself had shrunk from so close a copy of her ideal, and Ole demurred to the sending away to the big Departmental Store in Winnipeg. "Why could not her mother deal at the Colony store, or get a neighbour to bring up what was necessary from Minnedosa?" Ole demurred, but yielded on his wife's assurance that of course, Amanda would take her usual everyday wear, but must have something that would not make her feel different to the other young people she would meet in the English settlement on Sundays.

Jim's surprise expressed itself in its usual open fashion. "Why, Mrs. Swanson, what have you been doing to my little 'Rose of Sweden'? I hardly knew who this young lady was. I'll have to leave off calling you Amanda, and be calling you Miss Swanson, now," he added, as he turned to the blushing girl.

"Oh no, I hope not, Mr. Hardie, I shall always be Amanda to my old friends."

"Well, well, that's as I like it, but I'll have to look after 'the boys,' " he added laughingly, as he went to put Amanda's box in the buckboard while she said good-bye to her father and mother.

A kiss and a "Don't forget the old folks in 'Sweden,' " from her father, a warm embrace with a smile and a tear from her mother, and Amanda was on her way to the new world and the new life, with a timid anticipation of what it might have in store for her, mingled at the last with a deep love for those who had made her childhood's happiness, not only in the old farmstead in the woods, but with tender repenting of her wilfulness in mocking Ludwig's dreams of the future in the little log house by the lake shore.

CHAPTER IV

Life at Rosebank, as Jim Hardie's farm was called, was not by any means a bed of roses for Amanda for the first two or three weeks. It was not only that Jim and Dave were too busy in the harvest field to have much spare time to help round the house, but Mrs. Hardie was a little difficult, and slow to believe that any one could take over the routine of the house without a good deal of supervision, which at times was rather fretful. The strain of motherhood and the sense of being driven to keep up her work had come perilously near ending in a collapse of body and mind, for Jim, with all his readiness to help, yet failed to realise how great the strain and burden were. Her first impressions of Amanda were unfortunately not very favourable on the evening of her arrival, and in her "run down" condition, first impressions were slow to be displaced. Amanda's bright eyes and smiling lips were not the open sesame to Mrs. Hardie's good will that they had been to Jim's, and the trim English air of her sailor hat and the daintiness of her Oxford shoes were a distinct offence.

"What do I think of Amanda?" was her answer to Jim's confident question, when Amanda had gone to her little room, "what do I think? I think you have brought me a 'lady help,' Jim, instead of a 'hired girl.' She looks more like playing their tennis games down at the 'Dingle' than scrubbing my floors and milking the cows."

"No, no, mother," said Jim deprecatingly, "that's just Mrs. Swanson, she wanted her to be like the other folks on a Sunday. You'll see she'll be up bright and early in the morning, and as quick at her work as you when you were the smartest and prettiest girl in the settlement."

"May be, Jim," said Mrs. Hardie, a little mollified by the reminiscent compliment to herself, "at any rate, little Ted seems to have taken to her and she seems to be fond of the children; it will be something if she can look after them."

"Oh, it's you that must have the easy time, now, mother, she will do the work right enough when she gets used to our ways."

"May be, Jim," and so they left it for the night.

Jim was a little late himself the next morning, for the baby had been very restless in the earlier part of the night, and when he did fall asleep he overslept himself. So far at least he had foretold truly that Amanda's little room was empty as he passed by its door, and on going downstairs he found the fire lit, the kettle beginning to sing on the stove, and the milk-pails gone from their accustomed rack in the lean-to. Passing through the bluff to the corral he met Amanda bearing two foaming pails of milk, and with Frank and little Ted on either hand.

"Why, Amanda, you and the boys have got ahead of me this morning. Dave and I generally do the milking."

"Oh, I'm quite used to milking, Mr. Hardie; mother and I have been doing it all summer, while father and the boys have been busy with the clearing and the hay."

"Well, that's right," said Jim cheerily, "it's a fine thing for the farm when every one gives a helping hand; but Frank will show you the milk-pans and bring back the pails, and Ted will show you where the things are and help you to get breakfast. And, Ted, run upstairs and tell 'mother' we'll send her breakfast up this morning, and to have a good rest."

Ted delivered his message but by the time Jim returned to the house Mrs. Hardie was already downstairs, looking tired and rather peevish, for Jim's well meant suggestion that she should stay in bed and rest was not taken in very good part, though she had to admit to herself that Amanda looked more like work in her Swedish dress.

As days went on Amanda's bright helpfulness in the work of the house, and her ready sympathy with the children, won their way to Mrs. Hardie's heart. She found herself willing to forget to worry over the butter-making and the baking, and would go out into the garden and down the lane on sunny afternoons with the baby and little Molly. It was no longer an irritation to hear the shouts and laughter of the boys, as they played hide-and-seek with Amanda in the bluff after the "chores" were done. It did Jim's heart good to see colour stealing back into her cheeks and the brightness to her eyes, though it filled him with compunction that he had not realized sooner how hard the work and worry of the farm life had been to her before. "It's too bad of you—too bad—Jim Hardie," he said remorsefully to himself; "you're so tough yourself you never thought the little woman was wearing herself out," and he registered a quiet resolution that the little woman's life should never be so hard again, if he could help it.

In the meantime, day followed day, with little variety, though always with plenty of work to be done. Jim had hired two harvesters from Ontario to help in stooking and stacking his crop, but they were of little interest to Amanda and none to this story. They only appeared at meal times, when they ate largely, but in silence—such spare time as they had was usually spent down at the stables, where a rough bedroom had been fitted up for them in the hay loft. Occasionally a neighbour would come to borrow some farm implement, or a baking of flour till he could spare time to go to town, but the whole settlement was too much occupied in getting the crop harvested before frost came to have any time for social visiting.

So far there seemed little likelihood of the fulfilment of Mrs. Swanson's visions for Amanda, and though Amanda herself was quite innocent of any ambitious dreams for the future, yet her life did seem rather monotonous and lacking in fresh interest. The day itself was too busy to be dull, but when the "chores" were done and the children gone to bed she would wander to the end of the land, for the chance of a passing greeting with one of her own people returning to "Sweden" from town. Once or twice in this way she had been able to send little letters to her mother and messages to the boys and girls at home. There was always the chance of seeing a familiar face and if the chance lacked fulfilment, at least there in the quiet evening her thoughts could linger on the old homestead, and imagination fill in the details of what they would be doing there.

From the homestead to the little house by Otter Lake was a natural transition. "How lonely Herr Nielson must be there alone with only Trofast for company, and why need Ludwig go off so far to the Plains for work? What a stupid Ludwig he was to want to make more money to buy horses and to talk of building a larger house, as if money and horses and a big house mattered to her; and he might have known, but what did she want him to talk about?" and then there was a mist in the deep grey eyes and a blush on the fair face, like a dewdrop on a prairie rose on a May morning, and Amanda brushed the dewdrops away, though there was only the harvest moon rising over the bluff to see and guess at her tender thoughts. "But why need he have been so quick to be offended? and how handsome he had looked as he strode off through the bush." Then she would scold herself for being a little goose and trip back again to the house, resolved to think no more of such foolish things, but just to be content and happy with her work and the children's play.

One evening on her return to the house she found Jim sitting on the step of the veranda, smoking his pipe, and with him one of the English settlers whom she had seen once or twice at her own home, where he had come to buy cord-wood from her father. This was Bert Enderby, whose father, the younger son of a Leicestershire squire, had brought his fortunes, a young wife, and his ambitions to the Canadian West, in the glowing expectations of the first "boom." Those glowing expectations had never been fulfilled; lack of adaptability to the western conditions of life, frozen crops, and too ready a hospitality for all the young Englishmen who were settled through the settlement as homesteaders or farm pupils, wasted his substance, though they had not chilled his openness of heart or cheery faith in the country.

Bert, born and bred in the west, though he had his father's happy disposition, was the far better farmer of the two, and for the last four years had been steadily striving to unravel the tangled skein of land mortgages and chattel mortgages and lien notes, in which his father's easy nature had involved the fortunes of the family. In all these efforts Jim Hardie had been Bert's trusted adviser, and it was to him that he came for counsel in all matters relating to the work of the farm or the settling of a disputed mortgage.

To-night they both seemed in the best of spirits, for Jim was laughing heartily as Amanda joined them on the veranda.

"Good evening, Miss Swanson," said Bert, rising from the step on which he was seated, and raising his cap. "I am glad to see you have come out of your retreat in the woods. How do you like it here on the prairie?"

"I like it very much, thank you, Mr. Enderby, but I have not been very far from Rosebank," and Amanda was passing into the house.

"Stay awhile and listen to Mr. Enderby," said Jim; "he was just telling me a great joke when you came up."

"I was just telling Mr. Hardie about our new 'pup' that my father brought up from Minnedosa last Monday, and how 'green' he was."

"A green pup?" said Amanda innocently, and Jim roared with laughter.

"I beg your pardon, Miss Swanson," said Bert; "I mean a new farm pupil. You know my father sometimes takes young Englishmen as pupils to learn farming, and we have got into the way of calling them 'pups,' because they are so innocent of our ways and take such a lot of licking into shape for a settler's life. Well, on the first morning of his arrival, when my father came into breakfast, he asked where Mr. Vale—the 'pup'—was, and mother said he was not down yet, though they had heard him walking about upstairs. So up went father to his room and found him sitting in his pyjamas on the side of the bed.

" 'Breakfast's ready,' said father; 'you must hurry up and dress.'

" 'Ah—ah, Mr. Enderby—I have been looking round, but I can't find the bath-room.'

" 'The bath-room! Why, when Bert wants a swim he goes down to the little lake in the pasture field,' said father.

" 'Ah—ah—is there a bath-house there?'"

" 'Why,' said father, 'there's a little bluff where you can dress, and I guess that's the only bath-house between here and Winnipeg.'

"By and by Mr. Vale appeared in a swell knickerbocker suit and patent leather slippers, and we had breakfast. As soon as breakfast was over father got up and said:

" 'Come along, Mr. Vale, and I'll show you the stables, and then you can go down the fields with Bert and see what they are doing in the harvest —but where are your boots?'

" 'Ah—I left them at my door, they—ah—want cleaning.'

" 'Oh, hang it,' said my father, who is a little quick sometimes, 'you don't want clean boots to go through the stables, in this country our boots

22

get cleaned once a week, if they're lucky, and every one cleans his own.'

"The poor chap looked uncomfortable, but he and father got on better afterwards, for he does know something about horses, though he never hitched one up in his life.

"You see, Miss Swanson," Bert added by way of explanation, "he belongs to the rich class of people 'at home,' and he has never done a hand's turn for himself in his life; and it's pretty hard to get down to our rough-and-ready ways all at once."

"Well, well, it's too bad to leave the poor fellows so ignorant," said Jim, "and then to send them out here."

"Oh, he'll be all right," said Bert, "when he gets his 'greenness' rubbed off—he's a good-looking chap and knows lots in his own way—he can ride pretty well in an English up-and-down fashion and he's a good shot, and the girls say they never saw any one play tennis like he does, and the mother and he get along fine about books, and so forth; you know my mother has kept her English ways pretty well, Jim."

"Well, well, it's too bad," said Jim, to whom tennis and books did not appeal very much. "You must bring him down here, and amongst us we'll try and make him feel 'at home.' "

"All right, Jim, we'll come along some Sunday after church, and show Miss Swanson what 'a green pup' is like," laughed Bert, as he shook hands and went off with a cheery "so long."

CHAPTER V

Every old-established system, be it ever so corrupt, has some upholders at least among those to whom it is a source of profit, or to whom it affords a reputable release from irksome responsibilities, and so the "farm pupil" system is not yet absolutely dead in western Canada, though it has been long moribund.

As ten righteous men, could they have been found, might have saved Sodom and Gomorrah, so the western farmer who, *rara avis in terris*, has honestly tried to give value in real training for the premiums he has received, has kept the system from being an utter scandal. Not that on its merits, in any case, it deserves to live, for even when the farmer conscientiously does his best by the pupil, and the pupil brings a ready mind and willing hands to the task, it is still the worst imaginable system for converting a "green Englishman" into a practical Canadian farmer. The flaws are in the system itself, apart from the personality of the teacher or the taught, and they spring from conditions which are inseparable from western life.

It is impossible to learn to work a Canadian farm without learning to do the work down to every detail; and personal doing of the work is the only way of learning, it cannot be learned from books, or Agricultural colleges, or by watching some one else do it. The pupil who takes hold of the work is soon conscious of the fact that, if he were called "the hired man" instead of the pupil, he would be earning so many dollars a year by his labour, in place of paying a premium of four or five hundred dollars a year for the privilege of doing it. It seems to him too bad that a not wealthy father "at home" should be stinting the family life, that he may pay for his son being allowed to follow the harrows over the wind-blown, dusty acres all through the spring seeding, or that he may swelter under a July sun cutting brush on a new "clearing."

The inevitable question arises: the first "hired man" who is sent to work with him will put it bluntly before him, "Is it a square deal?" and the sense of injustice will kill all the zeal and enthusiasm he brought to his work. It may be his "boss" will have prickings of conscience at keeping him at the inevitable drudgery; he may release him from the rougher and more menial tasks; he may even encourage him to seek relaxation and pleasure in such society and amusement as may be found in the neighbouring town, with results even more fatal to the "pupils' " future, for when the glamour of pleasure comes in the reality of work goes out.

To attain success, the life of the farm pupil must be largely that of a farm labourer. Youth, health, and a good appetite may make it tolerable to those who have been country-bred "at home"; occasional opportunities for shooting and hunting may make breaks in its monotony; the prospects of future ownership of land is a very powerful incentive to many Englishmen —to a few these bring that steadiness of purpose and plodding industry which lead ultimately to success.

By a deplorable perversity on the part of English parents and guardians, those who lack most conspicuously the qualifications of temperament and training essential to a successful western life are the very ones to be most commonly met as farm pupils in the west. The derelicts of the public schools, of the services, of the learned professions, are launched on the waste of waters of the western prairies, ill-found, unvictualled, and lacking religious and moral compass for the hopeless voyage, and those who are responsible are amazed at the inevitable wreckage; forgetting that Mother Earth in our northern lands yields her fruits only to those who toil; forgetting that those who would lead a clean life in the west must bring to it a clean record from the past; change of environment alone will not effect a transformation of moral character.

Many young men are sent "out west" because they give no promise of being a credit to their people "at home"; some because, by their ill courses, they have already been a shame and grief to their fathers and mothers. Such an one was Roland Vale, though all the London lawyers, who had arranged his coming out to Mr. Enderby, had thought it necessary to tell that gentleman was, "that he was a fine, active young fellow, but had failed to pass his entrance to Sandhurst and was now past the age." And what lay behind that apparently natural and straightforward statement?

At sixteen Roland's father was asked by the authorities to remove him from the public school where, as the headmaster said, "He showed no aptitude for his studies, and no power of that concentrated effort so necessary for a successful career." Thence he passed to the charge of a gentleman who professed a special skill in dealing with backward youths, who "did not respond to the discipline of larger institutions." At twenty he was back again on his father's hands, an admitted failure. His father would have sent him packing forthwith to sink or swim in the colonies, but his mother pleaded for another chance to be given him before sending him forth into the world, and his father consented to a year's probation on the home farm, under the bailiff, before his departure, and for a time Roland's mother at least believed that her boy was going to turn over a new leaf.

In her and his father's presence he simulated, if he did not feel, an interest in his new life, and his ready answers when asked where he had spent the long summer evenings, that he had been down at the farm or out with his gun through the woods, aroused no suspicions. Their growing confidence was rudely shattered. Late one summer night Giles, the keeper, who lived with his wife and daughter in a cottage in the wood between the Hall and the bailiff's house on the home farm, appeared at the Hall and demanded to see the squire. On his departure Roland was summoned, and what passed none but Roland and his father ever knew. The following morning in a few stern words the squire announced to the elder children that Roland was going up to London that day to get a necessary outfit for the Canadian west, and that he would sail from Liverpool in two weeks time without returning home. None dared to question the squire, and from Roland himself the only answer that could be procured was that his father was "down on him," and was making a great fuss over nothing—"nothing more than lots of fellows did, without such a row being made."

Not one word of explanation did Giles give of his mission, but the next week his daughter left home to stay with an aunt in an adjoining county, and before her visit ended Giles and his wife were installed in a keeper's lodge on the estate of one of the squire's old friends a hundred miles away.

By the time Roland's ship was half across the broad Atlantic, such remorse as he may have felt for Nancy Giles' betrayal had passed away, and he was taking such amusement as he could get from his fellow passengers and the novelty of his surroundings.

CHAPTER VI

It was the afternoon of Roland Vale's second Sunday at the Dingle, and he was finding it, as he had expressed it to one of his old friends "at home," in a letter written before dinner, "deadly slow."

It was a broiling hot day with a cloudless sky, and the sun beat down with a pitiless brilliancy on the whitewashed walls of the old rambling log house. In the little pasture field in front the horses moved restlessly from the shelter of the bluff of poplars to the open sunshine, unable to settle the knotty question as to whether it were more tolerable to endure the blaze of the sun, or to be worried by the flies and mosquitoes in the shade. Half a dozen pigs alternated between wallowing in the muddy margin of the little slough by the stables and grunting and panting in such protection from the heat as they could find in the butt-end of a last year's straw stack.

The veranda on the east side of the old house was pretty enough in itself, with a screen of trailing wild hops and its rustic chairs and little home-made table, where Bert Enderby was writing letters while Roland, lounging in a hammock, grumbled now at the "infernal flies," which would not let him sleep, and now at the "rottenness" of the magazines, which were not interesting enough to keep him awake. Even his cigarettes, his usual refuge from being too much bored with his own or others' company, failed him to-day, for the tobacconist at Minnedosa did not sell the only kind "fit for a fellow to smoke."

Though his surroundings at the Dingle were new, it was a novelty entirely without charm; to him they were simply squalid. The work of the farm, about which Mr. Enderby and Bert talked most of the time, and in which they took an unfailing interest, to him seemed little better than the lot of a labourer "at home"; it passed his imagination to comprehend how two gentlemen, for he had to admit that in birth and breeding they were both that, could toil early and late in such menial labour and in such, to him, rough surroundings, not only cheerfully, but with a keen liking for it all.

And the food and the appetite with which these people ate! That day's dinner, for instance—the great roast of fat pork, with baked potatoes and boiled cabbage—with the thermometer about 100° in the shade. And a touch of humour turned Roland's disgust into amusement and he smiled to himself. "I wish the squire could have a couple of weeks of this kind of thing for himself." Then he wondered, "Did Bert really like it all, or was he just good-tempered and making the best of it?"

"I say, Bert, eh—don't you find this kind of thing rather slow?" and Roland indicated this kind of thing by a general wave of his hand, which took in the pasture, the horses and the pigs, and the outbuildings, which could be seen through the opening in the front of the veranda.

"Why, bless you, no," said Bert briskly; "it's never slow on a farm; there's such a lot to do and such a little time to do it in, and there's always something fresh turning up. Why, there are more possibilities and uncertainties, good and bad, in farming in Manitoba, than in any place in the world outside of the Stock Exchange and the race-track. Of course there is heaps of work, and lots of hard work at times; but no, certainly I should never call it slow."

"Really," said Roland, rather surprised at so much energy on such a subject on such a hot day, "really, ah——"

"It's all the way you look at it," said Bert. "Now to-day, when it certainly is a bit warm, what a comfort it is that it's Sunday, and one can take it easy!"

"Still," retorted Roland, "a fellow must do something, and it would take a lot of looking to find anything very gay and giddy in watching over-heated pigs grunting in a mud puddle."

"Well, perhaps the pigs are not very exciting," conceded Bert, "if they are not your own pigs that you have brought up from their infancy. If you don't mind the heat, let us go down to the lake and have a swim, and then we will stroll down to Jim Hardie's and see what they are doing there."

Roland agreed willingly enough, for he did not really mind the heat or a good deal of active exercise in any shape except that of work—work he disliked, because he never chose it for himself, but it was forced upon him by pressure of authority from outside. So far he had not found it too irksome at the Dingle, partly from its novelty, and partly because it was rather suggested than ordered that he should take a share in the daily round of farm life.

After their swim the two young men started off down the lane to the "town line" and entered the bush on either side, so as to have the shade of the trees from the hot sun. It was less than a mile to Jim Hardie's house and Bert thought it would be safer to prepare Roland a little for the visit. He knew Jim Hardie would be just himself, kindly and straightforward, and that, however much he might be quietly amused by Roland's "greenness," he would not betray his amusement, but Bert was not quite sure how the Hardie menage would strike Roland just fresh out from a refined English home, and with the engrained habit of his class of judging people by the merest incidentals of manner and speech.

28

"You'll like Jim Hardie, Roland, when you get to know him; but of course the people down there are regular Canadians."

"What do you mean by 'regular Canadians'?" asked Roland.

"Well, it's a little difficult to explain," said Bert. "You know we English people think a lot about the way a man's clothes are made, and about odds and ends of grammar. We are a little faddy about using a knife and fork and all that kind of thing. Now, Jim doesn't worry about his clothes so long as they are comfortable, and if it's cooler to sit down to dinner in his shirt sleeves, he'll do it, and you are quite welcome to do the same, and once in a while he may use his knife where we have a prejudice for employing a fork, in eating peas, for instance; but in anything that really matters he is just as much a gentleman as your or I."

"Well, I'll admit I have a prejudice when it comes to peas," said Roland, "but I'll not show any surprise."

"And he 'guesses' and 'bets his socks' occasionally, and little things of that kind; but he is as 'straight as a string,' and I never heard him use a rough word before his wife and children. Of course, he had very little of what you call education, but he's the best farmer and the best neighbour in the settlement."

"I see," said Roland a little superciliously, "one of nature's gentlemen —there is getting to be quite a lot of that kind of people 'at home' now, 'Labour' members and that sort."

"I don't know what 'that sort' are like in England, but the more there are of Jim Hardie's sort here the better," replied Bert rather sharply; "and you'll very likely see Amanda Swanson, who is helping Mrs. Hardie this fall."

"Amanda! Good heavens, what a name for a dairy-maid! I suppose she wears short petticoats and paddles round in bare feet."

"Don't be a fool, Roland," said Bert, who was getting rather ruffled out of his usual easy good-nature by his companion's banter. "Miss Swanson is no more a dairy-maid than my sisters, or than yours would be for a matter of that, if they were on a Canadian farm. She is the daughter of one of the Swedish settlers in the Scandinavian Colony, north of us, and, though her people were peasants at home, they are our equals here, and Amanda is quite civilized.

"Of course," he added rather maliciously, "she's not like the young ladies you are used to meeting 'at home,' but she will be very flattered if you take a little notice of her, and she can talk a little 'broken' English, you know; but here we are, and you'll see for yourself."

By this time they had come to the end of the bush and were crossing the little pasture field, from which a lane led them past the corral to the little bluff at the back of the house. Here, in the shade of the trees, they found the whole Hardie family and Amanda. Jim was lying on an old deer-skin robe, in his shirt sleeves as Bert had foretold, and with the last week's Winnipeg paper as an excuse for his afternoon nap. Mrs. Hardie, with the baby on her lap, was slowly rocking herself in the big rocking-chair, without which no Canadian farmhouse is complete, while the two boys and little Nellie were gathered round Amanda, who in a low voice, so as not to disturb their father, was reading to them "Lob lie by the Fire."

Amanda was one of that small number of people who have the chameleon-like gift of harmonizing with their surroundings. It always seemed perfectly natural that she should be doing what she was doing, and that she was doing it in the most charming manner possible. Had you met her the winter before on her way to school, walking briskly along the trail through the woods, clad in her dark-blue ulster of Hudson Bay blanket, with its red-lined hood drawn over her head, with here and there a fugitive lock touched with the silver hoar frost, with long red scarf girdling the folds of her coat to her shapely waist, her feet trimly clad in neat Indian beaded moccasins—these with her glowing cheeks and sparkling, laughter-loving eyes, seemed just the ideal presentiment of the daughter of the land of snows. Or, did you meet her on a dewy morning, late in May, bringing up the cows from the meadow for the milking, in the simple dress of a Swedish peasant girl, it seemed equally natural and charming, and she was, what Jim Hardie always called her, "the Rose of Sweden."

To-day, when all seemed more or less "mussed," as Mrs. Hardie expressed it, by the heat, Amanda alone seemed unaffected by it. It may be that Bert Enderby's promise to bring the "new pup" down to Rosebank had added, almost unconsciously, an additional touch to the careful daintiness with which Amanda always wore even the plainest and simplest attire; it may be that there was a girlish freak not to appear too "Norse" in the eyes of this countryman of Evelyn Raye's; or, after all, it may have been but the expression in outward form of nature's voice whispering in the heart of the young and pure and beautiful, which may be quite innocent of coquetry or of conscious desire to please.

"Well, here we are, Jim," said Bert, as Rowland and he reached the group under the trees, and Jim came forward to meet them.

"This is Mr. Vale, just out from England to learn how we live in the Woolly West."

"Glad to see you, Mr. Vale," said Jim heartily; "we always expect any one from the Dingle to be at home at Rosebank. This is my wife, Mr. Vale; Miss Swanson; and the rest are the kids," indicating the children by an inclusive sweep of the hand, "and now you know all. Ted, bring a chair for Mr. Vale—there's room for you, Bert, on the robe; now we're comfortable," and Jim resumed his place, anything in the way of social forms and "fuss," as he called it, being very distasteful to his unconventional tastes.

Bert was a great favourite with the children, and was soon listening to the boys' stories of the lots of fun they had had since Amanda came, and of how she was "just as good as a boy" in their games, while Jim, thinking that a farm pupil would of course be interested in the farm, entered on his favourite topics of the crops and the stock. Roland had an easy good-nature, which helped him to feign an interest even if he did not feel it, and while he listened to Jim was trying to readjust his preconceived notions of these people with the reality. While Mr. Hardie's shirt sleeves, Canadian colloquialisms, and occasional lapses in accepted forms of English grammar did not fit at all with Roland's notions of a gentleman, still less did his clear and capable descriptions of western farming, with his shrewd judgment of men, fall in with the impression which Bert had given him, that he would find in a Canadian farmer an up-to-date type of an English farm labourer.

By the time their visit ended Roland had wit enough to have discovered a few of the axioms of Jim Hardie's simple theory of the whole duty of man. A man willing to live without effort, on the results of another's toil, was a "dead head," to take advantage of another's ignorance in a deal was the mark of a "skunk," while Mr. Enderby and Bert were quoted as ideal neighbours, because they were in all things "as straight as a string."

But a greater riddle and one of far more interest to Roland was Amanda. What on earth had Bert meant by talking about her "broken English," and "being flattered by a little notice being taken of her"? The scraps of Amanda's English that reached his ears, from where she was laughing and talking with Bert and the boys, was as good as his own, and she herself —why, he found it hard to keep his eyes and attention from wandering too obviously from his conversation with Mr. Hardie. Here at least was some one who promised a relief from the "deadly slowness" of life at the Dingle; for the first time since his arrival Roland felt spurred to make an effort.

CHAPTER VII

Roland was growing rather weary of the greatness of the west, the rust in the oats, the iniquity of the grain buyers—unfailing topics of interest to Jim Hardie—and was glad when Bert broke into their conversation with the suggestion that he would like to take a walk round the fields, and see how the crops looked before dark.

"Of course, of course," said Jim. "Come, mother, if you and Amanda will give us an early supper, we can all go for a stroll around, and I'll show you those rusted oats, Mr. Vale. We might have a look at the horses while we're waiting for supper."

By the time the stables had been inspected and Bert's opinion taken of a team of broncos, which Jim had bought in town the week before, little Ted came to call them to supper, and they returned to the house. Mrs. Hardie prided herself on her cooking and was never caught unprepared for visitors on a Sunday, when the hospitable Jim would have been disappointed if some one did not "drop in." The big table was covered with a spotless cloth, the "best china" was set out, and there were pies and cakes and doughnuts in lavish abundance. Mrs. Hardie sat at the side of the table with the baby in her lap, and Amanda presided over the tea with Roland on her one hand and little Ted on the other.

"Sit down, Mr. Vale, sit down and make yourself at home. 'For these and all His mercies God's name be praised.' Come, boys, pass the bread-and-butter and the pie," and Jim seated himself at the head of the table and set the example of making himself "at home," by helping himself to cold meat from the dish, and passing the dish to Bert to do likewise.

At first Roland was rather embarrassed by the frequency with which he was invited to take a piece of this or of that, till he noticed that the English convention of finishing one thing before accepting another, was not observed, and that Bert had quite a varied assortment of cake and pie on his plate at the one time. As soon, however, as Jim was satisfied that Roland was being treated with due attention as a visitor, he and Bert turned again to farm topics, and Roland was free to devote himself to Mrs. Hardie and Amanda.

Roland always found himself more at home with the opposite sex. They were willing to take him more at his own valuation, and his good manners and good looks, both perhaps rather lacking in manliness and straightforwardness, won a readier way to their good graces than was the case with men like Jim Hardie and Bert Enderby, with whom they counted but little, if at all.

Mrs. Hardie, who in her girlhood's days had been the belle of the settlement, found his easy manners and ready, if superficial, sympathy with the lack of interest and variety in farm life very pleasant, and if, in reality, she knew little of a larger world, in which people lived for pleasure and not for work, it was flattering to be treated as if that larger world, were her natural sphere. Listening to his accounts of days spent down the river, of dances in the evening, of tennis on the lawn, of a life in which nothing seemed to count but "having a good time," it seemed to her as if her own youth had been wasted, and as if a hard fate had robbed her of the pleasure of living.

By the time supper was over she found herself consenting to a suggestion of Roland's that they might level and roll a little plat in the pasture, where he would put up a tennis net and teach them to play. Mrs. Hardie had always spoken rather scornfully of tennis and their "English" ways at the Dingle; but, before, she had always been "on the outside" and, secretly, rather jealous of the popularity of the Enderbys among the young people of the settlement.

Nor was Roland's evident admiration of Amanda distasteful to Mrs. Hardie; Amanda, if a Swede, was a Canadian, and for the time a member of her family. Though Mrs. Enderby honestly prided herself on her freedom from pride in her intercourse with her Canadian neighbours, yet was Mrs. Hardie conscious of a social line between the Dingle and Rosebank which she could never pass, and which, scorn it as she might, still rankled. The Dingle farm pupils were always encouraged to be on friendly terms with Jim Hardie, both for the sake of his own worth and for his skill as a farmer, but in the prospects of a "pup," who would desert the Dingle tennis courts and the Enderby girls for Rosebank and Amanda, Mrs. Hardie saw an opening for a very pleasant—well, not exactly revenge—but something as near to it as was permissible for a regular church member.

When supper was over a discussion arose as to who should go for a walk round the fields and who should stay at home and wash up the dishes and see to the milking. Amanda was anxious for Mrs. Hardie to go, saying that she and Frank could do the milking and that little Ted would help her with the dishes; but Mrs. Hardie was in a very gracious humour and insisted on Amanda making one of the walking party, and one of the farm hands volunteered to help Mrs. Hardie with the cows, and so it was settled.

The four set off together along the rough waggon road skirting the edge of the fence, which separated the crop land from the bluff and prairie on the other side of the snake fence.

They kept in one party till they reached the far side of the home fields —Roland a polite but very unwilling victim of Jim's desire to do the honours of the country to the newcomer, and quite innocent of any thought that a farm pupil might not be interested in rubbing out heads of wheat, which promised to be "number one hard," and in the devastations of rust on the oats, which would mean a loss of five bushels to the acre; but Roland had a skill in making opportunities when a pretty girl was concerned, which quite overreached Jim's simple mind in such matters. Jim was anxious to go on further to show Bert a "patch" of wheat on some new-broken land, but Roland discovered that he had a pebble in his shoe, and, by the time that was extricated, he pleaded that it had scraped his heel and he thought he would rather not go any farther, he would stroll back to the house.

Jim accepted the little subterfuge in perfect good faith. "Well, well, that's too bad, but we can't let you go back alone; you keep Mr. Vale company, Amanda, and Bert and I will catch you up before you get home again." Amanda accepted the solution as naturally as Jim, for though she felt a little shy of this well-dressed, easy-mannered young man, yet she had all the self-possession of the Canadian girl who had shared her work and play with her brothers and the neighbours' boys and girls, at school and in the farm life.

Bert Enderby had misgivings as to the desirability of the arrangement, but he could not very well suggest them, so he and Mr. Hardie climbed the fence and went off to the wheat, while Amanda and Roland turned back on the road to the farm.

"Do you never get tired of the crops and the cows and the rust and the frost and all that kind of thing?" asked Roland, as they strolled slowly along. "Do you know, it seems to me as if the people here fancied that the only thing nicer than work was more work, and when they have worked all one week, talk of nothing but the work they mean to do next."

"Oh no," laughed Amanda, "we have to work most of the time; but Mr. Hardie is so proud of his farm that he does talk about it a good deal, and of course everybody helps; and we are too busy in the summer time to think of other things."

"But you have not always lived in this kind of way?" pursued Roland.

"Oh yes, I have; only I see more people at Mr. Hardie's, and we do not work so hard at Rosebank as my own people do in the Colony. You know, I am a Swede, Mr. Vale, and have lived all my life in the woods to the north."

"Oh yes," said Roland, "Bert Enderby told me that there was a Swedish young lady at Rosebank, but, ah—he did not tell me—ah———" and Roland hesitated, for he could hardly suggest that he had expected to find a bare-footed dairy-maid in short petticoats.

"He did not tell you I was quite civilized," said Amanda, unconsciously using the very words of Bert's description.

"Oh no, I did not mean that," Roland said hastily; "but you talk English so well and look so—I mean——" and Roland found his explanation rather difficult.

"You mean that I talk English a little," said Amanda maliciously. "Oh yes, we have a school up in Sweden, and the children have to learn to read and write in English, you know."

"But you don't talk English like the Hardie children and Mrs. Hardie—and that book you were reading to them this afternoon."

"Oh, that was one of Miss Raye's books," said Amanda, with a slight blush, as she wondered how much attention he had paid to her reading, while he was supposed to be talking "crops" with Mr. Hardie.

"And who is Miss Raye?" queried Roland.

"Miss Raye was our teacher in 'Sweden,' and she boarded with us and was very kind in helping me, and we children and mother all talked English while she stayed with us, and she gave me all her books when she went home again."

"And Miss Raye was English?" asked Roland.

"Oh yes," said Amanda decidedly. "Miss Raye was an English lady, and her father was a clergyman in England, and she had to go home when her father died; but she writes to me, and may come out again some day."

"Why, I do believe I've heard of them," said Roland; "there was an old clergyman of that name at a little village called Scraptoft, four or five miles from my father's place."

"Yes, yes, that's it," said Amanda quite eagerly.

"And I went over there with my mother one holiday," continued Roland, "and there were two or three boys about my age, and a girl rather older, and we played tennis all the afternoon together."

"Yes, that would be Evelyn," said Amanda; "she often talked about them all to me. How wonderful you should know them all!"

"Well, you know, England is not as big as Canada," replied Roland, to whom this discovery suggested some uneasy doubts as to whether his own record might not follow him out to the west. "And do you often hear from her now?"

"Oh yes," said Amanda, "we write quite regularly, but she has moved to another part of England since her father died"; and Roland felt relieved.

"Oh, she would not remember me," said he; "I was only a schoolboy then and I have not been at home much since I grew up."

"Still it is nice to meet some one who knows any one one likes very much, if it is only a little," persisted Amanda, "and now you know the mystery of my English—and the rest that Mr. Enderby did not tell you," said Amanda, laughing, for she felt more at ease since the discovery of this little link with her beloved ideal, Evelyn Raye.

Now that he seemed secure from any unwelcome revelations from his own past life reaching Rosebank and Amanda, Roland talked freely enough of his English life at home, and Amanda's lively interest and quick understanding led him on. A ready imagination and the absence of troublesome scruples as to exact truthfulness are great aids to reviving recollections of past pleasures and half-forgotten scenes.

Amanda had never realized before how great a gap Evelyn Raye's departure had left in her life, the life of her thoughts and fancies. There is not much scope for idealizing life in the endless round of practical work in a Canadian farm house. Canadians give little thought to the mystery of existence, to analysing their own emotions or even to being conscious of the beauties of nature in forest, wild flower, or animal and bird life around them. These things are either useful and capable of being turned to practical account, that is to money value, or they are merely impediments to getting on, and are to be cleared away as speedily as possible to make room for prosaic utilities. Her one outlet for the expansion of her own nature Amanda had closed against herself, in her wilful trifling with Ludwig's love, a love that secretly she never doubted, though she had mocked his awkward, tactless way of trying to give it expression.

In her innocence of the world Roland's resemblance to Evelyn Raye, in voice, in accent, in manner, in easy readiness of speech—in reality only the merest accidents of similarity of social surroundings and upbringing—counted for far more than they were worth, and before they reached the end of their walk, she found herself talking of herself, her dreams of a freer, wider life than that of the bush and the prairie, with a freedom of which she herself was unconscious. To Roland that freedom and her unaffected interest in himself and in his old life at home were altogether delightful. Partly it reinstated him in his own good opinion of himself—an opinion rather damped by the unintentional way in which every one at the Dingle took it for granted that he was "green," and generally incapable in the only things which seemed to count—farm work. And again, no young man, sensitive to beauty of form and face and voice, could be untouched by Amanda's pure unconsciousness of her own charms.

He could not know how much of her sympathetic attitude to himself was the result of the regrets in her heart for her unkindness to Ludwig; he only saw a pleasant break in the monotony of his life, and was little given to anticipating the troubles into which his wayward and undisciplined pursuit of his own pleasures might lead him, for Roland was one of those many children of pleasure who disprove the truthfulness of the old adage, that "a burnt child dreads the fire."

CHAPTER VIII

Roland Vale returned to the Dingle full of enthusiasm for the new system of making a tennis court at Rosebank, and already enjoying by anticipation many opportunities of seeing again the lovely girl whose bright and sympathetic responsiveness promised so welcome a break in the monotony of his life. He never dreamt of meeting any opposition from the family at the Dingle; for one thing, since he was a child, he had always taken it for granted that he was to have his own way, and he usually had it. It was true he had never dared openly to disobey the squire, but Mr. Enderby and the squire were two very different persons.

At the Hall and in the village "at home" the squire was an autocrat, as absolute in his way as the Czar of all the Russias. Mr. Enderby was a little fussy and irritable, but withal an easy, kindly man; indeed, those who knew the Enderbys' household best hinted that Mrs. Enderby, with her unobtrusive, placid manner, was really the power behind the domestic throne.

Roland expected that Mr. Enderby might be as Roland put it, "a little touchy," if he were to take too much time out of the working hours of the day; but he reckoned on the handsome premium the squire was paying to keep him from much trouble in that quarter, and of Mrs. Enderby and the girls' co-operation, in his innocence, he felt quite sure. Mrs. Enderby would talk to him by the hour of his life and the people "at home," and the girls were always keen for a game of tennis in the evening. They would be delighted with the prospect of new recruits.

The one difficulty, which he never dreamt of, was any hitch on the score of Amanda's nationality or Mrs. Hardie's accent and Canadian figures of speech. The axiom of the west, which had been impressed upon him from the day of his coming by every member of the family at the Dingle in their different ways, was that "there are no social distinctions in Manitoba." It was with this preface that Mr. Enderby had set him to work to clean out the stable with the Barnardo boy, who did the "chores." "We could not keep a boy a week, if we had any difference," apologized Mrs. Enderby in an undertone, when the same salvage of a doubtful philanthropy took his place at the family dinner table.

"It would be so funny to your sisters, Mr. Vale, to see a lady scrubbing a floor," simpered Miss Daisy Enderby, when Roland found her on her knees in the kitchen engaged in that necessary, if rather menial, office.

"Mr. Vale will understand that there are no social distinctions in the west," snapped Miss Enderby, from the washtub.

Miss Enderby was thin and thirty, quite a nice, neat figure by the afternoon, in a ten-and-sixpenny English skirt and a white blouse, but rather sharp at the corners in the deshabille of the weekly wash. She had seen many "pups" come and go at the Dingle, and still had hopes—for Daisy. For herself, she was partially resigned to being an old maid, with the alternative of marrying a middle-aged Canadian farmer, well-to-do, but of unconventional habits of eating and speech. To Roland, Miss Enderby was very gracious in an elder-sisterly kind of way, and her participation in the tennis was a good deal of a sacrifice. If Daisy wanted this particular "pup," and as Miss Enderby admitted that he was a nice-mannered, good-looking boy, why, she should have him, if he was one to be had by the affording of tennis or other opportunities for falling in love.

Everything seemed favourable to Roland's new plans when he went down rather late for breakfast, on the Monday morning following his visit to Rosebank. Mr. Enderby and Bert were already at work, Mrs. Enderby was only just down, and joined him at the table, while Miss Daisy waited on them. He had not long to wait for an opening, for, after the usual morning greetings, Mrs. Enderby's first words were, "And how did you like the people at Rosebank, Mr. Vale? Is not Mr. Hardie's farm a fine example of what hard work and energy can do here? My husband and Bert think there is nobody like Mr. Hardie, so practical, and such a good neighbour to help when anything goes wrong—we always say we should be lost without him in the settlement."

"Oh, he was awfully hospitable, and all that kind of thing," said Roland, "and really took too much trouble to show me everything about the place; I never saw any one so keen on his work."

"But those are the people who get on here," said Mrs. Enderby.

"I suppose they are," admitted Roland, "but I don't—ah—quite see where the fun comes in."

"Oh, that is rank heresy in Canada," laughed Miss Daisy; "the fun doesn't come in, it's dollars that come in."

"But what's the good of dollars if you don't spend them?" protested Roland.

"Why they make more dollars, and you have the biggest crop in the settlement, and a huge barn that defaces the landscape for miles round, and 'the cattle upon a thousand hills.' "

"Don't be profane, Daisy," rebuked her mother. "Of course, such a life makes people rather narrow, but there is a great deal to be admired in Mr. Hardie, and he is not in the least obtrusive."

"Oh," said Roland, "I thought he was an awfully decent sort of chap, and he asked me to go down any time I liked, in fact."

"And is not Mrs. Hardie a wonder in the house?" interrupted Miss Daisy; "such lovely bread and butter, and always pies and cakes galore. Our 'chore boy,' was there the other Sunday and when he came back he said he never had such a blow."

"For shame, Daisy——" said Mrs. Enderby hastily.

"Well, he did, mother, and I guess he was right," retorted Miss Daisy.

"We certainly had a great spread," said Roland, "but Mrs. Hardie seemed very anxious to get a little amusement into the work; in fact, she was quite enthusiastic when I suggested they should have a tennis court down there, and we could work up a little——"

"A tennis court at Rosebank! Why, you must be joking," broke in Miss Daisy, with a satirical laugh.

"Who on earth would play tennis there? I'm sure Mr. Hardie would think it harder than work. The 'chore boy,' the 'hired girl,' Mrs. Hardie, and the baby; what a set they would make!"

"I don't see why they should not have a net down there," said Roland, flushing a little. "Mrs. Hardie seems awfully anxious to learn, and I'm sure Miss Swanson would make a good player. They could come up here till we got a court marked out down there."

"What are you laughing at, Daisy?" said Mrs. Enderby, bewildered, as that young lady went into screams of laughter.

"Who is Miss Swanson? I beg your pardon, Mr. Vale, for being so rude, but really," and she broke into a fresh peal, which did not ring quite true as pure merriment. "Miss Swanson is Amanda Swanson, the 'hired girl' they have down from Sweden. You should not be so sarcastic, Mr. Vale; mother thought you were in earnest."

"So I am in earnest," retorted Roland, who was rapidly losing his temper. "Why on earth should Mrs. Hardie and Miss Swanson not play tennis if they like?"

"Oh, by all means," said Miss Daisy; "but, thank you, Mr. Vale, for placing my sister and myself on the same level as Jim Hardie's 'hired girl.'"

"Why, ever since I came everybody has been telling me that there are no levels here—there was no level when I was set out to work with a 'guttersnipe' from Stepney Causeway, and Bert treated Miss Swanson with just as much respect as he does his own sisters, perhaps a little more."

"Of course, if Bert chooses to mix with such people he can," said Miss Daisy, with great contempt. "If you and he wish to gush over a Swedish doll dressed up like an English young lady——"

"Hush, hush, Daisy, you forget yourself," rebuked her mother. "I'm sure Mrs. Hardie would not have any one there who was not perfectly respectable, and Mr. Vale does not understand there are certain—well, not exactly social distinctions, but shall we call them limitations? in the intercourse of myself and daughters with people—very excellent people in their way—like the Hardies; and a 'hired girl' from 'the Colony' is of course impossible as a companion for girls whose grandfather was the Dean of Chester and very exclusive." Poor Mrs. Enderby was in rather a quandary. Mr. Enderby and Bert would never allow a slight to be put on the Hardies, and yet it would never do to allow Roland to become mixed up with this girl from "Sweden."

"Well, it will be jolly awkward for me," said Roland, cooling down a little, "jolly awkward, after my saying I would put up a net there and that we could all go down and play."

"Did you expect us to teach Miss Swanson English as well as tennis, Mr. Vale?" asked Miss Daisy, who was still feeling vindictive.

"Oh, there you're out, Miss Daisy," retorted Roland; "if Miss Swanson could play tennis as well as she speaks English, she would have very little to learn from any of us."

"What a paragon you have discovered, Mr. Vale! I'll go and tell my sister what a treat you have prepared for us; I'm sure she will be as charmed as I am," and Miss Daisy retired to the kitchen, with a high colour and her nose in the air.

"Do not be put out, Mr. Vale," said Mrs. Enderby, after Daisy had left the room, shutting the door behind her with much emphasis. "Of course, you could not tell how things are out here; there are no social distinctions among the men, but your father would not like you to see more than necessary of such people as Miss Swanson."

"Oh, it's father, is it, Mrs. Enderby? It was to suit him I came out to this howling wilderness, and now I'm here I intend to suit myself, at least as concerns whom I play tennis with."

"Of course, of course, Mr. Vale," said Mrs. Enderby hastily, for it would never do to jeopardise a fat premium for a trifle; "but you might tell Mrs. Hardie the girls are too busy this week as the threshers will soon be coming and we'll see what can be done."

"Oh, be sure, I'll say nothing about them, the social lines are too fine for me to explain," replied Roland. "I'm going down this afternoon, and certainly don't mean to tell the best-dressed, best-spoken, and best-looking girl I've seen since I left England that she is an uncivilized savage," and with this parting shot Roland picked up his cap and went out to join the men in the field.

CHAPTER IX

During the harvest season the usual routine of work and meals at the Dingle was varied, so as to allow as much work as possible being done in the fields. In place of dinner at twelve and supper at six, and no further work, except the milking and the "chores," dinner was at eleven, and supper at four, and then Bert and the "chore boy" went out to the field again till dark, while Mr. Enderby helped with the milking and fed the calves and pigs.

Usually Roland was given the option of going out with Bert or spending the evening round the house, which meant sitting out on the veranda with Mrs. Enderby and talking "old country," or else chatting with Miss Daisy while she washed the dishes, and then playing tennis till dark with her and Miss Enderby.

By supper-time on this particular Monday all signs of the morning's warm discussion had passed away, under the quiet influence of Mrs. Enderby, who warily steered the conversation from any dangerous channels. Roland still felt a little sore and disposed to "have it out" with Miss Daisy, but she, under her mother's restraining eye, was only prim and demure, and Bert and his father were too much absorbed in the crop and the approaching threshing to be conscious of any subtle under-currents of feeling.

As soon as supper was over Mr. Enderby whistled for his dog and went off to the bush to "hunt" the cows, which often wandered a long distance in search of pea-vine and vetches in the wood, now that the shorter grass of the prairie was becoming dried and burnt up by the long spell of hot fall weather; and when Bert turned to Roland with the question, "Are you coming out again?" Mrs. Enderby answered for him.

"Oh no; Mr. Vale has had enough work for to-day, and I am going to ask him to take a note for me to Rosebank, to see if they are going to kill a 'beef' for their threshing, and if we can get half of it for our own."

"Oh, all right, mater," said Bert, "and you might tell him, Roland, that one of us will come with a team to help him draw his grain from the thresher to his granary."

"Very well," answered Roland; "I'll just change and be ready for your note, Mrs. Enderby, in a few minutes"; and he went upstairs, whistling a scrap of a tune, just to show Miss Daisy that he was not in the least embarrassed by her aside to him.

"Don't forget your racket, Mr. Vale."

41

Roland had brought a tennis net, a dozen balls, and a spare racket with him from England, not expecting civilization to be advanced to the tennis point in the west, and these he determined to take down to Rosebank; if the Enderby girls chose to be disagreeable, he would show them that he could do without their help. The net and its posts were rather awkward to carry, and he felt conscious of the bulginess of the balls in his "blazer" pockets as he set off down the land to the road. Miss Daisy was nowhere in sight, but he felt sure she was watching him from some hidden corner, and that he was affording a subject of ridicule to her sharp tongue.

Once out of sight of the house, and in the path through the woods leading to Rosebank, he recovered his good humour. After all he would see more of Amanda, if the others were not there, and that was the principal thing.

The barking of the old collie announced his approach to the house, where he was met at the door by Mrs. Hardie with the friendliest welcome.

"My, it is good of you, Mr. Vale, to carry all those things down on such a hot day. Do come in and have a cup of tea; the men are off to the field again, but Amanda is just tidying herself and will be down in a minute, and the boys will carry the net down to the pasture when they come from school."

"No tea, thank you," said Roland, "we've just had supper. Mrs. Enderby asked me to bring this note down with me; something about the threshing."

Mrs. Hardie took the note and ran her eye over it. "Oh yes, they want to get some meat from Jim when he kills. Then mother says, 'So sorry the girls are too busy for tennis this week'—it's something new for Daisy Enderby to be too busy for tennis when there's a young man in the neighbourhood—'it will be nice for your boys to learn to play while they are young,'" and the corners of Mrs. Hardie's mouth hardened a little. "'Of course, it is not much pleasure for a good player like Mr. Vale to play with beginners, but he is very good-hearted.'"

Roland flushed with vexation as Mrs. Hardie read out the last sentence. "Indeed, I shall enjoy it very much, and I'm sure, with a little practice, Miss Swanson and you will play as well as they do up there."

"Well, it really is very kind of you, Mr. Vale, and if we are too clumsy, you must just give us up as a bad job. Here comes Amanda."

Though he would not have admitted it for the world, Miss Daisy's remarks about "Swedish dolls" and "hired girls" had not been without their impression on Roland, and as he walked down to Rosebank he had wondered to himself whether he had not been too impulsive in forming his judgment of Amanda, but his first glance at her as she entered the room reassured him. "Hired girl" or not, there was nothing common about her or suggestive of the least effort to seem anything different to what it was perfectly natural for her to be. Her pink-and-white print frock was as plain as that of a nursery maid, but it was fitted trim and daintily to her figure. Roland had seen many gaudy vagaries in head-gear among the girls with whom he had played tennis at home, but never had he seen anything which seemed to him at once so quaint and yet so natural to the wearer as the simple Swedish handkerchief of whitest lawn, gathered to the form of her shapely head, by its ribbon of pink, the end of which nestled in a bow beneath her chin.

"Why, Amanda child, what have you got on your feet?" exclaimed Mrs. Hardie. "Did you think it was a toboggan slide we had in the pasture?"

"Oh, no, Mrs. Hardie," laughed Amanda, holding out one foot a little and blushing; "but Miss Raye had a pair of little shoes without heels, that she said she played tennis in at home, and this was the best I could do."

Now, there is nothing so becoming to the wearer as a true Indian moccasin, for it shows in every line and curve the symmetry of the foot within, or the lack of it. The true Indian moccasin, made by the squaws in their teepees, bears no more resemblance to the coarse, clumsy moccasins of the factory in eastern Canada, than a Parisian shoe to a hobnailed boot. And Amanda's moccasins were the daintiest of their kind. Ludwig had brought them from the Indian Reserve the winter before, as a Christmas present; perhaps that was why they had found a corner in her little box, for she did not expect the snow to come before she was back at home again in Sweden.

"I should think they would do," said Roland, looking at the little foot admiringly, "only they're too pretty to wear."

"Well, let us go and have our first lesson, Mrs. Hardie; I'm all anxious to begin," said Amanda, moving to the door. "Here are the boys coming from school, and they will want to come too."

The whole party were soon at the pasture, where Jim had that morning rolled the smoothest plot before going to his work, and with the help of Amanda and the boys the net was soon up, and the lines marked out with the white tape Roland had brought with him, and then the instructions began. First Roland played a game with Amanda, and then Mrs. Hardie tried. It was not very good tennis, but there was plenty of fun and laughter, and every one enjoyed it immensely in their own way and for their own reasons.

The two boys chased, and tumbled over one another in racing after the balls, when some erratic and too vigorous stroke of Mrs. Hardie's or Amanda's sent it flying far out of the court. Mrs. Hardie after one or two games found it rather too warm and tiring, but found consolation for her unwonted efforts in Roland's evident admiration of Amanda. It was worth while being hot and tired to get even with those Dingle people and their English airs. Amanda enjoyed it unaffectedly for the sake of the game; she wanted to learn to play, and her quick eye and deft wrist made her an apt pupil, and she never dreamt of being ashamed to run and jump; and every movement was graceful, because she had no dread of being otherwise. And Roland—he simply let Mrs. Enderby's hints and his own doubts fly away where they would, and gave himself up to the charm of his new attraction. "Bother the Dean of Chester and his granddaughters," "the old squire was safe enough at home and far away, and here was the brightest, prettiest girl he had ever met, and he meant to make the most of it," and Roland never looked beyond the engagement of the present moment. Analysis of his own feelings and motives was the last thing to give him pause in the pursuit of his own way.

Mrs. Hardie was too much of a Canadian to let pleasure interfere with farm work, even the peculiarly pleasant pleasure of detaching a Dingle farm pupil from his allegiance to the Enderby girls; so, as the sun began to sink behind the bluffs, the boys were sent over the pasture to bring home the cows, and the rest of them turned back toward the house.

"If you don't mind, Mrs. Hardie, I'll leave the rackets and balls here," said Roland. "I am going to walk down to Dawson's for the mail, and per-haps we can get another game some evening before long."

"Of course, you can, Mr. Vale; I'll just put them in the lean-to, and we shall be glad to see you any time you like to come down."

"You may be sure I'll come," replied Roland heartily. "Good-bye, Mrs. Hardie; good-bye, Miss Swanson;" and he lifted his cap and started down the lane leading from the house to the town line.

CHAPTER X

Roland had only gone a little way, and was just stopping for a minute to light a cigarette, when he heard a light step behind him, and turned to meet Amanda.

"Oh, Mr. Vale, Mrs. Hardie says, would you mind asking if there is a letter for Herr Hardie; she forgot that the boys were to have gone for it after school?"

"Of course I will, and if there is a letter for 'Herr Hardie,' " with an amused smile, "I'll bring it up to the house as I come back."

"Oh, no, that would be too much trouble," said Amanda quite seriously, "one of us will meet you at the end of the lane, and then it will not be out of your way. So long, Mr. Vale," and she was already on her way back to the house.

Half an hour's brisk walking brought him to Dawson's, the settlement post-office, where a mail-bag was brought once a week from Minnedosa. Mr. Dawson was the nominal postmaster, but being, as he said, no "scollard," he left its management in the hands of his wife and daughter. The mother, a sharp-featured, sharp-tongued little woman of sixty or so; the daughter, rather slow of speech and heavy of frame like her father, but her stolidity hid a world of unsuspected sentiment—sentiment true and nourished by the romantic stories of the literary supplement of weekly Canadian papers, which were sent as complimentary copies to her father by virtue of his office as postmaster.

To the two women the arrival of the mail-bag was the event of the week, and the sorting of the letters a delightful source of surmise and conjecture as to the private affairs of those to whom the letters were addressed, and each enjoyed it in her own way. Old Mrs. Dawson had an abiding conviction that most of her neighbours were in financial difficulties, while Miss Mary Ann let her imagination run riot as to the sentimental possibilities that might be hidden within the missive that passed through her hands. The mail-cart on its road to the next post-office twelve miles away in Sweden, passed Roland as he turned in at old Dawson's gate, and by the time he reached the house the weekly orgie had just begun. A chair was set for him by the "bit of fire" in the stove, for the evening was chilly, and "old Dawson" was told off to entertain "the young man from the Dingle" till the letter-sorting was completed. Old Dawson was one of the "old timers," plodding but unprogressive, who had never adapted the ways of an "Onteerio" bush farm to the bustling ways of the west. For the past few years his son had taken the active charge of the homestead, and he was a tolerated, rather than the honoured, member of his own household. He did not greatly chafe under the narrowness of his sphere of life, he still had his two weekly plugs of tobacco, the one to smoke and the other to chew, his bottle of patent medicine, and the *Weekly Mail and Empire*, and these met his most conscious wants. The farm work he left to his son, the care of the post-office and the family observance of religion to the women folk. He had one hero, John A. Macdonald, one saint, William of Orange, and one saint's day, the 12th of July; and one deep-seated religious conviction—that the Pope of Rome was the embodiment of the Prince of Darkness.

Roland submitted with as good a grace as he could to "old Dawson's" drawings on these rather depressing topics. Fortunately the old man was not as exacting on the attention of his victim as the Ancient Mariner, and was quite satisfied with an occasional note of agreement with his drastic judgments on things political and spiritual.

What did, however, chafe and vex Roland's spirit was the dilatoriness with which the sorting of the letters went on, for he was afraid that it lessened his chances of seeing Amanda at the lane end on his return, but fidget as he might, the two women were not to be hurried in their enjoyment of their weekly sport. From time to time, in the intervals of "Old Dawson's" monologue, scraps of subdued conversation would reach his ears as each letter was scrutinized by two pairs of eyes before being put in its pigeonhole in the office desk.

"Here's another letter for Old Man Jones, the third in three weeks, from Massey Harris; they'll be looking for the money for that binder he got last year." "Who does that second girl of Enderby's know at Maple Creed, Mary Ann?" "Don't you mind the young fellow, mother, that was learning farming there, last year. I did hear as how——" and the voice dropped too low for Roland to catch the rest. "Who's Roland Vale, Esq.? He seems to get——" "Hush, mother, the young man"—and the young man was conscious of being indicated by a backward turn of Mary Ann's thumb. "Miss Amanda Swanson," at Jim Hardie's. "That's the 'Swede' hired girl." "Well, some folks are lucky. I can mind when Jim—— Why here's another letter for her from the old country; who does she know there?" "Oh, it'll be the 'schoolma'am' as used to be in Sweden, and the other from Portage may be from that handsome young Swede fellow"—and again the voices dropped and Roland's ears, now sharp enough, could only catch something about "Swedish picnic," "boat together," "Guess he had to," "May be he'll marry her," and so they rolled poor Amanda's reputation under their tongues with low-voiced, but infinite gusto.

It was over at last, and with "Here's the Dingle mail, young man, and some for Hardies," Roland was free to depart, which he did in a lively state of exasperation at his long delay—and exasperation not soothed at all by the last fragments of conversation about Amanda and her letter from Portage.

It was now quite dark, except for a faint glow of light from the west, and though the day had been quite hot, the air was already sharp and keen. The pace at which Roland walked was more the result of his vexation than of any hope of finding Amanda awaiting his return, but fortune was kind to him, for when he reached the gate where the Rosebank lane came down to the "town line" there was the outline of a figure showing light against the deeper shadows of the land, and it was Amanda's voice that greeted him.

"Why, we thought you must have got lost, Mr. Vale, or else there was no letter for Herr Hardie."

"Oh no, I did not get lost, but those old women up there were an unconscionable time in sorting the mail."

"And is there a letter for Herr Hardie after all?"

"Oh yes, there is a letter for Herr Hardie, and two for Miss Amanda Swanson."

"Two for me! Oh, whoever can they be from?" exclaimed Amanda.

"I'm sure I don't know," replied Roland, rather shortly, for the note of eagerness in Amanda's voice did not escape him; "but those inquisitive old cats seemed to discuss every letter in the bag, till they knew whom it was from, and what it was about."

"But what did they say about mine?" asked Amanda, quite innocently.

"Why, they said one was from the schoolma'am that used to be in Sweden."

"Oh, that will be from Miss Raye; that will be a treat. Please give it to me, Mr. Vale; and the other will be from mother."

"Will it, Miss Swanson? Is there no one else to write to you? Miss Dawson said it came from Portage, and seemed to connect it with 'Sweden' and a picnic and a boat." It was too dark for Roland to see the quick rush of colour to Amanda's face, but he was conscious of a swift change in her voice and manner. "You are quite right, Mr. Vale, about these old women. Thank you for bringing the letters. Good-night."

Roland resumed his way to the Dingle in a generally disgusted frame of mind—with the Dawson women for their "infernal gossip," with himself for laying a trap for Amanda, which she evidently resented, and with himself for caring so much whether Amanda was vexed or pleased, and whether there was "a handsome Swede" in the background or not. It galled his pride of birth and nationality to think that he might have been anticipated in Amanda's heart by a "common Swede fellow," as he said to himself, and while the thought did not diminish aught of his growing passion it placed it on a lower plane.

The roll of a few miles of prairie at the source of a little creek may determine the whole future course of a mighty river—the impulse to a purer love than he had yet known, that had come to Roland from his first impressions of Amanda's beauty of form and mind, was checked and turned into a more dangerous and coarser channel, by the inductive suggestions of Mary Ann and her anxious, too-ready tongue.

CHAPTER XI

The general feeling of discontent with which Roland woke the next morning was not dispelled by the reading of the letters from home, which he had received the night before, and which he left unread till morning, partly because the coal-oil lamp, which he had in his own room gave but a dim and uncertain light, and partly because his anticipations of their contents did not fit in with his infatuation for Amanda. And he was so far right, that he derived but little pleasure from their perusal. First came a curt missive from the squire, enclosing a cheque for ten pounds, and informing him that a similar sum would be sent every three months for pocket money, so long as satisfactory reports of his conduct and work was received from Mr. Enderby, who would also pay and forward to the squire reasonable accounts for clothing and such like.

The squire hoped that he would make the best use of the opportunity given him to redeem the past, and to make some amendment for the grievous disappointment he had been to them. Roland scowled as he read it—"if the squire thought he was going to be treated as a truant schoolboy, with 'old Enderby' for schoolmaster, he was much mistaken." Then came a loving, rambling letter from his mother, half petting and sympathy for her poor boy, in the rough and wild life, as she imagined it of the west, anxiety lest he should get wet and not change his clothes, warnings not to be too venturesome out hunting, and above all to propitiate Mr. Enderby, so that good reports might come to his father, and then, perhaps—who could tell? —in a year or so he might come home again to his mother—this, and much more, of love and tenderness, all winding up with a pathetic postscript, begging him for her sake to go to church when he could, and to say his prayers at night, and not to vex the squire.

Poor Roland was barely twenty-one, the child of emotions and impulses not altogether bad. He read again the squire's letter; it was as cold and friendless as the bare whitewashed log walls of his room—not for his sake was he going to give up what little life and excitement were to be found in such a dead-alive hole as the Dingle. But his mother—she really loved him, and cared what became of him; but the rest of them "at home" did not understand him, why, not half as well as Amanda.

The unconscious bringing together of his mother's love and Amanda's sympathy was that which had poisoned his mind the night before. Finally he decided, honestly enough for the moment, that he would not make opportunities for seeing Amanda; the tennis must go, and if he did see her, he would just be friendly and nothing more, and for the Enderby people and his daily work, he would make the best of it. The last resolution he confined strictly to the pleasure it would give his mother, if good accounts of him were sent home from the Dingle.

He knelt down and said a prayer, the first for a long time past, just the simple little verse he had learnt as a child, and went downstairs, feeling happier and lighter-hearted than he could have told why. Everything seemed to fall in to help his new purpose, and to make his path easy.

Little Frank Hardie had just come up with a note from his father, to say the threshers were coming to Rosebank the next morning, and asking Bert to go down, and help him to kill a "beef." As Roland entered the room, Mr. Enderby was wondering how they could do without Bert's help for the day, as there were still a few acres of oats to stack, and the threshers were to come to the Dingle as soon as they had finished at Jim Hardie's.

"I'll take Bert's place," said Roland willingly, "if you will build the loads and the stack, Mr. Enderby, the 'chore boy' and I can do the pitching."

"Oh, thank you, Vale," said Mr. Enderby, "it will make a hard day for you, but it will help us out of a difficulty."

"Oh, that's all right," replied Roland; "I'm strong enough, and it will get me in good training for our threshing when it comes," and he followed Bert out of the room to the porch. "I say, Bert, you might tell Mrs. Hardie I'm sorry I can't get down for any tennis to-day; I half promised Miss Swanson I would go down after supper."

"Oh, you need not worry about that," said Bert, laughing, "nobody will have time to think of tennis, either there or here, till the threshing is all over—they quite understand work first, play afterwards down there."

It was as Mr. Enderby had foretold—a hard day's work for Roland. The weather, however, had changed since the day before. There had been a slight touch of frost during the night, and with a north-west wind, there was a chill in the air, although the sky was still cloudless. By steady work, and by foregoing the usual early tea, the last load was stacked by six o'clock, and by dusk the horses were stabled and fed, and all the "chores" done for the night. It was a new and pleasant sensation for Roland to feel that he had already done a good day's work, and though he pretended to himself to think little of it, he was really a good deal gratified by Mr. Enderby's hearty slap on his shoulder as they sat down to supper. "There's nothing like hard work to give you an appetite, my boy." Miss Daisy, too, was all friendliness again, having decided for the present, at least, not to surrender Roland to those sly people over at Rosebank, without a struggle.

When supper was over, and the dishes washed and put away, Roland suggested that he should keep a promise made the week before, of teaching the girls to play "bridge," and they were soon seated around the table. Mrs. Enderby and Miss Enderby to play Roland and Miss Daisy. Mrs. Enderby usually offered a mild resistance to the girls playing cards, looking on the game generally played in the west of euchre and poker as being American and low, and possibly distressing to the shade of the Dean of Chester, but "bridge" was quite *comme il faut*, and figured in the society items of the best papers.

Roland was a good player; he did most things well, which were free from any suspicion of work or utility. Mrs. Enderby and Miss Enderby played whist in an old-fashioned way, and Miss Daisy was an apt pupil with a dash of gambling in her disposition, which made the game exciting, though it might have been disastrous if their counters had represented any money value.

They were so wrapt up in their game, that it was nearly ten o'clock, late hours for a Manitoba farm house, when it was broken up by the return of Bert from Rosebank. He was surprised to find any one out of bed, and rallied his mother good-humouredly on allowing such wild dissipation. He had had a very busy day, first in helping to kill and dress the "beef," and then in giving Jim a hand to put up bins in his granary. Then, of course, he had stayed for supper, and a smoke and a chat about the arrangements for the morrow.

The stir of Bert's return woke up Mr. Enderby, who had nominally been reading the *Farmer's Advocate* in an easy chair by the stove, and who was much scandalized at the lateness of the hour.

"Come, girls, come, girls, off to bed with you, or we'll never get breakfast in the morning. What are the plans for to-morrow, Bert?"

"Why, Jim wants to get two men and a team, father, if we can manage it; one of his harvesters left him to-day, and he is a man short to pitch."

"Well, well, that's awkward; I cannot go from home, and we could hardly send the 'chore boy' with the team."

"I know," said Bert doubtfully, "I thought perhaps Roland might not mind going, he could drive the team drawing grain from the thresher to the granary, and if he found that too slow, change off with me for a time, and try pitching."

"Oh, Vale can pitch well enough; he's worked like a Trojan to-day, but ____"

"I will go, Mr. Enderby," interrupted Roland. "Shall not mind in the least," and so it was settled, though Miss Daisy made a little pout to Roland as she said "good-night," and Roland, as he went upstairs to bed, was not without misgiving that going to Rosebank to help to thresh was not quite the way to keep his good resolution of the morning; at least, if it brought him in temptation's way, it was not of his seeking.

CHAPTER XII

Before Amanda reached the house, her curt dismissal of Roland was re-pented of, it was too bad to punish him for Mary Ann Dawson's gossiping tongue, and had he not brought her a letter from Ludwig, a letter safely tucked in the bosom of her blouse, to be read when she reached the seclu-sion of her own little room. Poor Ludwig! perhaps he was coming home, how glad she would be to see his handsome face again, and to hear again the Norse tongue, that she seemed to be forgetting among all these English-speaking people. How proud and shy the great big fellow was in telling her of his love. Perhaps his letter would be more daring, and her eyes were bright, and her cheeks glowing at the anticipations of her fancy as she opened the door at Rosebank.

"Why, what a colour the girl's got," exclaimed Jim Hardie, as Amanda entered the house with the other two letters in her hand; "sure the 'Rose of Sweden' is in full bloom to-night; I'd like to know what Mr. Vale has been saying to you at the end of the lane," he added teasingly.

"Oh, he only stopped for a minute to give me this letter for you, Herr Hardie, and I have one from my old teacher, Miss Raye," and Amanda threw it on the table carelessly, while she took off the wrap she had on her shoulders, and hung it behind the door.

"Why, the threshers will be here to-morrow night," exclaimed Jim, who had glanced over his letter. "They expect to pull in after dark, ready to start the next morning, and I did not expect them till the beginning of next week. Here's a to-do, and no 'beef' killed, and my granary bins all to fix and everything."

"That's just like you, Jim," said Mrs. Hardie reproachfully, "to go and spring the threshers on me without warning. How do you think I am going to feed that great hungry crowd at a moment's notice? You men never think."

"Well, well, mother, it's too bad altogether, but it can't be helped. They were to have gone to Cameron's first; but there, 'old man' Cameron is sick, and they are coming here."

"And me with a week's washing to soak in the lean-to. I might have known when I didn't wash on Monday that something was sure to happen —and not a bit or bite of anything baked in the house, and you know what the threshers are if they don't get the best of everything; everybody in the settlement will hear of it."

"It's too bad, too bad," said Jim sympathetically, "but we must make the best of it. Ted must go up to the Dingle in the morning to see if Bert can help me kill a 'beef,' and Frank can take a note up to the post-office, and ask Mary Ann Dawson to come down and help with the washing and baking."

"Mary Ann Dawson is not going to put her clumsy hands into my flour —the pie-crust would be like rocks; and as for the washing, it would take me all winter to get the things a decent colour again."

"Well, well, mother," said Jim deprecatingly, "every one knows there's no baking like yours, but you and Amanda can do the fine things, and let her do the rough work, and save you getting too tired."

"Oh, I suppose she could do the 'coloured' and pare the potatoes, and such like. Never you marry a farmer, Amanda, unless you want to be worried all your days"; but there was a returning good humour in Mrs. Hardie's voice—after all, she did not dislike the rush and excitement of the threshers; but it would not do to let Jim think so.

"Well, it's no use standing here talking," went on Mrs. Hardie; "you'll have to bring down a bag of flour from the storeroom, Jim, for we'll have to do a big baking. And, Amanda, you can bring in the cream from the dairy, and set it by the stove, ready to churn first thing in the morning, and then you'd best get to bed, for we'll all be tired enough before to-morrow night, let alone before the threshers are gone, and I'll write the notes for the boys to take, and set the bread, and that's all we can do to-night."

It was not long before Amanda found herself in the seclusion of her little room, and free at last to read her two letters. Naturally she read Evelyn Raye's first—from the same primitive instinct which leads a small child to store the currants on the side of its plate, till duty has been done to the less interesting portion of its pudding. Not that Ludwig's letter was for a moment forgotten. It lay well within sight in the little circle of light from her lamp, where she could give it a little nod and smile every time she turned a page of Evelyn's letter, as though to say, "I know you are longing to speak to me, but be patient a little—love is all the greater for waiting!"

And Evelyn's letter was a long letter, full of description of her new home and new duties and new friends. Though she thrilled with impatience, Amanda would not slip a single word, and at the last sheet she became really interested, for Evelyn said that perhaps the next year, she might come back to Manitoba again, with a brother, who was full of schemes to homestead in the west, with Evelyn for his housekeeper, "and would Amanda ask Mr. Hardie, or perhaps young Mr. Enderby, whom she spoke of in her last letter, to advise him as to where he should look for a homestead, and how much money he would need for a start on a farm?"

Even when Evelyn's letter was read carefully through to the last word, Amanda could not forbear coquetting a little longer with herself before yielding to her longing to listen to Ludwig's wooing. She must needs tie her little prim square handkerchief about her neck, let fall the waving glories of her hair over her shoulders—nay, she even turned out the contents of her box to find the old starched sun bonnet, which she never wore at Rosebank, and tied it over her head, with its bows beneath her chin, in her wilful make-believe of how Ludwig was to find her when he came through the garden wicket (of her chamber door) to seat himself by her side on the rustic bench (of her little cot) to tell her of his love—and then with a laughing, mocking glance at herself in the little mirror hanging beside her on the wall, she at last opened her letter—"now, Ludwig, it is just your own little Swedish rose that is listening to you."

Poor Ludwig was not equal to such flights of imagination—the depths of the ocean cannot explain itself to the brook babbling over the pebbles—and Ludwig's passion for Amanda became inarticulate through its own intensity. Just as on the night before he left the house, when he attempted to tell his love, he had sought refuge from his sensitive reserve by branching off into prosaic common-place about his plans for buying a team of horses, and his father's loneliness in the long winters, so now he was in a worse case in trying to tell his love through the unaccustomed medium of pen and ink.

It was a long letter, written on poor paper of a cheap writing-pad in the caboose of the threshing gang, which Ludwig had joined after the harvesting in the Plains was over. It was a long letter, and had cost him most of the hours of his Sunday's rest; but it was very far from the letter which Amanda's quick imagination had pictured, when Roland Vale put it into her hand at the lane end.

Poor Ludwig, who was absolutely heart-sick with the longing to see Amanda, who sat down to his writing with the desperate intention to reveal all his love to her, found he had set himself a task beyond his powers. With a perversity impossible to any one but a too diffident lover, he repeated his already deep offence of talking of dollars, when Amanda was thirsting for epithets of tenderness, and of substituting his father for himself as the one who needed Amanda most.

It was very rough and uncomfortable with the threshing gang, most of whom were Galicians; but he had made up his mind to "tough it out" till the end of the season for the sake of the big wages ("he thinks of nothing but his miserable dollars," said Amanda to herself). Now, however, he had changed his mind, and hoped to be at home again in a couple of weeks, and Amanda's heart beat more quickly, but he went on to write that he was "very uneasy about my father, and the little house at Otter Lake," and

Amanda tapped her little foot impatiently on the floor. "Twice," the letter continued, "fires have been started in the bush behind the house, and on the night before he wrote, my father was roused by the dog barking, and on going out found the haystack in the little meadow by the lake burning. My father never had an enemy, and is never afraid, but it has made me very uneasy, and as soon as this month is out, I shall start for home again. He tells me he was down at your father's place the other day, and your mother said you might stay on at Herr Hardie's till spring, and that you were making a lot of new friends among the English people down there. She seemed quite pleased to think you would not be satisfied to go back to the old quiet life in 'Sweden' again. I shall call at Herr Hardie's on my way home, and hope you will not be sorry to see your old friend."

Poor Ludwig! after Roland Vale's ready tongue and freely admiring glances, his involved awkward phrases, and ill-concealed jealousy cut but a poor figure. In her heart of hearts Amanda knew how deep and true his love was, but she was longing for its expression in passionate vows of love, which to him were an impossibility. Her disappointment turned to angry reproach again, his thinking of money, of his father's haystacks, and his implied contempt of new friends. "If he likes to be horrid—he can be," Amanda said to herself, and so cried herself to sleep.

CHAPTER XIII

Though from loyalty to her sex and to farmers' wives in general, Mrs. Hardie had felt it her duty to scold and fret at the announcement of the unexpected word of the threshers, she had not the least doubt in her mind but that she would be fully equal to the emergency, and her spirits rose to the occasion. The threshing is the great event of the year on a Manitoba farm; it forms the most engrossing topic of every gathering of neighbours' wives in the fall of the year. It is the fashion to speak of it as a great trial, and weariness of the flesh; as the crowning profit of the "men folk's general selfishness and lack of consideration." If there is a bountiful harvest, it is not, as one might expect, matter of congratulation and thankfulness, but an additional grievance which will prolong the visitation of Providence, and may even result in having to keep the threshers over Sunday—the adding of insult to injury. Should the crop be but scanty and perhaps touched by frost, then—so the aggrieved housewife declares—the threshers will eat more than the harvest is worth.

The wise husband, like Agag, "goes delicately" when he broaches the subject of the advent of the threshers to his wife. In any case he is sure to make a mistake, there is no safe channel between Scylla and Charybdis of a too cheerful aspect, and a too deprecating sympathy in the approaching trial. Yet there is nothing so secretly dear to the heart of a true western farmer's wife as a successful threshing. She accepts it as the supreme test of her capacity to "run the house." To come through the threshing with flying colours is to establish a name and reputation, which will be an object of envy to every other woman in the settlement, and a tradition among threshing gangs for years to come. To fail is rather worse than a moral delinquency—it is a confession of incapacity. If the housewife fails in the matter of the quantity or quality of "the grub," then the husband is an object of contempt in the eyes of the women, and of an insulting sympathy on the part of the men.

At the threshing the western-born farmer's wife usually comes to her own, and settles some old scores with her less capable "Old Country" neighbours. And she settles them none the less effectually, because she is full of expressed neighbourliness and offers to help them in their difficulties. Jim Hardie's was always a favourite place with the threshers. Jim's energy and good temper kept things running smoothly at the work, and Mrs.

Hardie always gave the squarest of "square meals," well served, piping hot, and on the table at the blow of the whistle to stop work.

This year Mrs. Hardie had a double incentive to make the threshing a success. She had not only a reputation to sustain, but she intended the difference between their threshing and the way things were done at the Dingle to be most obviously marked—to the latter's disadvantage.

The Dingle people, though matters had improved the last year or two, since Bert took the management more into his own hands, had never quite achieved the spirit which is essential to a successful threshing. Mr. Enderby was too fussy round the machine, and the girls, though they worked hard and had plenty of food of all kinds, could not, as the threshers expressed it, "run the show." Once in the early days, Mr. Enderby had suffered the inexpressible indignity to a western farmer of being called aside by the "boss" of the gang after dinner, and being told, "If you can't do better than this at supper, Mister, we shall have to pull out, the boys won't stand it"; and after supper the gang "pulled out," and he was left with the remainder of his stacks unthreshed. This unheard-of event fixed the date for all kinds of reminiscences, when "old hands" were smoking in the caboose before turning in, and many a yarn would be prefaced with, "Do you mind the year when 'Big Ben' pulled out from old Enderby's?"

Mrs. Enderby never appeared in public at all at the threshing, she could never bring herself to so far forget what was due to the exacting shade of the Dean of Chester, as to pour out tea and hand round smoking dishes of meat and potatoes, to the noisy, loud-laughing and jesting crowd, to whom the conventional politenesses of the table were a thing unknown. She thought she had done all that could be expected of her, when she offered her daughters as propitiatory sacrifices to "the ways of the country."

Though Amanda woke with a dull sense of unhappiness on the morning after receiving Ludwig's disappointing letter, she was too true a western girl to dream of humouring her feelings in the face of the pressing duties of the day. She jumped out of bed, and dressed quickly at Mr. Hardie's first call, and after rousing the two boys, hurried downstairs to get ready the breakfast, and to heat the water in the big boiler for the washing.

The "chore boy," after being fortified with two rounds of toast and a thick slice of cold pork, was despatched with the "buckboard" and pony to fetch Mary Ann Dawson, and by the time they returned the white wear was hanging on the line, and the churning done.

Mary Ann and the "coloured" were relegated to the lean-to, with the "chore boy" to turn the washing-machine, and Mrs. Hardie and Amanda were left with a clear field to begin the baking. First there were two large pans of dough to be mixed and set to rise till they should be ready for the oven after dinner, and then the two settled down steadily to make "pies" and cakes, sufficient for a rough estimate of twenty men, three times a day for two days—with a reserve, in case any breakdown of the threshing-machine should prolong the visitation to a third day.

Now a western pie is not a pie at all, in the ordinary sense of the word, seeing that it is baked on a large tin plate. Sometimes it consists of two layers of paste, with the differentiatory material between; sometimes it is merely a large open tart. The variety is limited, only to the maker's skill and available materials. Most farmers' wives were satisfied in the early days, if they had an abundance of pies filled with raisins and currants, or dried apples. Since times had been better the threshers had become more exacting in their tastes, and rather disposed to turn up their noses at the old-established stand-by.

For the past year or two Mrs. Hardie had added to her reputation by drawing freely at threshing time on her stores of home-made raspberry and wild strawberry jam. It cost her many pangs, when she thought of the hot, back-aching hours she had spent in the hay meadows, picking the strawberries, to see the results of her labours engulfed by the hungry men of the "gang," but those who would reign must pay the price of sovereignty. This year she was determined to set a new standard that should be a crushing contrast to the best that the "Dingle folk" could attempt. Not only was her paste of the flakiest that deft fingers and unsparing fresh butter could devise; she even went beyond all threshing precedent, and made three dozen of lemon pies, such as were usually reserved for very special high days and holidays.

When Jim and Bert Enderby came in from killing and dressing the "beef" for a lunch-dinner at noon, Jim was filled with admiration and compunction as he saw the long rows of pies set out on the big table, and the hot, tired faces of the two women.

"Why, little woman, you're just wonderful, wonderful; the threshers will think they have come to a wedding. You'll have to have another to help you and Amanda, when the right boy comes along to pluck 'the Rose of Sweden'—but you shouldn't work so hard; we'll have you both 'tuckered out' before the 'gang' comes."

"Oh, if it has got to be done, it may as well be done properly," said Mrs. Hardie, with an air of resignation; "only you'll have to do with cold meat and bread and cheese for your dinner, we've had no time to fix potatoes and pudding."

"Oh, don't trouble about us, Mrs. Hardie," said Bert, "we shall do very well; and I am coming to the threshing to-morrow, and shall have my share of the good things then."

"That reminds me," said Jim. "Can two of you come to help us from the Dingle? I'm going to be a man short—that long-legged chap we called

Steve, who has been with us all harvest, wants to quit to-night. He has been 'working' with the threshers at two or three of the neighbours', and I expected him to stay on till the end of the month; but some one of his folks is sick in Ontario, and he's bound to go right off."

"Oh, I daresay we can manage. My father can hardly get away, but Vale could drive a team all right; he's a good driver."

"I'm thinking," said Jim; "he's not much used to hard work. Playing his tennis games with the 'wimmen' folk is more in his line."

"Oh, he's never had to work. But he's handy enough if it takes his fancy, and he's fond of horses."

"Well, if he wouldn't mind, it would help me out," said Jim.

"I'm sure he won't mind," broke in Amanda innocently. "He said yesterday he'd like to come to the threshing if he wouldn't be in the way."

"Well, if he's in the way at the machine," said Jim, "we'll know what to do with him. We'll just send him to the house to help you, only I'm afraid the two of you might forget all about the cooking."

"Oh, there will be no time for any foolishness to-morrow," said Mrs. Hardie, rather sharply, for Amanda blushed at Jim's remark, and Mary Ann Dawson, who had been steadily working her way through a very substantial meal, gave a subdued giggle, and looked at Jim in a very knowing way.

"That young man does have a power of mail," remarked Mary Ann. "He was that fidgety yesterday while mother and me were sorting the letters, and were just wondering, innocent-like, who was writing to Miss Swanson here."

"Let me take the baby, Mrs. Hardie; I've finished my dinner," broke in Amanda; and in the stir of her getting up from the table, the thread of Mary Ann's remarks was broken, for Jim and Bert rose at the same time to fill their pipes before going out to their work—though Amanda's embarrassment and rosy cheeks were not lost to Mrs. Hardie's observant eyes.

Mrs. Hardie and Amanda devoted the afternoon to baking the bread and the making of cakes—Mary Ann, rather to her secret indignation, being left to the washing of all available plates and dishes, the cleaning of knives and forks, and the paring of large quantities of potatoes and carrots ready for the morrow. She consoled herself somewhat by a diligent catechizing of the "chore boy," who helped her, as to the whole manner of life of the Rosebank family, their degree of intimacy with the Dingle folk, and how often Roland Vale had been down to Rosebank. The "chore boy" was loquacious, a secret worshipper of Amanda, and proud to find his conversation of so much interest. By supper-time Mary Ann had all the material to supply her with the post-office gossip for a month to come. She was rather resentful of the subordinate position evidently to be assigned to her at the threshing, but her greed for sentiment and scandal led her to give a ready assent to Mrs. Hardie's request at night, that she would come down every day till the threshing was over.

CHAPTER XIV

Roland Vale's keenness overnight to volunteer for the threshing rather lost its edge when he was aroused the next morning at daybreak by Bert, and turned out to find a cold chilling morning, the view from his window cut off by a heavy fog, in which the rising sun was marked by a dull crimson blur in the east. By the time he got downstairs, he found Bert had fed the horses, and was preparing breakfast, as the rest of the household were still in bed.

"We'll have to hurry up, Roland," said Bert, as he placed two steaming plates of porridge on the table, and sat down, "the whistle to start threshing will blow in half an hour—but make a good breakfast; we'll get nothing more till noon, and we'll have lots of work."

"Oh, I'm not hungry," said Roland, who pushed his porridge away after two or three spoonfuls. "I'll have some bread and butter; I can't eat a heavy meal at this heathenish hour in the morning."

"Well, you'll wish you had," said Bert, getting up for a second supply of porridge. "Have some of that cold pork. There's nothing like fat pork on a cold morning; it stays with you better than porridge."

"It won't stay with me," retorted Roland shortly, he found Bert's cheerful good-spirits exasperating. The rough-and-ready way of getting breakfast, which Bert accepted as a matter of course, to him was simply squalid and distasteful.

The tablecloth carelessly thrown over one-half of the table, the litter of newspapers and the girls' sewing on the other end, the light of the coal-oil lamp struggling with the dull rays of the morning through the windows, the ill-carved joint of pork on a greasy dish, Bert helping himself to fried potatoes out of the frying-pan—it was all "beastly" to Roland, and with a muttered oath to himself he got up from the table, lit a cigarette, and sat by the stove till Bert finished his meal. He had not long to wait, for Bert's breakfast, if hearty, was hasty, and in a few minutes they were rattling in the waggon over the rough lane to the "town line," Bert keeping the horses on a sharp trot in the hope of reaching Rosebank before the threshing began, it being rather a point of honour to be "on hand" at the blow of the whistle to commence work.

They fell a little short of attaining that desirable end, for the faint sound of the whistle reached them as they turned in through the Rosebank pasture to take the short cut to the house, and as they passed the corral the "chore boy" hailed them with the information that the threshers were starting on the wheat on the new breaking, which meant another half mile's rough driving before they came to the scene of operations. It was rather a weird scene, for the mist still hung heavily in the lower air, and the engine smoke showed with a lurid light through the gloom. The separator was drawn in between two large stacks of wheat, to the top of which men were scrambling with the aid of their forks to throw down the first sheaves to the table, where two band-cutters stood with sharp knives ready to cut the twine binding the sheaves before passing them into the separator. Jim Hardie had just given the "boss" of the gang the signal that all was ready to start threshing, as Bert and Roland drove up alongside two other waggons by the side of the separator.

"Good morning, Bert; morning, Mr. Vale," shouted Jim, coming out of the mist and smoke by the engine, "you're just in time, and everything is going fine. If you'll 'pitch' for a while, Bert, I'll take the first trip with Mr. Vale, to the granary, and then he'll know all about it," and Jim, first throwing into the waggon a dozen or so empty bags from a pile near by, jumped into the waggon and took the reins from Bert, who was soon on the top of one of the stacks to be threshed.

With a little manœuvring of the waggon in Jim's skilful hands, it was backed up to the separator, the spout delivering the grain swung over the waggon box, and the wheat running into the bag held to receive it.

Their bags were soon filled, and then they started off with their load, across the stubble to the granary, their place at the separator being taken by another waggon. At the granary they found one of the gang to help to empty the bags, and to shovel back the wheat in the bins. They returned to the machine on the trot, passing on their way a second load of wheat, and a third waggon was just ready to start for the granary as they drew up to take its place.

It was stirring, exciting work, and Roland's grumpiness soon wore off. After a short struggle with the fog, the sun emerged victorious, and was shining brightly in a cloudless sky; the air, keen and invigorating, made quick and lively movement a pleasure. Every one was working with will, and Roland's mercurial temperament responded readily to its environment. He had a spirited team to drive, and of horses he was really fond, and for once he felt that the offensive term of "a green Englishman" could not be applied to him.

Long before noon he wished that he had taken Bert's advice at breakfast-time in better part, and the blowing of the whistle just as he returned with his empty waggon to the separator was a welcome sound. Every one stopped work at once—the "pitchers" jumped or slid down from the stacks, and scrambled into his waggon for a ride back to the house.

After stopping for a minute at the door to let the threshers get out, Bert and Roland drove round, and by the time they returned, the rest of the gang were already seated at the table. There was little talking and less ceremony. Mrs. Hardie, Mary Ann Dawson, and Amanda moved swiftly from the kitchen to the "living-room" where the table was set, bringing in smoking dishes of vegetables and steaming jugs of tea. At the little table on one side, Jim carved away steadily at a huge roast of beef, which was placed as carved on the table, and there every one helped himself and passed it on to his neighbour.

At another time Roland would have been disgusted at the lack of what he would have considered the ordinary decencies of civilization, but to-day he was too hungry to be squeamish, and he helped himself to potatoes with his fork and to salt with the blade of his knife, as if it were quite the natural thing to do.

With the removal of the meat, and the bringing in of clean plates for the plum pudding and the pies, there was a lull in the rattle of knives and forks, and Roland had time to look about him, and to take in his surroundings. To his eyes they seemed indeed a rough-and-ready crew, which was natural enough, for there is nothing more difficult than to judge from first impressions the social standing and material prosperity of the individuals forming the average threshing gang. All were warmly and roughly clad, all seemed equally intent on making a "square meal," and most of them seemed on familiar terms with one another, for it was "Jack" here and "Bob" or "Mac" there—surnames and the conventional "Mister" seemed quite at a discount.

Yet Roland could not help noticing that if any of them addressed Amanda or Mrs. Hardie there was deference of manner and courteousness of tone, which to him seemed incongruous with their rough-and-ready way of addressing each other—he had yet to learn that in the west the essentials of a gentleman are quite apart, not only from garments and table manners, but also from the niceties of grammar which in the "Old Country" may be more seriously injurious to social claims than moral delinquencies. One or two fair-complexioned young fellows did indeed call Amanda by her name, and seemed to Roland to be unduly familiar in calling to her to fill their cups, or to bring them some pie, but she did not resent it in the least. One young "oaf," as Roland mentally dubbed him, even put his arm round her waist, as she reached over him to take a dish from the table. And he only received a laughing rebuke and a pinching of his ear. The fair-complexioned lads were old schoolfellows of Amanda's back in "Sweden," and the one so over bold was a cousin, whom Amanda had played with since she was a baby. But Roland did not know that, and relapsed into disgusted gloom till the meal was over.

After dinner there was a spare half-hour before resuming work, during which the gang broke up into little groups outside the house for a chat and a smoke. Here Roland was joined by Bert Enderby, who had sat at the other end of the table during dinner.

"Well, Roland, what do you think of threshing?" asked Bert, as he filled his pipe; "pretty hard work, isn't it?"

"Oh, I like it well enough," replied Roland, "but I don't think much of some of the gang; they're too free-and-easy for me."

"Why, what do you mean?" asked Bert, surprised. "I thought they were a very well-mannered lot; of course, they don't stand on ceremony—but I didn't hear a rough word, not in the house."

"Oh, it's not that," said Roland, "but some of these rough-looking louts called Miss Swanson by her Christian name, and one even put his arm round her waist."

"That was her cousin, Carl Swanson," replied Bert, laughing; "of course, Carl and the other Swede boys in the gang know Amanda as well as I know my sisters."

"Oh, of course, then that makes it different," said Roland inwardly much relieved, though insensibly to himself, it put his feeling towards Amanda on a lower level to find that her place by birth and upbringing was among what he, with his English prejudices, regarded as just "common working people."

He had, like many other young Englishmen of his class, a moral code, based on distinctions of social standing, which would have saved him from giving Amanda a dishonourable thought so long as in his own mind he put her on the same footing as the Enderby girls, or his own sisters; but if, after all, she were only a peasant girl—more lively and captivating than any girl he had yet met—why, of course—and he did not put the sequence of ideas into words, even in his own mind. When Bert went to the stables to water and hitch up the team, he strolled into the house, where the "wimmen folk" were now having dinner; and until the whistle blew to return to work, he kept them laughing with his light-hearted fun about the quantity of good things the threshers consumed, and the serious silence in which they settled down to a meal, as if it were a race against time.

Mary Ann Dawson and Amanda went to the door to watch him start off with his team, and the women were fairly delighted with his face and easy manners "so friendly like," as he expressed it; but Amanda was not quite so sure whether she liked the change from his careful courteousness of the tennis court to the "Good-bye, Amanda, I mean Miss Swanson; be sure and keep me a big pie for supper," with which he jumped into his waggon, and followed the rest of the gang, already on their way back to the machine.

CHAPTER XV

The good luck which favoured the beginning of the Rosebank threshing stayed with it to the end, though it was well on the third afternoon before the shrill and continued shrieking of the whistle announced that the last sheaf had passed through the cylinders of the separator. But this prolonging of the anticipated duration of the threshing was not owing to any serious breakdowns on the part of the machinery, but to a case far more agreeable to Jim Hardie, and one which reconciled Mrs. Hardie to the putting up of a third dinner—the yield of bushels to the acre exceeded by far Mr. Hardie's cautious estimate of his crop before the threshing began. When Jim had gone over his fields with Bert Enderby, while they were closely dotted with the stooks of well-grown, ripened grain, he had gone so far as to venture the remark that he thought it would turn out pretty "tidy." The tally of bushels handed to him by the "boss" of the gang went far beyond "pretty tidy"; it was a record crop, not only for Rosebank, but for the whole settlement.

Though there was no decent pretext for the "gang" to stay at Rosebank over Sunday, there was a general feeling that it was hardly worth while to start on a fresh job so late in the week. So it was decided to move over to the Dingle and get everything in shape for an early start on the Monday morning, and then to lay off for the rest of the afternoon. Those of the gang whose homes were in the settlement went home, and the young fellow from "Sweden" borrowed a waggon and team from Jim and struck north; promising to return by sunset on Sunday evening. This arrangement suited Bert Enderby very well, as it would leave only three or four Galicians to be provided for at the Dingle, and they would stay in the caboose except at meal times, when they could be fed in the kitchen. At his suggestion, too, his mother had sent by him on Saturday a very friendly and neighbourly note to Mary Ann Dawson, asking her if she would help them through their threshing. "My son tells me," wrote Mrs. Enderby, "that it is quite wonderful the way in which everything runs smooth with you in charge," and Mary Ann had risen readily to the flattering bait, and had promised to come and "see them through."

Roland slept late on the Sunday morning; he was honestly tired with the steady work at the threshing, and Bert gave such a good account of his energy and willingness, that Mrs. Enderby issued orders for him not to be disturbed till nearly dinner-time, which was put back half an hour on his account. "Poor Roland! he must have found their rough ways a trial at Rosebank," said Mrs. Enderby to her husband, who rather fussed at any departure from their usual hour, to sit down to table with Galicians, who never wash and cannot speak a word of English, "and his aunt married to a Gold Stick in Waiting to the House of Lords—or something quite nearly related to the peerage. I know what the poor boy's feelings must have been, and even Mr. Hardie, though he is so kind and good when we need help— even he helps himself to butter with the same knife that he cuts his meat with."

"Oh, I don't think you need worry about that, mother," said Bert, laughing. "I fancy Roland was too hungry to be fastidious, and he seemed to make himself quite at home down there, and a little of the rough-and-ready will do him all the good in the world."

"Perhaps so," admitted Mrs. Enderby doubtfully, "but I can feel for his poor mother, if she knew. Perhaps, after all, it's not so dangerous as his going down there for tennis with that young—ah—Swedish person."

"Well, mother, your anxieties will soon be over," said Bert, good-humouredly. "The threshers will be gone, I hope, in a couple of days, and I fancy the 'young Swedish person' will return to her native wilds at freeze up, which won't be long now; and, any way, I am going to see Jim Hardie this afternoon, and have a talk about our hunting trip, and Roland will go with us on that, and be safe out of harm's way for a while."

At this point Roland appeared, and they sat down to dinner, and the conversation fell to Bert and Mr. Enderby, who talked "yield to the acre," "smut and rust," and probable "grades" till the meal was over.

Sunday afternoon at the Dingle was usually a quiet one. Mrs. Enderby retired to her room, nominally to write letters. Mr. Enderby lay down on a home-made lounge in the end of the dining-room, which, partially screened off by a pair of curtains, was called his "study," the *Farmer's Advocate*, which wooed the drowsy god of slumber on weekday evenings being replaced, as was more seemly and equally effectual by a volume of "plain" sermons. The girls washed up the dishes in the kitchen, and then went upstairs to make themselves tidy, which, with a little surreptitious novel reading, usually took up most of the time till the early supper. Roland followed Bert out to the stables, where there was a little work to be done in the way of watering the cattle and feeding the pigs.

Bert hoped that when this was done Roland would return to the house, as he did not want him to go down with him to Rosebank. He was more uneasy than he would admit to his mother about Roland's admiration for Amanda, and he had been quick to see during the last two days that Mrs. Hardie was quite willing to encourage Roland's infatuation, though he did not guess the motives that lay behind her encouragement.

He devoutly wished Amanda were safe again among her own people, but he judged truly enough of Roland's disposition to realize that any show of opposition would only render him more persistent—perhaps after all it would be safer to take him with him, rather than for Roland to fancy he had been purposely left behind.

So when he had prolonged the work as long as he could without Roland giving any sign of leaving him, he remarked casually:

"What are you going to do for the rest of the afternoon?—I am going to drop over to Rosebank for a while to have a chat with Jim about our hunting trip. Will you come along?"

"Oh, I don't mind if I do," replied Roland, equally casually. He too had been watching for a way of escape, for Mrs. Hardie had dropped a hint on his leaving the house on the day before—"we shall not be so busy to-morrow, if you like to come down." Bert's suggestion relieved him of any need to find an excuse for his visit.

The two young men received a very hearty welcome at Rosebank, where every one, as Jim Hardie said, was "taking it easy," after the rush of work of the past few days.

As the day was chilling, a little fire had been made in the big box stove in the living-room, the children had been sent upstairs with liberty for such subdued play as should not disturb their father's nap on the lounge. Mrs. Hardie and Amanda were sitting by the stove discussing the latest edition of "Eaton's Catalogue," the best-read literature of the west. If a Canadian farmhouse has a book on horse-doctoring, and "Eaton's Catalogue," and a Bible, it has a library. The conversation was at first general, and of the crop and the threshing, but they soon separated into two groups—Roland joining Mrs. Hardie and Amanda by the stove, while Bert and Mr. Hardie were discussing their plans for the deer hunt.

His yearly "hunt" was Jim's one great holiday—the one pleasure for which he would let the routine of steady work slide, even for a day, and for the taking of which he made many deprecating apologies to his "little woman."

For the past few years it had been Jim's custom to go up to "Sweden" at the first snowfall after the open season for deer-hunting began, and to make his headquarters at Ole Swanson's, or Christian Nielson's, returning home as soon as he was successful in shooting "the single" deer, to which each hunter is restricted by the game laws. This year the hunting was to be on a larger scale.

Jim had purchased in the spring a quarter-section of timber and meadow land on the north shore of Otter Lake, on which he had built a rough shanty and a stable. These, which were primarily intended as a shelter for himself and team when putting up hay in the summer or cutting wood in the winter, needed but little to make them sufficiently comfortable for the not very exacting requirements of western hunters. It was decided that as soon as the Dingle threshing was over, Jim and Bert should make a preliminary trip to the shanty, taking with them a camp stove, cooking utensils, and a store of provisions, sufficient to last the party of three for a couple of weeks, as in addition to the hunting they intended to do a little trapping and fishing before returning home.

Bert and Jim had been too absorbed in their own plans to pay any attention to the group round the stove, though Jim was conscious that it would require a little diplomacy on his part to reconcile his wife to his going off to the bush for two weeks. Mrs. Hardie usually exacted a *quid pro quo* in some shape or other on the rare occasions when he left her out of his calculations. Though hitherto he had only dropped a few tentative hints about the deer-hunting—such as wondering whether they would get an early snowfall, or a chance suggestion that a little deer meat would be good after so much beef and pork—Mrs. Hardie read his thoughts like a book, and had already decided on the price he was to pay for his holiday.

Now, though the soul of hospitality in a free-and-easy, neighbourly way, Jim loathed a fuss which upset the regular work of the farm; above all did he hate anything which could seem to his poorer neighbours a matter of display or pride in his prosperity. He liked well enough for a few neighbours to drop in for a game of "Pedro," or even if a couple of sleigh loads of young people came for a "surprise party," and insisted on an impromptu dance to the music of his fiddle—but beyond this he would never go.

"Well, mother," said Jim, getting up from the lounge and drawing a chair up to the group by the stove, where a subdued but steady flow of conversation had been going on for some time, led by Mrs. Hardie. "Well, mother, what are you and Amanda here so busy about? The 'wimmen folk' are never too tired to talk, are they, Mr. Vale?" he added jocularly.

"Well, now just listen to that," exclaimed Mrs. Hardie, "as if you and Mr. Enderby had not been so wrapt up in your crops and things, that you forgot all about us—'wimmen folk' indeed."

"Now, we didn't say a word about crops, did we, Bert?" said Jim, who saw an opening for bringing up the hunting trip, under the protecting cover of Bert's and Roland's presence; "we were just talking a bit about running up to the bush for a day or two to see if we couldn't get a deer, and to let Mr. Vale have a little sport after all his hard work at the threshing."

"Hark to that now, Mr. Vale," said Mrs. Hardie, mockingly; "you'd think Jim was that unselfish he didn't care whether he went himself or not. There's 'the men' every time—it's work, work, work, and you never see them for five minutes, and as soon as there's a chance for a little pleasure, off they go by themselves to the woods, hunting and living like Indians, and we 'wimmen folk' may be left to ourselves."

"Come, come, little woman, don't be too hard on us," said Jim; "Mr. Vale will be thinking I am a terrible fellow."

"Well, isn't he now, Mr. Vale?" asked Mrs. Hardie, turning towards Roland; "you just see what he'd say if I want a little trip of my own."

"Sure, mother, we'd like it fine, if you and Amanda would come and run the shanty for us while we go hunting."

"Thank you, Jim Hardie," replied Mrs. Hardie, with great scorn. "Since when have you had a 'squaw'? You'll want me to live in a 'teepee' next."

"Oh, that's just his joking," interposed Bert Enderby, who knew that Jim's fondness for hunting was rather a sore point; "you really must forgive Jim this time, as it's more my fault than his."

"Well, I suppose, I must, if you say so," relented Mrs. Hardie, "but you must let us have our little bit of fun before you do."

"Sure, little woman, you can have anything you like," said Jim eagerly; "it's glad I am for you to have all the pleasure you can—it's little enough I'm thinking, with the work and children and all."

"There, I told you so," broke in Amanda. "I knew he would let us have it."

"Have what?" asked Mr. Hardie, bewildered and looking from Amanda to Roland.

"Why, just a little dance now the threshing is over, and before I go back to 'Sweden,' Herr Hardie," said Amanda eagerly. "I've been telling Mr. Vale of the fine times we have at home in the winter, with dances every week, and the sleigh rides home by moonlight."

"Well, well, I suppose we must let the young folk have their way," said Jim doubtfully, "if mother here does not mind the fuss and bother."

"Oh, she says she doesn't mind a bit," said Amanda, "and I'll do the work."

"Yes," interposed Roland, "and I can come and help decorate the room and get the floor ready."

"It seems to me, Bert, that you and me are the outsiders this trip," said Jim, good-humouredly. He did not like the price that he foresaw he must pay for his hunting trip, but it was too late to grumble now, and happily for his peace of mind, he did not realize how actively his "little woman" had "run the show." If it was to be done, he wanted it done well; so it ended in Mrs. Hardie, Amanda, and Roland being given a free hand in making all the preparations, Jim only stipulating that all the young folks of the settlement were to be given "a bid," without any difference of a social kind. Roland was in the highest spirits all the way home to the Dingle. Amanda had been all gaiety and smiles—his good resolutions had flown to the winds; and if Bert was rather grumpy about it, "why, let him be." Two western notions Roland had accepted very readily and intended to make his own—the right "to run his own show" his own way, and the right outside of working hours "to be his own boss."

CHAPTER XVI

After much discussion between Mrs. Hardie and Amanda, it was decided that the dance should be on the Monday week, after the Sunday spoken of in the preceding chapter. This would allow a clear week for a general house cleaning and the doing of the necessary cooking, and would bring it to the evening before the first day of the deer-hunting season, when if there should be the necessary snowfall, Jim and the hunting party would leave for the bush.

While not intending to relax anything of the free hand which Jim had given her, Mrs. Hardie felt that it was desirable that he should suffer as little as possible from the preliminary upheaval of his domestic arrangements, and from the discomforts of the return to ordinary ways after the dance was over. On the Monday and Tuesday Jim was away at the Dingle threshing from daylight to dark; on the Wednesday he left home in the early morning with a load of wheat for Minnedosa, bringing back not only the supplies for the hunting trip, but also a big box of groceries for the cooking for the dance; and on the Thursday he and Bert Enderby went north to fix their camps, not returning till the Friday night, all of which kept the "men folk"—by which Mrs. Hardie meant Jim—out of the way.

By this time a great change had taken place in the weather—the long spell of bright clear days, with sharp frosty nights, was broken—by one of those swift panoramic shifts in which the Manitoba climate delights, the fall gave place to winter. The ground, which had been alternately freezing in the night and thawing during the day, was in one bitter night congealed to iron—and then came a day of leaden sky and thick-falling snow. As weather it was vile, but it was full of promise for the success of the hunting, and by this time Jim was too full of spirit of the chase to mind either the discomforts of the elements or the disorder of the house.

The freedom for preparing for the dance, which came to Mrs. Hardie and Amanda through Jim's preoccupation in his approaching hunt, came also to Roland, from the confusion attendant on the threshing at the "Dingle." Thanks to Mary Ann Dawson's assistance, that ordeal was passed without disorder, and Roland's energy in helping with the work while it lasted consoled his frequent and long absences at Rosebank during the latter part of the week.

Miss Daisy, indeed, made certain slighting allusions to the approaching festivity.

"Of course Bert and Mr. Vale might find such an 'omnium gatherum' amusing," she remarked disdainfully, when the bid came for the entire family in the shape of a very formal note of invitation from Mrs. Hardie. "It will be a new experience for you, Mr. Vale," she added with a quizzical laugh; "you'll see the greatest collection of the beasts of the field to be met with outside of Noah's Ark or a travelling show."

"For shame, Daisy," said Mrs. Enderby hastily; "you know everything is always quite respectable at Mr. Hardie's, even if it is so different to our English ideas."

"Oh, yes, Mr. Vale, it will be quite respectable," retorted Miss Daisy, who was too sore at Roland's evident eagerness to be easily put down by her mother's deprecating apologies. "Oh, yes, it will be eminently respectable, and Mrs. Hardie will comfort herself in strict accordance with the etiquette column of the *Family Herald*. Mr. Vale—ah, will you and Miss Mary Ann Dawson take your places for the first 'square' with Mr. Jake Murphy and Miss Cline Pederson for your *vis à vis*—ah—you have not met them before—allow me—Mr. Roland Vale, Miss Pederson, Mr. Jake Murphy," and Miss Daisy completed her pantomime with a sweeping curtsey.

"Hang it all!" exclaimed Roland angrily, "you were making all manner of fuss over Miss Dawson while she was helping you with your threshing. It was 'Mary Ann, you are so kind, Mary Ann; do come in the parlour and rest awhile,' and now why the—why should I not dance with her, or you with Jake Murphy for the matter of that?"

"Thank you, Mr. Vale, but I draw the line at a 'hoe down,' " and Miss Daisy sought her usual safety, in a retreat to the kitchen before her mother's rebuke could fall for her use of the last expression.

The upshot of all this was that, after doing his stable work after dinner, Roland went off nearly every day to Rosebank, and remained there till late in the evening, usually going straight to his own room on his return. Poor Mrs. Enderby had her hands full between condemning Roland's absence from work to her husband, and keeping the appearance of a truce between Miss Daisy and Roland when they met at meal times; moreover, she grieved much secretly at the suppositional feelings of Roland's mother, if she could know how he was degenerating from the standard of his "gold stick," and other relatives "at home."

If Roland was in a constant state of irritation while at the Dingle, he was fully compensated by the friendliness of his welcome every time he went down to Rosebank. Not only was Mrs. Hardie his firm ally in every suggestion he made for the success of the dance, but Amanda herself was a new and altogether more charming and tantalizing Amanda than she had been in the earlier and more formal days of their companionship.

Roland did not understand in the least the reasons that lay behind the change in Amanda's manner to himself, nor did his impulsive and undisciplined nature seek to look beyond a change that he found altogether to his liking, since he had put his own responsibility for its future consequences on one side as a thing beyond his control. Great as had been his attraction towards Amanda at their first meeting, and sensitive as he had been to her beauty, her unconscious refinement of speech and manner and dress had set her in his mind among those of his own social class; but he had not the innate strength of character to maintain her there in his own mind against the scornful sarcasm of Miss Daisy, and the obvious familiarity of such of her own people as he had met at the Rosebank threshing.

What there remained to him of scruple vanished before the frank yet half-coquettish familiarity and light-heartedness with which she treated him during those few days of preparations for the dance. In the early days of that fatal lesson in the "Old Country" the English peasant girl had defended as best she could, the citadel of her honour at every step, yielding at last to a word of her own, to one who, for such as she, felt no word of honour sacred. Amanda felt no fear, for she realized no danger, and for her there was no danger. To her Roland belonged to something apart from her experience of life in the past, of her anticipation of life in the future, just as her admiration and affection for Evelyn Raye was apart from her own place in the world.

All the pleasure she found in his descriptions of his life at college and at home, his mockery of the girls at the Dingle, and of Canadian ways, his quaint terms of English slang, it was a constant source of amusement to her, but she never took it as more serious than the reading of a fairy tale. If his word of admiration and a glance of the eye took at times a warmer tone than she had encountered from the "boys" with whom she laughed and danced at home in Sweden, she put it down to his English ways, and never gave it a second thought; indeed, could Roland have known it, her very light-heartedness at this time was altogether a thing apart from himself, and his growing passion.

Her pique with Ludwig for his disappointing letter had not lasted beyond the night it came, and her resentment passed with her tears. For a day or two she had said to herself that he should not have a single word of answer, to punish him for being such a "silly, silly fellow, when he might have known." But when Herr Hardie gave his consent to the dance, the last spark of her vexation died away, and she had sent to Ludwig a long note of invitation. "If he could tear himself away from his work, and was not in too great a hurry to see if the haystacks at Otter Lake were quite safe, he might stop at Rosebank on his way home, and perhaps have just one dance with a little Swedish girl, who hadn't quite, only nearly, forgotten a big, foolish fellow, who once fished her out of Otter Lake."

Happy as she had been at the Hardie's, there was a deep longing to be once more among her own people. The half play, half earnestness of her "girl and boy" tenderness for Ludwig, hidden in so much tantalizing waywardness when they were so often together, had deepened into a deeper and steadier stream of love. The very eagerness of Roland's growing and more obvious admiration, though they had won nothing of response for himself, gave birth in Amanda a greater longing to see Ludwig's handsome face again, to hear her mother tongue, and to find the realization of her dreams of happiness in the sure possession of that heart which she had long known, despite her wilfulness, was all her own.

CHAPTER XVII

By the time the evening of the dance came, things had worked round to a rather more comfortable footing at the Dingle. Miss Daisy still remained firm in her refusal to go to the "hoe down," though she relented sufficiently to write a civil little note to Mrs. Hardie, excusing herself on the ground of a cold caught at threshing. Miss Enderby, whose English pride was beginning to yield to more material consideration, had on the Sunday evening before acceded to the request of Mr. Dugald McLeod, that he might be allowed to call for her with his cutter, and take her to the dance. Mr. Dugald McLeod was the alternative to Miss Enderby's permanent spinsterhood, alluded to in a previous chapter.

For some months past he had fallen into the way of dropping in at the Dingle on Sunday evenings, ostensibly to have a talk with Bert and his father. So far he had not made much progress in his courtship, which was of a cautious and Scottish type, but it had come to be generally understood in the family that Miss Enderby was the attraction, and Miss Daisy's attempts to tease her sister on the subject were not met with any very resolute disclaimer. Roland and Bert walked down to Rosebank together. Bert cared very little for dancing, but there was usually a bedroom set apart for cards, and he was very anxious that the Hardies should not suspect any unwillingness on the part of the family to respond to their invitation.

They were the first arrivals, as Roland had promised to be down early to give a few final touches to the decorations of the big room, and to light the Chinese lanterns on the veranda, which had been shut in by hanging sleigh robes and quilts so as to force a retreat from the crowd, and heat off the dancing room. They were welcomed by Jim himself at the lean-to door, full of hospitality, though rather embarrassed by the formality of his Sunday clothes and the unaccustomed restraint of a highly starched collar.

"Come in, Mr. Vale, make yourself 'at home'; you and the 'wimmen folk' have the place fine between you. You look after him, Bert, and see he has a good time and dances with all the prettiest girls. I'm going to look after the horses, and see they get stabled and fed; it's more in my line. You and me will get a quiet game of 'Pedro' in the boys' room by-and-by, when the young folk get started with their dances."

Bert and Roland passed into the big room, where they found Mrs. Hardie and Amanda and Mary Ann Dawson.

"Now, it is real good of you to come so early, Mr. Bert," exclaimed Mrs. Hardie, as they entered. "It's too bad Miss Daisy couldn't come, and where is Miss Enderby?"

"Oh, she's driving with Dugald McLeod," said Bert, "and will be here in a little while; Roland and I walked on ahead."

"That's right, Mr. Vale. Now, do you and Amanda get those lantern things 'fixed' before the folk come, and perhaps Mr. Bert will help Mary Ann here carry in some of the supper things from the dairy, and put them on the big table in the lean-to."

"Oh, I've got them all on a little stand on the veranda, Mr. Vale; they are all ready, if you will hang them up, and light them," and Amanda led the way into the veranda, followed very willingly by Roland.

"It's too bad you should have so much trouble, Mr. Vale," said Amanda, as they found themselves alone in the veranda, and Roland proceeded to open out the lanterns and to light the candles.

"It's too bad you should call me Mr. Vale to-night, Amanda, when you look simply lovely," replied Roland, dropping his voice.

"Oh, nonsense, Mr. Vale—well, Roland, if you will have it so," as Roland made a deprecating grimace at the "Mr. Vale."

"And I'm to have as many dances as I like?" urged Roland.

"Oh, indeed no—what would everybody say if a gentleman just out from England were to dance more than twice—well, three times—with a little Swedish girl?"

"Oh, hang everybody!" said Roland; "you know there won't be another girl here that I want to speak to."

"Oh, I don't know that at all," said Amanda. "There will be ever so many—yes, ever so many nice girls here to-night."

"There'll be just one lovely girl that I shall see," said Roland, "just one lovely rose, and it must be my rose to-night."

"But there will be the 'boys' from home, and Mr. Bert, and, yes, I must make Herr Hardie have a dance with me—and perhaps—'somebody else';" and Amanda's voice took unconsciously a softer tone, as she said the "somebody else."

At this moment Mr. Hardie called from the other room, "Hurry up, Amanda, there's sleigh-bells—the folk are coming," and Amanda hurried away before Roland could ask who the "somebody else" might be.

The whole place was soon in confusion, with the arrivals following quickly upon each other. Amanda took the ladies upstairs to Mrs. Hardie's room to take off their wraps. Mr. Hardie was busy at the stables helping "the boys" to unhitch and stable their horses, the cows and young cattle being turned out to the straw-stacks for the night to make room for them all.

The two fiddlers had arrived, bringing with them Rube Duncan, a young man much in request at all such gatherings for his skill and humour in "calling off" the "squares"; and Mrs. Hardie was moving here and there, welcoming the guests and introducing Roland to such of the young fellows as he had not met at the threshing.

At first there was rather a stiffness and formality. The young ladies took their seats round the room, flushed and over-conscious of possible disarrangements of their white muslin frocks. The young men, being welcomed by Mrs. Hardie, showed a tendency either to sidle into the lean-to or to form groups for self-protection in odd corners of the room; but this passed away when the fiddlers took their stand on a little raised platform, and the "caller off," mounting a chair by their side, called out in a raucous voice: "Gents, take your partners and promenade for the dance."

Amanda was Roland's partner for the "square," and she piloted him skilfully through its intricacies, though it was quite beyond his experiences of English dances. The "sing-song" of the "caller off" was of no assistance to him, as he could only catch a word here and there, and its free-and-easy colloquialisms had no meaning to him.

He had mentally dubbed the young men of the party as a lot of louts before the dance began, but he was simply amazed at the way they danced. It was dancing of a very vigorous order, but every one seemed perfectly familiar with the complicated figures, and the young men especially took it very seriously—most of their faces being marked by a grave and conscientious air, as if it were a matter of duty rather than of pleasure. There was none of the casual, lounging, it's-too-much-of-a-bore air to which Roland was used "at home," none of the wild romping of the "kitchen lancers." He had come prepared to be amused by the ways of the natives, and found to his disgust that he was rather out of it.

After the first dance the general air of awkwardness on the part of the young men and of self-consciousness on the part of the girls wore away, and dance succeeded dance with great vigour. Early in the evening Bert Enderby escaped to the card-room upstairs, and relieved of the feeling that he might be observed by what he was pleased to consider might be one of his own class, Roland resolved to make the most of his opportunities with Amanda. After the first "square," he did not attempt them again, but she was his partner in nearly all the waltzes, in which he was more at home, and she seemed quite to have forgotten the limit of three, which she had placed before the dance began. There was a lightness of her foot and a brightness in her eye, that were not solely due to her Norse love of music and dancing; she had had a message from Ludwig.

It came thus wise: she had just been dancing with Roland, and as they were standing by the entrance to the lean-to the outer door opened, and a young man came in, fur coat and cap.

"Oh, there's my cousin Carl!" exclaimed Amanda. "Excuse me, Mr. Vale; he may have a message from home for me," and she slipped away.

"Oh, Carl, I'm so glad you've come. Is there any one else with you from home?"

"Helloo, Amanda! I guess I'm pretty late. No, there's no one else. I've just come up from town in my jumper."

"Oh, I thought perhaps—I mean, I didn't know;" and Amanda tried to hide her disappointment.

"Well, it's too bad," said Carl, laughing. "Especially when you thought you didn't know, but I did see some one in town, who said he might pass by here some time before morning."

"Now, Carl dear, don't tease, there's a good fellow," whispered Amanda.

"Well, Amanda," said Carl, dropping his voice, "I did really see some one; he'd just come into town from the south, and he'd been driving all day, and I told him he'd better put his team in the barn and give his horses a rest till to-morrow."

"Oh, how could you be so horrid, Carl? When——"

"Well, I guess he's not very careful of his team, or else awfully anxious about his father, for he said he'd just put them in for a couple of hours, and then strike for home."

"Without coming in here?" exclaimed Amanda, with a quick flash mounting to her cheeks.

"Well, you see, he had only his rough clothes on, and he said there would be a lot of smart English folk here."

"What do his clothes make when he knows——"

"Well, so I told him, and he's going to pull into the lane, and just come up and have a look in, in case any one might be around that he knew."

"Now, you horrid teasing boy, why couldn't you say so right away?" said Amanda, laughing and blushing; "you don't deserve a single dance, but you shall have one just because——"

"Just because the other fellow isn't here."

"Oh, I know we none of us have a 'look in' when——"

"Here, don't you dare to say another word, Carl, or you shan't have a bit of supper either——" and Amanda ran off to join Roland, who was waiting for her by the door.

CHAPTER XVIII

Supper-time came and passed, and still no Ludwig. Once in the middle of a dance with Roland, Amanda heard the jingle of sleigh-bells pass the door.

"There he is," she cried involuntarily.

"There's who?" asked Roland.

"Oh, I don't know," she stammered, "perhaps some one from home."

"Well, you seem very anxious," he said jealously. "I suppose you will drop me when he comes."

"Oh, no, you know I won't, Mr. Vale—Roland—when you have been so good to me; see it's only the Dennis boys who were here at the thresh-ing. Now this must be the last dance for quite a long time," she added, as the music stopped; "I have promised Cousin Carl a dance, and two or three of the other boys from 'Sweden.' "

"Well, I shan't dance with anybody else," said Roland rather sullenly. "I'll go and have a smoke with the Dennises; I guess they won't care much for this kind of thing," and he crossed the room to the lean-to, where the Dennis boys were being welcomed by Mrs. Hardie.

Tom and Jack Dennis were old Dingle pupils, who, after two years' training at the Dingle, had been started by their father to farm on their own account. Their father had bought them a farm, with a good house on it, and had given them a very generous measure of help; but it seemed as if his money and provision for them were to be thrown away. They had had their farm for three years now, and were farther from making their own living than when they began. They kept "back" in a comfortable fashion—doing their own cooking and washing—the latter a diminishing quantity as time went on. The Dingle was still the best influence in their lives, and up to the last month or two, they had usually gone there for Sunday, and kept up some measure of self-respect, but latterly, partly from the dullness of their lives, and partly from their ill-success in their farming, they had been seek-ing for distraction in more frequent visits to town. There at least they could get company, and some kind of excitement—the company was not of the best, that of the hotel bar; and the excitement came from bad whisky; but to them it seemed better than the deadly dullness of their own place.

The Enderbys had not encouraged their visits since Roland came, as they did not want to throw him in their way, and Roland from perversity had struck up rather a friendship with them. They were older than himself, of his own social class "at home," and there was something attractive to him in their ill-regulated, shiftless manner of living, and their freely expressed contempt for Canadians, and the whole d——d country. Once or twice they had asked him to go over for a Sunday, but Mr. Enderby had always put difficulties in the way.

"Hello, Vale, old man, you must be having a 'bully' time," said the elder Dennis, as he joined them. "Pretty rank outsiders most of them—ain't they?"

"Oh, it's not so bad, as you know," replied Roland; "some of the girls are not bad looking, and they can dance all right; the men are a pretty rummy lot."

"Well, dancing is not in my line," said the younger Dennis—Jack —"it's too much like work. I say, Vale, come for a turn outside; it's beastly hot in here, and then we'll have a smoke, and, if we can get a quiet corner, will have a game of cards by ourselves."

Roland fell in with the suggestion. If he couldn't dance with Amanda, he wasn't going to let the Dennises see him dancing with Mrs. Hardie and Mary Ann Dawson. They lit their pipes and passed out of the house together.

"Come along, Vale, down to our jumper in the yard," said Tom Dennis. "We've been to town to-day, and I put a bottle of 'all right' in the horse blanket, and we'll just have a 'go' apiece, to keep us from catching cold, you know."

"I say, Tom, how are you going to get the cork out?" asked Jack.

"Oh, I have a corkscrew," said Roland. "They gave me a regular tool-chest of a knife when I came out—here it is," and he handed it to Tom, who soon drew the cork.

"Take a pull, Vale—it's this Canadian Rye—it isn't too hot to swallow," and Tom handed Roland the bottle.

Roland had no love for spirits, and indeed had not tasted anything of the kind since he left England; but he hadn't the courage to refuse or to decline a second "go" before returning to the house, when they had finished their smoke.

The three young men passed through the lean-to into the house to go upstairs to the card-room, Roland noticing with disgust that Amanda was dancing with one of the "boys" from Sweden. In the card-room they found Bert Enderby and Mr. Hardie having a smoke.

"Glad to see you," said Mr. Hardie to the Dennises. "Come and have a quiet game with Bert here. Him and me have been talking over our plans for our hunting, and I must go downstairs again and see if the young folk are having a good time; so we'll leave at noon, Bert?"

"All right, Jim; Vale and I will be ready when you come round with the team."

The four sat down round the table, and Tom Dennis picked up the cards.

"What's it to be, boys, bridge, or euchre, or what?"

"I guess it had better be pedro," said Bert. "I don't play bridge, and I don't think Vale here plays euchre."

"We may as well have fifty cents on the game," suggested Jack Dennis, "just to give us an interest."

"Let's make it a dollar," broke in Roland, who, in the heat of the little room, was becoming hot and flushed from the effects of the unaccustomed whisky. "A dollar a game, and I'll bet you a couple of dollars, Bert, that Tom Dennis and I win three games out of five."

"Oh, Jack and I will play you, but I won't bet on it; and Jim Hardie would be awfully put out if any one played cards for money in his house. Besides," added Bert, "I have no money to lose."

"Just as you like, Bert," said Tom Dennis, who knew Bert meant what he said. "You come over to our place some Sunday, Vale, and you can have a game without any Sunday-school restrictions."

Roland submitted with rather an ill grace, his mood had become reckless, and he was ready to quarrel at the least sign of Bert putting any restraint upon him, but Bert had noticed his flushed face, and the heavy odour of liquor in his breath, and was not going to give him any pretext for a dispute. At the end of the fourth game Bert put down the cards.

"I guess we may as well quit now," he said to Tom Dennis. "Vale and you have won three games, anyway, and I have to be up early, and I want to get some sleep before we go to the 'bush,'—are you coming home with me, Vale?"

"Oh, you needn't wait for me, I have another dance promised," said Roland. "I know my way from here to the Dingle by myself."

"Just as you like," said Bert. "Good-night, Tom, good-night, Jack"— and he went off downstairs.

"Well, I guess we may as well be striking the trail too," said Tom as soon as Bert was gone. "You might as well come and have another sip at the rye, Vale, to liven you up for your dance." Roland followed them downstairs, and out of the house to the jumper.

"I'll get the horse, Tom, while you give Vale a drink; leave a 'go' for me in the bottle"; and Jack Dennis went off to the stable.

"I guess you find it pretty slow at old Enderby's, Vale?" said Tom. "He's an awfully decent sort, and so's the old lady, if she could forget her uncle, the dean, and a lot of 'rot' of that sort."

"Oh, yes, they are all right," said Roland. "But Bert needn't think he's going to run me just as he likes."

"Oh, it's his way," said Tom good-naturedly. "Bert's a rattling good chap, but a little prim, you know. Here's good luck to your 'hunting,' " and he took a long pull at the bottle, and handed it to Roland. "Don't be afraid of it."

Roland was afraid of it, for his head was still a little dizzy; but not so afraid of it as of seeming not to be a man in the eyes of Tom Dennis, so he gave two or three big gulps at the bottle before handing it back.

"Now in you go to your dance, before you get cold with your bare head. Good-night, Vale. I'll go and see what's keeping Jack with the nag," and Tom started off to the stable.

As Roland returned to the house, he passed two or three young fellows with a stable lantern, on their way to the yard. Evidently the party was breaking up, so he hurried his steps. On entering there was a crowd of young people in the lean-to, where Mary Ann Dawson and Mrs. Hardie were giving some of the girls a final cup of hot coffee before they went out into the sharp, frosty air. As he paused for a minute to look round for Amanda, he heard the voice of the "caller off" from the big room. "Now, boys, one more extra before we go"; and the fiddles struck up a lively waltz.

He pressed in through the crowd in the lean-to. Three or four couples were dancing, but there was no sign of Amanda, so he made his way into the veranda. He found her with one of the hanging robes drawn back, looking out into the night, and hurried to her side. She started and let the robe drop at his feet.

"This is my last dance, Amanda."

"Oh, is it you, Mr. Vale? I thought you had forgotten me!"

"Is that why there are tears in your eyes, Amanda?" he asked.

"Oh, nonsense, it's just the frosty air. Why should there be tears in my eyes?" she added half defiantly. "Whom should I cry for?"

But the tears were there, for pride and love had been struggling in poor Amanda's heart for the last two hours. "Why"—again and again the question came—"why does Ludwig not come?—why does he leave me? has he gone by without caring enough to come in and see me, just for one little moment?" Then pride came to her rescue. "If he doesn't care, neither do I," and she took Roland's arm, and turned back to the big room.

It was the last dance, and the fiddlers were bound to have, as they said, a good fast finish. By the time they had circled the floor two or three times, Roland's head was reeling, and even Amanda, hardened little dancer as she was, was giddy.

"Oh, do let me sit down: oh, I am so giddy," she whispered, and he half led, half supported her to the veranda, where she sank on a lounge, and Roland by her side. She was half unconscious that his arm was still around her waist, that her head was resting on his shoulder, and that his face, flushed with whisky and passion, was close beside her own. Reckless of all, his lips were pressing to her own when she opened her eyes, and there —there in the opening of the robes by the veranda steps, there was Ludwig. Ludwig with face drawn and stern, and a very passion of rage in his blue eyes.

"Oh, Ludwig, Ludwig, have you come at last?" she cried, and started to her feet, and, breaking from Roland's arms, she staggered blindly across the floor, but he was gone. When she had torn aside the robe and stood upon the veranda steps, there was nothing but the moon shining in the quiet snow, and the wild rattle of sleigh-bells down the land, and Roland was by her side, confused and angry.

"Oh, leave me, leave me; I cannot tell you why"; and she darted back into the house, and into the thronged lean-to, where the last lingering were singing an uproarious, "For she's a jolly good fellow," in honour of Mrs. Hardie.

Roland elbowed his way through the throng, but he could not find Amanda; so getting his coat and cap he made his way unnoticed into the outer air, and took the path leading through the bluff by the corral—the way he had come that first afternoon with Bert to Rosebank. Every bad passion was in his heart that could be fostered by lust and strong drink, fostered and now foiled. Inflamed with whisky, infatuated with a love, now utterly degraded with jealousy, for he had caught a momentary glance of that stern, white face in the opening robes, he half walked, half staggered down the path. There, by the bars leading into the town line, he came upon Amanda, with head bowed down upon the frost-covered rail, and sobbing as if her heart would break.

He hastened to her side, and endeavoured to put his arm about her shrinking form.

"So my Rose of Sweden, I have caught you—you won't slip away from me so readily again." And Amanda leapt back from his arm and stood, flushed and panting.

"Oh, Roland, how can you, you that have been my friend—how can you, how dare you touch me so?"

"How dare I? I dare anything—now I have you here and alone—yes, and you shall be mine for all the damned Ludwigs in Sweden," and with outstretched arms he leapt upon her.

With open palm, and swift-striking arm, with the courage and strength of outraged innocence striking its last blow, she smote him full across his inflamed and passion-branded face, and ere he recovered from its stinging force she was away, with the swiftness of a hunted deer, away along the winding path through the bluff, through the now empty house, safe in the security of her little room and sobbing, sobbing with fear and anger—and her lost love. Was it for this she had tried too far the cord of love woven by the peaceful waters of Otter Lake—so long, it seemed "so long ago"?

CHAPTER XIX

Roland slept long and heavily into the far hours of the morning, after the ill-fated dance, his mind slowly returning to consciousness under the repeated knockings of the Dingle "chore boy" at his door.

First, was the bodily awakening to the throbbing pain of a splitting headache, and a dry and burning throat, the fruits of the raw undiluted whisky. Then came a general sense of mental misery—that sense of disaster having overtaken him—which so often precedes the realization of the details which led up to, and crowned disaster with hopelessness. One by one the events of the preceding evening took their place in the monument of his mad folly; but his sense of resentment against Amanda was far keener than any sense of shame for the part he had played himself. His cheek still tingled from the swift sharpness of that blow, and he put back the curtain from the window, and faced himself in the little mirror hanging on the wall. What dull and bloodshot eyes! And, yes, there was a bright streak of red across his cheek. "The little vixen, after leading him on—and then to be cast aside for a common Swede fellow. By Gad! she shall pay for it," and he turned away from the glass and proceeded slowly to dress. Then came other thoughts of the unpleasantness of his own position, both at the Hardies and at the Dingle. "How much would Amanda tell, and Bert?" Anyway he would get away to the bush, and perhaps it would have blown over before they returned from their hunting.

The house was in too great a bustle, from Bert's preparations, for much attention to be paid to him when he got down in time for the early dinner. Bert discreetly made no allusion to the dance, and the rest put down his heavy eyes and white face to the late hour of the night before. Jim Hardie was along before the meal was over, and with hurried good-byes to all, they were soon in the sleigh and on the bush.

Mr. Hardie and Bert took the only seat in the sleigh, a rough piece of board, but Jim made a comfortable place for Roland on the bottom of the sleigh-box among the robes and blankets which they were taking for bedding at the shanty, for he had noticed Roland's dull and wearied face.

"You look pretty well 'tuckered' out, Mr. Vale. You dancing folk have to pay up next day for your fun; the wife is fairly worn out this morning, and the little Rose just opened her door to say 'good-bye' to me before I started, and the poor little body looked just like a ghost, she did—a rose with the dew gone, and the blush of it faded, with her cheek and her big eyes as if she hadn't slept for a week. But lie you down, lie you down, lad, and pull the robes over you, and you'll be so warm as a——" and Jim completed the familiar western comparison expressive of cosy comfort.

Roland was only too glad to escape further remarks on his appearance, or the necessity of discussing the dance. He drew a corner of the robe closely over his face, and soon fell asleep—a broken, restless dozing at first, in which the sleigh-bells mingled with fitful dreams, passing at last into a heavy slumber, from which he was awakened by the sudden stopping of the sleigh, and Bert shaking him.

"Wake up, Roland, wake up; here we are at the shanty. What do you think of this for a 'shooting box' in the west?"

"Why, where are we?" asked Roland, sitting up and rubbing his eyes. "How long have I been asleep?"

"Well, I guess you've been asleep for well-nigh four hours," answered Jim, who was unhitching his team, "well-nigh four hours by the sun. And where are you? You're sixteen miles up in 'Sweden,' and this shanty here is 'The Hunter's Rest'; that's what I christened it, when I was putting it together last hay-time. Now you go in and make yourself at home, and put a bit of fire on, while Bert and me fixes the horses up comfortable, and then we'll have supper and a look round before we turn in—it's 'early to bed, and early to rise' with the hunters isn't it, Bert?" and Jim led off his horses to the rough stables beyond the shanty, followed by Bert, carrying the horse blankets.

Jim had chosen well the site for The Hunter's Rest. It stood on the rising ground at the head of a chain of sloughs, or little shallow lakes, the margin of which, from the fringe of reeds by the water-side to the spruce-covered slopes of the steep hills on either hand, formed the hay meadows. At the south end of this little valley, half a mile from the shanty, the hills drew together, leaving only a narrow ravine, through which, after the spring thaw and after the June rains, the overflow of the slough found its way, with many turns and twists, to the greater waters of Otter Lake.

The shanty was only far enough back from the slough side to gain the shelter of the spruce of the hill at its back. It was roughly built of in-hewn logs—roughly but warmly; for the crevices between the logs were tightly packed with moss; rafters of smaller logs, thatched with reeds and coarse grass from the lake edge, formed its roof. A few boards strongly nailed together served for a door, on one side of which was a little square window. Roland, in sooth, did not think much of The Hunter's Rest from the outside, though he had to admit when he entered that there was an air of neatness and comfort about the interior. It was all in one room, some fourteen feet wide and eighteen feet long. Its height of nine feet or so in front sloped away with the roof to less than six feet at the back. The prairie served for floor, its grass worn away to the bare earth, dry and smooth, for Jim and his hired man had lived there for a month in the haying.

At the one end were two berths or sleeping bunks, running the width of the shanty. At the other end was the stove—an old-fashioned cooking stove, which Jim had picked up for a few dollars at a sale. Along the wall at the back ran two or three rough shelves, on which were ranged a mixed assortment of pots and pans, plates, and cups and saucers. In one corner a large packing-case served as storeroom for provisions, while in the other were neatly piled some bags of oats, which Bert and Jim had brought up on their trip the week before. An old kitchen table and two or three chairs, discarded from Rosebank, completed the furnishing of The Hunter's Rest; but, rough as it all was, everything was suggestive of Jim's neat and handy Canadian adaptability, and in his eyes it was all that the most exacting could desire for a bush camp.

Though not very expert in such matters, Roland succeeded in lighting the fire, and it was burning brightly by the time Jim and Bert re-entered the shanty. Bert was quietly cheerful, after his manner, but Jim was in the highest spirits, as gay and irresponsible as a schoolboy on the first day of the holidays.

"Now, Vale, you must have a real good time. We'll drop the 'Mister' here in the bush, if you don't mind, and you just call me, Jim; you must have a real good time. We live a bit in the rough when we come hunting, but it's fine when you get used to it; no work, no dollars to worry about, plenty to eat, and always hungry. Bert here and me will look after the horses and the cooking; you've nothing to do but put in a good time," and Jim kept on talking as he prepared the supper.

"It'll be great if this is the last pork to fry till we're back home again," he went on as he turned the thick slices in the spider, with a great sound of spluttering and sizzling. "Won't it be immense, just immense, if it's a great juicy rump steak of moose by this time to-morrow? I mind the first time I came deer-hunting; it was with old Christian Nielson from down at Otter Lake. We just brought an old ox and a sled to bring up our tent and grub; and the first day, while we were off hunting, the old ox got loose, and poked his nose under the tent flap and eat all the flour, and we had nothing but deer meat and tea for a week; but it was fine"; and Jim kept up a stream of reminiscences, broken only with injunctions to Roland to "eat hearty," till supper was over.

While Bert went out to feed and fix up the team for the night, Jim washed the dishes and made up beds in the bunks for Roland and Bert, announcing his own intention of having a "shake down" on the floor. The three of them then lit their pipes and went for "the look round" before turning in. They took their rifles with them, "just as they shouldn't see anything," as Jim said, and skirting round the foot of the hill behind the camp, they made a circle back again to the shanty, coming across frequent deer-tracks, though none of them quite recent.

Jim, however, was quite satisfied. "The deer are here all right," he said when they got back. "We'll turn in for a good night's sleep, and we'll be on their tracks bright and early; you just sleep till we call you, Vale, and leave the waking-up to me."

They prepared for rest by the dim light of the stable lantern, hanging from the roof—a very simple preparation, consisting of the removal of their moccasins and outer garments—and then Jim and Bert knelt down simply, and as a matter of course, to their prayers, an example awkwardly followed as to the outward act by Roland, though there was no spirit of prayer in his heart. Jim and Bert were soon sleeping soundly, but it was long before he shared their quiet rest.

It was not only the sense of unaccustomed physical discomfort, from the hardness of the bunk and the roughness of the blankets, that kept him awake. There was a dull sense of separation from the clean and wholesome peace of conscience of his companions—that sense of moral isolation which is more cruel than solitude on an untrodden desert.

Twice he was on the point of sinking into unconsciousness, only to be startled to a terrified wakefulness by the blood-curdling howl of a coyote near by the shanty, and its piercing note of misery seemed as if it might have been the expression of his own troubled heart. At last, after what seemed to him hours of misery, he sank into a deep and unbroken rest.

CHAPTER XX

The eastern sky was rosy with the promise of the rising sun, when the three hunters left the shanty the next morning. Soft wreaths of mist still hung along the sloughs to the south, but the spruce-capped summits of the western hills had already caught the first rays of the sun, and the snow on every bough of spruce or twig of saskatoon scrub, scintillated as with myriads of purest diamonds.

During the quiet hours of the night there had been a fresh fall of snow, resting softly, like a thick coverlet of eider down, along the meadow before the shanty, though but little of it had reached the ground in the bush, where it had been intercepted by the wide-spreading, feathery boughs of the spruce and the pine. No lightest branches of the highest trees, the stillness of nature was absolute. It was a scene of surpassing and mysterious beauty, and the three men stood before the shanty door for a few minutes in an almost awed silence. In the western men it was a spirit of reverence, its quietness fell upon them like the embodiment of the peace of God; but to Roland it only spoke of loneliness, entire and unbroken by any sense of fellowship with nature or the Eternal Spirit who caused nature to be.

Jim was the first to break the spell of beauty, a little awkwardly, for he was conscious of quietness, which he felt was not quite in harmony with—as he would have expressed it—"a plain everyday chap like himself." Not that he despised the feelings which lie at the back of a sense of natural or spiritual beauty, rather he felt himself unworthy of them. He allowed himself to muse over many things, as he followed the plough on its furrow, or wielded the axe in long solitary days in the bush; but the expression of sentiment he delegated in his own mind to the "wimmen folk," and the minister whose vocation he judged it to be.

"Boys, but it's a grand morning." That was Jim's tribute to nature. "But we'll get better hunting if there was a wind." That was the reawakening of the sportsman. "I guess, Bert," he continued, "we'll go north through the big timber; it's so mighty still, that the deer will hear us if we snap a twig or step on a dead bough. We can strike an old surveyor's line a bit back, and then we won't be so likely to make a racket."

They entered the bush in Indian file, Jim leading, then Bert, and Roland last. It was slow, laborious work, for there was often a thick undergrowth of small scrub to be crawled through, fallen trees to be climbed over, and treacherous muskegs to be skirted; but at last they reached the surveyor's line, a narrow cutting running east and west through the woods, and here it was easier travelling.

They had followed the line in silence for two or three miles, and Roland was mentally dubbing deer-hunting "a rotten show," when Jim suddenly stopped, and, holding up his hand as a signal for caution, waited till they came up to him.

"Look at that," he whispered to Bert, pointing to what to Roland looked like the big hoof-prints of a cow, in the fresh snow; "look at that—it's a bull moose, and a big fellow too, you bet; look at the spread of his hoof."

They followed the marks a little way along the line, when they branched off into the wood to the north, and Jim stopped again for a whispered consultation with Bert as to the best method of procedure. It was decided that Jim should go off alone to the west, gradually circling in again to a point about a mile north of where they stood, a performance which seemed wildly impossible to Roland, though the other two spoke of it as simply as going down a street. Bert and Roland were to follow the moose tracks in the snow, with many adjurations from Jim on the necessity of absolute silence, and of keeping their eyes "skinned."

Jim slid off into the bush with the speed and secretiveness of an Indian, while Bert and Roland prepared to follow the tracks of the moose, after Bert had warned Roland to be on the alert for the slightest signal, as there would be no waiting for him to get a shot when once the deer was sighted. The two kept close together, and did not travel very quickly, as silence was more imperative than speed. It was evident that the moose was as yet unalarmed, as in places it had stayed to browse on twigs and shoots of the undergrowth. At the end of half a mile or so, the tracks led across a little opening in the woods, and here Bert, before leaving the shelter of the bush, crouched down, an example followed by Roland.

Just as Roland was about to stand upright, cramped by the uneasiness of his position, Bert raised a warning hand and slowly raised his rifle to his shoulder. For a minute he paused, taking a deliberate aim—though still there was nothing visible to Roland's straining eyes—crack, the rifle rang out sharp and clear; crack, with a dulled echo the report came back, and with a mighty bound, a big bull moose burst from the skirt of the opposite bush into the clearing, where it stood with head tossed high, and snorting loudly from its distended nostrils.

"Quick, Roland—fire," shouted Bert, jerking his empty shell from his rifle, and preparing to fire again. "Quick, before he rushes."

Roland had started to his feet at the first shot, and now, taking a hasty aim, he discharged his Winchester, and without waiting to see the effect started to run towards the moose, which was still snorting and stamping angrily upon the ground. He was half across the clearing, when he stumbled and fell, losing his grip of his rifle, which was jerked by his fall into the snow. He had not scrambled to his feet before the moose rushed—he had one moment of panic fear, and the rifle of Bert rang out a second time, and the deer came down with a terrible crash, pierced through the heart.

"You've had a pretty close call—are you hurt?" called out Bert, as he came running up, his rifle still smoking. "Another minute, and he would have pounded you to death."

"Oh, I'm all right," said Roland, though he looked sick and white, "I'm all right; but who thought the brute would rush like that?"

"Oh, a wounded moose is a pretty dangerous customer, and we should have warned you—you need not be ashamed of being shaky after such an experience," for Roland was looking vexed and ashamed. "He's dead enough, now; see where my first shot hit him above the shoulder. I was too high; I thought the clearing was wider. We must call Jim up, and bleed the deer, and get it ready for trailing back to the shanty."

Just as he spoke Jim broke through the bush to their left; he had heard the three shots, and had followed the sound of the reports. He was in, for him, a wild state of excitement and delight at their success, and full of understanding and sympathy for Roland's mishap.

"It's too bad, too bad, Roland should not get the first deer, but we'll give him the first show next time," he said, in an undertone to Bert, as they proceeded to get the deer ready for taking to camp—a piece of business in which Roland did not join, a "horrid, gory job" Roland described it to himself, "too much in the butcher line for me." However, he stamped round to keep himself warm, and had a smoke while it was being done in a very complete and master-like manner by Jim with Bert's assistance.

"Now for the shanty and dinner," said Jim, when it was finished to his satisfaction, "and I'll cut out some deer meat, and give you your first taste of hunter's fare. Bert and me will come back later on, and I fancy we can get pretty nearly in here by an old bush trail with the stone boat and one of the team, and then we can take the hide off and cut up the carcass at the shanty."

It was midday by the time they reached their camp, all very hungry, and Roland tired and sore from the long tramp in moccasins, which he had never worn for a long tramp before. By the time dinner was over he was very stiff, and the warmth of the shanty made him drowsy after the keen, frosty air of the bush. So it was decided that he should stay in and rest while they went back to trail in the moose.

"I'm thinking you'll find it lonesome," said Jim to Roland, while Bert was out at the stable getting the horse and stone boat ready for their trip back for the moose, and he himself was washing up the dinner dishes. "It's all right for Bert and the likes of me; we are used to it now, but I doubt you find it too rough—your mother, now, would think it terrible, just terrible, for her boy to be living in this Indian fashion"; and his voice was full of kindly sympathy, for he felt Roland's evident depression to be a rebuke to his own enjoyment of their "camp life."

"Oh, I shall be comfortable enough," replied Roland. "It's awfully good of you and Bert to be bothered with a 'greenhorn' like me," he added, with some compunction at his own irresponsiveness to Jim's evident anxiety to give him "a good time." "I shall be all right by myself, and perhaps by-and-by I'll take a turn round with my rifle. What would you think," he added with a laugh, "if I were to find and shoot a deer on my own while you were away?"

"It would be great—great, and you'd have something to tell them when you wrote home," said Jim; but he added. "Don't go far into the bush yourself, or maybe we'll have to be hunting you when we get back. It's fine enough now, but I'm afraid of these very still days after a snowfall; it might be a howling blizzard before night, and the bush is a bad place to get lost in. You might skirt along the bush to the end of the sloughs, and then follow the old creek course down the ravine for a bit—it's a likely place to run across an elk or a 'jumper,' and as long as you keep in the ravine you are sure of finding your way back to the meadow."

At this moment the voice of Bert was heard shouting from outside, "All aboard," and Jim, picking up his rifle and an axe, hurried out of the shanty with a hasty "good-bye, and luck to your hunting" to Roland, who followed him to the door, and stood watching them till they turned the foot of the hill, when he turned back again into the shanty and closed the door.

CHAPTER XXI

Roland's first sensation on re-entering the shanty was one of relief at being alone. He was still conscious of a sense of physical lassitude, due not so much to his long tramp through the woods, as to the panic of fear that had possessed him for the brief moment between the rush of the wounded moose and the crack of Bert's rifle. He had never lacked in nerve and courage in boxing and football at home, and he was a fearless rider, but this was something quite beyond any previous experience, and he felt vexed and humiliated by it. He was glad too to get away for a time from Jim's exuberant high spirits, which smote no response from his own feelings. As was natural with him, the heat of his resentment against Amanda had cooled down almost as quickly as it had arisen, and he was chiefly busied in seeking the easiest way of escape for himself from the awkward position into which he had been hurried by his ungoverned passion.

Putting on some more wood, he drew up to the stove an old easy chair, one of the derelicts from Rosebank, shabby but comfortable, and sat down for a quiet smoke. He had brought up with him to the bush the last bundle of magazines and papers from "home," and for a time he amused himself in a listless way, with reading a scrap here and there, and looking at the pictures. Then he recollected that he had only hastily glanced over the last letter from his mother, which Mary Ann Dawson had brought up from the post-office on the evening of the dance, and he drew it from his pocket, and slowly read it through. It was full of all the little doings of the quiet village at home, full too of anxious love for himself, full of pleadings that he would reconcile himself for a time to the roughness and monotony of his new life.

The squire had received very favourable letters from Mr. Enderby, and she herself one from Mrs. Enderby, expressing the pleasure she found "in welcoming to her family circle one who, by his courteous manners and re-fined speech, brings back very pleasant reminiscences of the happy hours of my childhood, which were spent with my uncle, the late Dean of Chester," and Roland laughed as he read it, in spite of his depression. The squire too showed sign of relenting, touched by Mr. Enderby's praise of his willingness to work and of his skill with horses. His name was no more en-tirely tabooed at the Hall, "only, my dear boy," the letter closed, "only watch over your hasty impulses, remember who is thinking and praying for you here, and God may send you home again to your loving mother."

Roland's eyes filled with tears as he read. "What a cur I was to grieve her so when I was at home, and now, if this last damnable folly should reach her ears, it would break her heart."

And slowly he reviewed his life of the past few weeks—his infatuation for Amanda and its disgraceful climax. But that might be never known. Bert might have his suspicions, but that was all; and Jim evidently was entirely innocent of what had passed—his open nature would have shown at once, if such a thought has ever entered his mind. And Amanda? She would not forgive him, perhaps, but he judged truly she would never betray his madness—she would be too proud, and she was going back to her own people; and his thought wandered on, "She'll marry that great rough wild-eyed Swede. Confound him, I hate to be beaten by a common fellow like that."

Backwards and forwards his good and evil angels swayed in mortal strife in his wayward heart, and for the time the advantage lay with the spirit of good. "I'll start a letter to mother now," he said at last to himself, "that will help to keep me straight," and he took from his travelling-bag the little writing-case, which had been her last gift on the night he left home. The very opening words as he wrote them, "My darling Mother," seemed to help him, and he launched out into a long account of the trip to the bush, with a ridiculous description of the shanty and its make-shift furniture, of the kindness of Bert, and Jim's anxiety to give him "a good time." He touched lightly on his escape of the morning, and wound up by saying that he would add a little to his letter every day till their trip was over. "And now," he finished, "good-bye, mother, don't worry, you shall see your boy again some day. I'm off for a little tramp with my rifle before the others come back? If I shoot a deer 'on my own' I'll send the head for father to put up in the Old Hall. Love and good-bye to you all for to-day. Your loving, Roland," and he laid down his pen and put his letter in the writing-case and returned it to his bag.

After putting more wood in the stove he picked up his rifle, and went to the door of the "shanty." He was surprised to find how the afternoon had slipped away. The sun was getting low over the western hills, and a change had come over the weather. The sky was still clear overhead, but a heavy cloud of dense, indigo darkness was slowly rolling up from the south-east. There was no breath of air in the little valley where the shanty stood, but the upper branches of the spruce on the hillsides were stirring restlessly, and ever and anon the sound of a long sighing seemed to pass through the woods behind the shanty—a sound so weird, so mysterious, that Roland shivered, though not conscious of cold, as it passed along and died away among the reeds by the little lakes. Had he but known it, these were warning signs of approaching storm to the hunter in the woods, clear and vivid as the colours of a rainbow after a May shower. On either side of the sun were "sun dogs"—the attendants of the spirit of the tempest.

But Roland was innocent of all woodman's lore. He was sensitive to the spirit of mystery and loneliness, and strode off through the untrodden snow, along the foot of the western slope of hills, anxious to escape by motion from its own thoughts and feelings. He paused when he reached the end of the meadows, and half thought of turning back to the shanty. Then came the recollection of Jim's last words—there might be a stray deer along the creek bed up the narrow ravine, and he determined to follow it a little way. He would like to shoot a deer "on his own"; it would restore his self-respect, and dull the edge of any good-humoured banter from the others about his "buck fever" of the morning. So he plodded on, though the walking was rough and difficult among the scrub that edged the creek bed.

He heard a sound to his right: surely that was the snapping of a dead branch; and he crouched down by the side of a fallen tree. Nearer and nearer the sound came; now he could distinguish a dull snorting as of some wearied and hard-pressed creature. He knelt by the fallen tree, in breathless silence, and slowly brought his rifle to his shoulder just as a fine elk with branching antlers emerged from the scrub, and slowly crossing the creek bed began to mount the opposite bank. Now was the moment, and with a steady grip of his rifle he pressed the trigger. Crash! on the moment of the crack of his rifle, the deer gave one convulsive bound high into the air, and then fell backwards into the bed of the creek. Forgetful of his lesson of the morning, Roland rushed madly forward up the creek; but there was no danger this time, the deer lay still and lifeless, pierced through the heart, for the bullet had sped true.

For a moment, forgetful of all else, he stood in the pure exultation of the hunter, and feasted his eyes on the size and beauty of his prey. Then came the thought of the morning's scene—he must finish his triumph in a sporting manner, just to show Jim how much he had learnt; so he drew his long hunter's knife, and was about to cut the throat of the elk, when, without consciousness on his part of how or whence it came, his arm was struck sharply by the barrel of a rifle, jerking his knife from his hand far into the snow, and a voice clear, but low, cried out: "Drop that knife, the deer is mine." Roland started back with an oath of alarm and anger, and looked straight into the eyes—of Ludwig Nielson.

CHAPTER XXII

When Ludwig galloped his horses down the lane from Rosebank on the night of the dance, he was urged by a desperate resolution to put as great a distance as possible between himself and the temptation to commit some irrevocable deed of violence and revenge. He had seen, as he believed, the evidence of Amanda's betrayal of his love with his own eyes. What though she had teased and tantalized him in her wilful way, when he had endeavoured to win from her a plain and simple acceptance of his love; yet had she accepted it by glance of eye and lingering touch of hand a thousand times since they were boy and girl together at school. Now he was to be cast aside like a broken toy; his faithful, honest devotion was to count nothing against the good looks and smart clothes of this alien to his rank and race. He had hated the idea of Amanda going down among the English people in the settlement, and had foreboded no good from it, and now the worst had happened.

He had seen her, without an effort of resistance, almost reclining in his rival's arms; and the starting to her feet and crying out his name, what were they but alarm at his discovery of her falseness? Never again would he trust his life's shaping to a woman's smiles. He was grievously wounded, not only in his love, but in his pride; the note of invitation to the dance became an insult, the coaxing words added by Amanda an outrage; words that he had repeated to himself a hundred times on his way up from Minnedosa, letting his imagination run riot in its anticipations of the joy so soon to be his, and this was the end of it all.

Yes, the end, for he could never settle down to the old quiet life by Otter Lake. How intolerable would the old routine of land toil on the farm and in the woods become, with the inspiration that gave it all its happiness gone for ever. How should he tell his father, the good old man who had not a thought beyond his happiness? He felt as if that deep and quiet sympathy would only accentuate and sharpen the bitterness of his own sense of loss. He must get away again as soon as might be from the old home; forgetfulness could never come amid the old surroundings so full of memories and associations of the past. Little by little the heat of his anger died down, to be followed by a dulled sense of misery; the horses, excited by the fierce shout of his voice and the keen cut of the whip with which he left Rosebank, gradually slackened their speed; the sleigh-bells gave only an occasional tinkle; the moon, that had been high and clear when he left town, was lowering towards the west, and was half hidden by light, low-drifting clouds.

His road now lay through the woods, the outlying bluffs of bare, leafless poplar were passed, and he was again in the full, sombre shade of the pine and the spruce. The gloom and silence were fitting to the gloom of his own thoughts and the silence of his heart, where no voice of hopefulness whispered of hope or love or happiness. Suddenly a piercing cry, almost human in its appeal, broke the silence, and a coyote crossed the track only a few yards in front of the horses, bearing in its jaws the crushed and mangled form of a bush rabbit. At Ludwig's shout the wolf dropped its prey, and slunk off into the woods, leaving its lifeless victim a little ball of snowy fur, flecked with blood, by the side of the trail.

The accident, trifling as it was and familiar to his experience, gave a new course to Ludwig's thoughts. His quick Norse imagination, nurtured on all the old weird legends of his people, seized on this tragedy of the suffering of nature, and moulded it to a new meaning.

"What if Amanda had been but as this little innocent creature of the woods, pure and innocent of thought of wrong? What if she, in childish innocence of lust and evil, had been seized upon by that ruthless wolf of an alien people? What if the purity of her maiden soul were already flecked with the blood-red drops of the violated purity of life? If," and his heart almost stilled its beating at the intensity of his thought, "if that be so, the wolf shall die, though I follow his bloody trail through a thousand miles of forest, and my own life be spent in tracking the beast of evil to his last den."

The increased darkness of his road seemed to match the gloominess of his thoughts. He had now left the main trail through the colony, and was following the narrow track cut through the woods that led to his father's house.

The wearied horses plodded along slowly, the newly fallen snow was light and untracked, and every now and again they would stumble on some hidden stump. The sky was overcast, and the line of snow showed but faintly before them through the dark masses of the spruce on either hand. Never had the road seemed so long to Ludwig. At last the trail spread out into the little clearing of his father's fields, and he could see the dim outline of the little log house and its outbuildings. With a jerk of the reins and a shout to the horses he roused them into a trot, and at the first tinkling of the sleigh-bells he heard the deep baying of Trofast, and a minute after the big Dane came bounding to meet him, the first angry notes of his bark changing to wild delight when he recognized Ludwig's voice.

Leaving the team standing by the wicket-gate, Ludwig strode up to the house, quieting as best he could the excited hound, and as he reached the threshold the door opened, and his father appeared with a lantern.

"Welcome home, my son, welcome home," and Christian embraced and kissed his son. "Welcome home; I knew by the sound of the good dog's bark that it could be only you."

"Yes, it's me, father, and glad to be home again. Give me the lantern till I put away the horses, and I will soon be in; but go back to bed again. I've had a long day, and am pretty well tired out."

"But you'll want something to eat and a fire, my boy, after your long drive in the cold?"

"Oh no, father, it's nearly morning. I'll just turn in for a few hours, and get a sleep, and then we can have a long talk after breakfast. I'm just too tired out to eat or talk now," and Ludwig's voice was indeed very weary.

He took the lantern from his father's hand, and turned back to the garden path. Tired as he was, he lingered over his task of unhitching his team and taking them to the stable. He did not wish his worn and haggard face to come under his father's quick-reading eyes, till sleep and time for a little thought had prepared him to face the future with a brighter and better courage than he felt possible for him to-night. When at length he re-entered the house, he threw off his outer clothes and, extinguishing the lantern, found his way to his bed, and was soon in the weary slumber of a body and mind equally exhausted.

Ludwig slept far into the morning, and was awakened by a light touch on his arm, and opened his eyes to find Trofast standing by his bunk with uplifted paw. The good dog could not understand why his master, usually astir at the first break of day, was lying there long after the sun was shining in at the little windows of the log house.

For some minutes Ludwig lay and let his mind travel back over the events of the preceding night, and at first his thoughts were full of bitterness; but by degrees the peace and quietness of the old home softened his heart. His eyes rested on the little picture of his mother, and he thought of the years of quiet strength and cheerfulness with which his father had borne the wrecking of his life's happiness. Should he be less brave to bear? Did all that strength and cheerfulness call for no sacrifice on his part? He would not hide his sorrow from his father's eyes—to attempt that he knew would be vain—but he would bear it as his father's son; and Ludwig got up and proceeded to dress.

A bowl of water, freshly melted snow, stood on the little stand by the door; a clean, if rough, towel was hanging on the wall by the side of the little mirror; the little table was set for breakfast; the fire was burning brightly in the stove; the freshness and cleanliness of it all was refreshing, after the coarse roughness of the past few weeks, spent in a threshers' caboose. It was good to be home again, and Ludwig went and opened the door and looked out. His father was just returning from the stable, half humming, half singing to himself a little snatch of an old-time Danish song of the sea, and Ludwig knew that his father's heart was glad at his return.

"Good-morning, father; it is a treat to hear you singing the good Danish tongue again, and to be back at the Otter Lake among the hills and the spruce, after being on the big lonesome prairie of the plains."

"And it's good to have my boy home again, for it's been rather quiet here for us without you, and Trofast has been looking for you every time there has been the sound of a waggon wheel or a sleigh-bell down the trail. But you are here safe again, and we'll go in and thank the good God, and then have our breakfast, for you'll be hungry enough."

They entered the house together, and Christian, hanging up his cap, took down the old Bible from its stand. The morning chapter and prayer, his father kneeling by his side before the little picture of his mother, had been part of Ludwig's life as long as he could remember. So simple and entire was Christian's sense of his wife's spiritual presence with him at all times of his life, that it had become a part of Ludwig's faith even from his childhood, the sense that there was always the unbroken family of father, mother, son, before the throne of God.

In his moments of repentance for boyish faults, usually faults springing from his hot, passionate temper, Ludwig had never separated father and mother from his thoughts as he sought reconciliation and forgiveness. The restraining influence of his father's presence was as great, perhaps, but no greater than that of the mother, whom he had never seen but in that faded picture of the bride of more than twenty years ago.

Christian's prayer that morning was the outpouring of gratitude to God for the restoration of the unity of the family, the bringing back of the child of their love to the waiting hearts of his parents.

CHAPTER XXIII

After breakfast Ludwig and his father had the "good talk" of which the former had spoken the night before, and with the softening influence of the old home upon him, Ludwig did not find it so difficult as it had seemed by anticipation. He began his narrative at the beginning with the day he left home. His work with Gus Anderson had been pleasant enough, and his first intention had been to return back to "Sweden" at "freeze up," but he had been tempted to prolong his absence by an offer from Gus to sell him the team with which he had been ploughing, if he would pay Gus a hundred dollars cash, and the balance in the spring, after he had sold the big pile of cord-wood which his father and he had cut down the winter before. But to do this it was necessary for him to earn more money before he returned home, and so he had hired with the threshing gang. Then he told of his uneasiness from his father's letter, and of the note of invitation from Rosebank, and his sudden resolution to come back at once.

Poor Ludwig found his task more difficult when he came to tell of his drive up from town, and of the shattering of his dreams when he looked through the hangings of the Rosebank veranda, but he told it through to the end with every detail—Amanda's abandonment to Roland Vale's embrace, the flushed and heated passion of Roland's face, Amanda's swift recognition and startled cry of Ludwig's name—and Ludwig's voice grew tense with feeling as he told of all his thoughts as he drove homeward through the woods.

Christian thought long in silence before he answered the eager questioning of his son's eyes. He read again the note of invitation from Rosebank with the innocent words of coquetry which Amanda had put at the end. At last he spoke slowly, but with conviction, as he tapped his finger impressively on the words where Amanda spoke of Ludwig's anxiety for his father and of the Otter Lake.

"The little Amanda is never false; she is quick of temper and high spirit, like yourself, my boy. It may be she is jealous of your speaking so much of your father and the like, but she would never betray you. You were late in your coming, and the night was far gone, the little maid was wearied and full of disappointment, it may be of resentment at your seeming neglect; who can tell? And the young man you speak of—the idle sons of the rich have no honour when they love, as they call it, the daughters of the poor—I grant you he may be base in thought and purpose; but think it not of Amanda, that she could be aught but pure and true of heart."

"Then you think, father, that all my black thoughts may only be a bad dream, and that Amanda may love me still?" broke in Ludwig impulsively. "Why was I so mad in my haste to think the worst, and never to give Amanda the time for a word? And now perhaps she will not forgive me; but shall she be left there alone and unprotected, away from her own people?"

"I do not think you need to fear for that," said his father thoughtfully. "Herr Hardie is a good man, and would guard her as a daughter, if he thought she were in danger; besides, she is soon to return home, and, if I mistake not, the young man whom you saw is already far away."

"Away, and how do you know?" asked Ludwig eagerly.

"I saw young Jenson this morning; he was going for wood with his oxen, and he said that he heard at the dance that Herr Hardie, the young Enderby, and another Englishman were going up to Herr Hardie's shanty for the deer-hunting, and I don't doubt that the young Englishman is the one whom you saw last night, for Amanda had spoken of such an one in her letters to her mother, saying that a young Englishman, learning to farm with the old Herr Enderby, came often to the Herr Hardie's. Stay quietly here for a few days, and I will go over to Ole Swanson's and hear, perhaps, when Amanda returns home."

Ludwig assented rather unwillingly, delay and patience were always difficult to his impulsive nature—still, it was something to have a new hope in his heart, when all before was so full of doubt and misery. It would be much, if only Amanda were once safe again among her own people.

From speaking of Amanda, Christian went on to tell his son of the reasons which had made him so unwilling to leave the little house by the Otter Lake for any length of time. It was not only that there had been the fires in the bush and in the hay meadow, for there were often fires in the woods after long dry weather in the fall of the year, but he was convinced that the fires were not the result of accident or of a careless lighted match thrown by some passer along the bush trails. More than once lately he had been aroused in the night by Trofast, who had his kennel by the porch, barking furiously as if some strange and unfriendly presence was near.

"But who, father," urged Ludwig, "who would wish you harm, you who have nought but friends in the whole of 'Sweden'?"

"Nought but good friends, as you say, Ludwig, among our own people, but I have thought it might be one of the Indian folk who have been wandering through the woods."

"Why, you have always been so kind to them, and often given them food and powder and shot, when they have come to the lake to shoot the wild fowl."

"Have you forgotten the Indian lad, old Black Hawk's son?"

"What! the young rascal I broke the bow over the day before I left home? Surely such a boy would not dare," said Ludwig incredulously.

"Maybe I am wrong," said his father doubtfully. "Neither he nor his father have been to the house since you left, and the old man often used to come for a bit of tobacco or a little tea, and I still see every day the smoke from their 'teepee' up the lake."

"Well," said Ludwig, "I'll go and look them up one of these days, and if I find them hanging round here at night, Trofast and I will chase them to their camp, and make them give an account of themselves. But I think it's all fancy, father, just from you being left here alone, and the fires were just an accident."

"Maybe—I hope so," said his father. "But you and Trofast are both a little hasty, and must not be too ready to make enemies of the Indians; they have long memories for injuries."

"Oh, I won't hurt them," said Ludwig lightly. "To-morrow I will take a turn through the wood with my rifle, and if I shoot a deer you shall give them half of it. They'll be your friends fast enough if you give them some deer's meat, and now, father, come out and let me show you my team of horse. We'll have a little work to do at the stable to make it warm and comfortable for them for the winter," and Ludwig led the way out of the house.

CHAPTER XXIV

Ludwig spent his first afternoon at home in making the stable warm and comfortable for his new team. It was the first time he had owned horses of his own, and he was full of pride in his new possession. In the estimation of "Sweden" the settler who drove horses was on a distinctly higher plane than the man who drove oxen. Indeed, besides more material advantages, Ludwig had hoped that his possession of horses might propitiate the good graces of Mrs. Swanson, who, he was conscious, did not look very favourably on his suit. Interest in his work, and his father's evident happiness in having him home again, kept his mind from dwelling on his own troubles, and when he went to bed at night, it was with some revival of his former keenness in hunting that he looked forward to the morrow. But with the morning came a change in his plans and feelings.

On taking his horses down to water at the hole cut in the ice by the edge of the lake, one of them proved to be dead lame. Ludwig found on examination that its fetlock had been deeply bruised, probably by some snag hidden by the snow on his journey through the woods, and it was much swollen and inflamed. The morning was spent in applying hot fomentations and such simple remedies as were at hand to the wounded part, and by the time he had done what he could for his horse his own desire for the hunting had gone. His dejection of the previous day, which had yielded somewhat to his father's sympathy and quiet hopefulness, returned, and the mishap to his horse seemed only a fresh reminder that he was marked by fate for misfortune.

It was more to please his father by an apparent interest, and to be alone with his thoughts, that in the middle of the afternoon he took down his rifle and hunting-knife from the wall, and went, as he said, for a turn through the bush before supper—bidding his father not to be uneasy if night should have fallen before his return. Trofast, who had bounded up from his mat by the stove as his master took down his rifle, slunk back again, and crouched down with an air of deepest dejection at the sharp, curt tones in which he was bidden "Lie down, dog"; and it was with an unwonted weakening of his usual quiet confidence in the benignant power of God that Christian Nielson watched the listless fashion in which Ludwig, after pausing for a few moments at the wicket-gate, took his way across the opening, and was lost to sight in the spruce bluffs by the lake shore.

For some time the old sailor stood by the open door, unconscious of the frosty keenness of the winter air, with an occasional quiet and friendly word of sympathy with the crestfallen hound, who, from his mat by the stove, was watching the door, in the faint hope that some relenting of his master's severity might set him free from the iron bond of obedience in which he had been trained. But no call or whistling summons came, and Trofast's last hope fled when Christian slowly closed the door, and began to busy himself with the small domestic duties of the house.

For half a mile or so Ludwig strode moodily along, following one of the many paths that ran along the lake shore, for owing to the long dry weather of the fall, the smaller sloughs were dried up, and the cattle came from many of the settlers' homesteads to the lake to drink. Wrapped in his thoughts, and noticing but little whither his way was leading him, it was with a start of surprise that, on stepping from the sheltering trees of a bluff, and coming out into a small clearing, he saw only a few yards away the forlorn and dilapidated teepee of old Black Hawk.

Down by the lake shore two Indian ponies were pawing away the snow to get at the dead and frozen grass beneath, a roughly fashioned sledge was in front of the opening of the teepee, and here Old Black Hawk himself was busily engaged in repairing the sledge-box, which carried all his Lares and Penates in his wandering from one camping-ground to another.

For a moment Ludwig thought of retiring back into the shelter of the bush, and of skirting through the woods till the clearing was past; but, as he hesitated for a moment, a dog came barking from the teepee, and Old Black Hawk looked up quickly from his work. With a sudden change of purpose Ludwig strode across the few yards of open ground till he stood by the old Indian's side.

"Moving camp, Black Hawk?" asked Ludwig, pointing to the sledge at which the old man was working—but a grunt of a non-committal character was the only reply vouchsafed, for Black Hawk was not at all sociable in his dealings with the white man, and disdained any knowledge of their language unless there was a prospect of a gift of tobacco or gunpowder.

"Going deer-hunting?" continued Ludwig, pointing to the north, and tapping the barrel of his rifle. Black Hawk raised, as it were for a moment, the corner of the veil of blank inexpressiveness, which had fallen over his face at his first sight of Ludwig.

"Black Hawk no hunt deer," and he bent over his work again.

"Crusty old rascal; I'll be bound you are after no good," said Ludwig to himself. "Have a smoke, Black Hawk?" he added aloud, and the old Indian so far relaxed his stolidity as to reach out his hand for the plug of tobacco which Ludwig held out to him, and which he thrust into a pouch under his blanket.

"Catch many rats?" asked Ludwig, pointing to some traps lying by the side of the sledge. "Plenty rats, eh, Black Hawk?"

"Much cold, no water," and Black Hawk embraced the whole horizon by a wide wave of his arm, and then relaxing under the influence of the unexpected tobacco, pointing to the east, he went on: "Black Hawk go big water—fish—Manitoban—white man give Black Hawk plenty meat—plenty"—and he held up the grimy old blanket that fell from his shoulders.

"Oh, you're going fishing to Lake Manitoba for the winter, and expect the priests at the Mission to look after you—you've a long way to travel. Do you start to-day, Black Hawk?" And by a little pantomime Ludwig suggested the falling down of the tepee, and pointed to the ponies.

Old Black Hawk shook his head emphatically, and pointed to the black bank of cloud coming up from north-east. "Plenty snow, plenty storm." And three times from east to west the old Indian marked the daily passage of the sun across the heavens.

"I believe the old fellow's right," said Ludwig to himself, divining his meaning, and for the first time conscious of the rising breath of wind whispering among the tree-tops. "Three days' storm, Black Hawk—well, so long," and he turned as if to leave, and then wheeling quickly round, and laying a heavy hand on the Indian's shoulder, he looked him straight in the eyes: "Black Hawk, who fired the hay by the lake?"

For one briefest moment a venomous flash lit the old man's eye, followed by an absolute death of all intelligent expression. Shaking off Ludwig's grasp he bent over his sledge, and picked up again his hatchet, muttering: "Black Hawk no talk English—Black Hawk no know."

Ludwig realized that his coup had failed. "Well, Black Hawk, English or no English, if I catch you or that young imp of yours round the place, look out." And there was a note of menace in his voice that needed no knowledge of speech to interpret its meaning to the old Indian, who did not raise his eyes from his work till Ludwig had passed out of sight into the woods.

The interview had not soothed Ludwig's spirits, and though he had little expectation of seeing any deer so far down in the settlement, he determined to make a sweep round the south side of the lake, and to return home by the western shore—crossing by the ice when he came opposite his home. The four or five miles of tramping would wear off, maybe, some of the soreness of his heart and temper. But, in hunting, fortune comes often to those who least seek it, and so it was with Ludwig. He had just determined to leave the bush and make his way home across the lake when, only a few yards from his path, in the thick saskatoon scrub where they had lain down, three elk, a buck and two does, started to their feet. For one brief, but fatal moment, the buck stood to sniff the breeze. Led to the chase from his boyhood, Ludwig's rifle was already at his shoulder, and with a hasty aim he fired.

With a bound the elk crashed through the undergrowth, and though it was at once lost to view, Ludwig was satisfied that it had received a deadly wound, for its path through the bush was marked by a trail of blood. Night was at hand, the sky was dark and lowering, and already heavy flakes of snow were thick in the air. There was no time for the leisurely waiting till the deer should weary in its flight, and lie down to stiffen and to die; he would, as he had done once before, put his mind and speed against that of his prey, and follow as swiftly as he could the blood-marks on the snow. At some clearing in the bush he might come in sight of the wounded beast, and a second shot would complete its course.

All Ludwig's listlessness was gone; the fiery keenness of the hunter was coursing through his veins. Pulling his cap hard down over his head, and tightening the belt of his leather jacket, he ploughed into the thick spruce. Twice he caught a momentary glimpse of the wounded deer as it crossed small clearings in the bush, but both times, quick as he was in handling his rifle, it had disappeared again before he could get even a running shot.

By openings and old trails, which he crossed, Ludwig knew that the chase was taking him far to the north of the lake and his father's house. The snow was falling more thickly, and it was growing darker under the heavy plumes of the spruce; but the danger of being lost in the woods or overtaken by storm never suggested a thought of abandoning the pursuit. He paused for a moment as he came to a steep ravine. At its foot was the bed of the creek near Herr Hardie's shanty. If only the deer would turn and follow its course to the meadows, he would get a good shot at it in the open. Hark, he could hear it; by its dull and heavy gasps, it was well-nigh spent.

In the very glow of his anticipated triumph a rifle shot rang out, so sharply that it seemed only a few yards away, followed by a crashing of dead branches, and a dull thud at the foot of the ravine. So sharp and near was the report, so tense was every nerve, that Ludwig sprang backward as if he himself had received the fatal bullet. For a moment he stood as though dazed, then swiftly, and with a rush of sudden anger, he realized the truth; not so would he be robbed of his hard-won reward.

With silent carefulness he made his way through the scrub to the bed of the creek; there in the narrow rocky bed between its banks, some forty yards down its course, lay the deer, and bending over it, hunter's knife in hand, was the robber of his spoils. With bounding steps from stone to stone of the creek bed, Ludwig was by his side, an upward blow of his rifle sent the hunter's knife flying far away to be buried in the snow, and with a voice quiet in passion, "The deer is mine" he said.

CHAPTER XXV

Mutual recognition came to the two men in a flash, recognition that brought even a fierce sense of joy to their hot and passionate young blood. Here was a fitting time for the strife to the death of love and lust; here, amidst the primeval surroundings of forest and storm, was to be fought the primeval strife for the possession of the coveted mate. Each was conscious in his own heart that much more than the possession of the deer was involved in the solution of its ownership, though Ludwig was determined that no other cause of strife should pass his lips; never should Amanda's fair name be soiled by bandying words with such an one as he judged Roland Vale to be.

The characteristics of their blood and upbringing showed in either of the young men, as they stood for a brief moment gazing each into the other's eyes—Roland's flashing and passionate, full too of scorn and contempt; Ludwig's with a dull and sombre gloom, for he was holding a supreme control over the fire of jealousy that had been consuming him for the past three days, and the struggle for self-mastery left his features drawn and colourless.

Roland was the first to break the silence with loud and angry voice, as he held up the arm that had been struck with the rifle.

"What the devil do you mean by hitting me like that?" and he turned back the cuff of his hunting-coat, showing a red wheal across the white skin of his wrist. "Damn it, fellow, what do you mean?" he repeated.

"The deer is mine," said Ludwig slowly, and he placed his foot on the neck of the dead elk that lay between them, and he went on more slowly, as if he found it hard to find the words of the alien tongue, "The deer is mine, by every hunter's law. He that shall wound the deer, to him the deer belongs."

"First wound be hanged! There in its side is the shot that brought it down," retorted Roland, pointing to the gaping wound where his dumdum bullet had found its way to the dead creature's heart.

"And whence then comes all this blood that is already dry, and clotted to its side?" asked Ludwig.

"I don't care a hang where it came from," said Roland loudly. "When I shoot a deer I'm going to have it. It would be a mile away by now, for all your shooting would have done to stop it."

"That is not so," and Ludwig's voice became quieter and slower in its even monotony. "The deer was wounded to the death, and spent with the loss of the blood and of its life. Herr Englishman, the deer is mine."

Roland's hot courage was retreating before the still persistency of the other's claim, he began to realize, though not to admit, its force; he realized too the disadvantage at which he stood to enforce his own right of possession. His rifle he had leaned against a fallen tree some yards away, his knife was lost in the snow. What were his chances? "But the beggar shan't have it all his own way, if he can feel under that thick hide of his," for Roland had been betrayed to a very false conclusion by the slow quietness of Ludwig's speech.

"See here, you fellow, I'll take the head, and you can have the carcass, I don't want to eat beastly deer's meat all winter."

"I care neither for the head nor yet for the carcass of the deer, but the deer is mine by hunters' law, and mine shall the deer remain," and Ludwig slung his rifle over his shoulder and pulled round his belt as if to reach his hunter's knife. "Stand back, that I may cut open the deer before it be stiff and cold."

"Hang your hunters' law! I want the head, and it's no good to you. Look here, I'll give you ten dollars for it," and Roland pulled out some money from his breast pocket. "I'll take the head and," in his irritation he could not keep back the lying retort, "you can take the deer—and the rest of my leavings."

"Your leavings?" and Ludwig, who was already stooping over the elk, sprang upright with a fierce cry; "your leavings, Herr Englishman? How mean you by that?"

"I mean what the devil you like to think I mean," for Roland's temper rose hot again to the change in the Dane's face and voice.

"You shall say that mean here and now, or, by the living God, Herr Englishman, you or I leave not the spot alive," and a rising ring came to Ludwig's voice, and a flashing light to his eye. "Your leavings, Herr Englishman, answer."

Roland started back a step, daunted by the fierceness of voice and gesture; he shrank from the unequal strife, but stubborn pride would not let him withdraw at the threats of this—to him—low-born peasant.

"I mean you can marry the girl if you like—and if she will have you. I wish you joy of your bargain for she's a devil of a temper of her own. Keep the deer by your hunter's law," and with a swift leap he sprang to his rifle, and as his hand grasped it he turned with a mocking laugh, "Keep the deer by your hunter's law, but by God by the same law the girl should be mine."

With the bound of a wounded lion, Ludwig was upon him, ere he could raise the rifle and lay his hand upon the trigger, and grip of iron was at his throat, and the glint of uplifted knife flashed in his eyes.

The Berserk rage of his forefathers was upon Ludwig; gone was all the restraining power of mind and will; a wild torrent of passions raged through his heart: be it truth or falsehood the Englishman should die. The knife was raised high above his head, and then, swift as the first flash of lightning in a summer's storm, the sight of his helpless enemy passed from his vision, and in its place, clear to its last detail, came the little log house by the Otter Lake; and, as though he were looking through its open doorway, there was the little lake, the open word of God, and his father kneeling with uplifted arms to the cross that stood beneath the little faded picture of his mother's bridal morn.

Swiftly as it came the vision passed, but God had heard and answered the parent's prayer. The knife with a sweep of the uplifted arm was hurled far down the bed of the creek, the grip on Roland's throat relaxed, and with a wild cry Ludwig leapt up the steep slope of the ravine, and plunged into the woods, heedless of storm and the gathering gloom of night; heedless of wound and scar from fallen tree or intercepting bough. Escape, how it might be or where it might be, was all he sought—escape from broken faith and from every lost hope—from the dark shadow of the guilt of murder.

Slowly Roland arose from the ground on which he had sunk in half unconsciousness from the fierce grip of Ludwig's hand about his throat. Picking up his rifle, which lay half buried in the snow at his feet, he stumbled with uncertain steps down the creek bed towards the meadows. Gone was every thought of passion, a great weariness of mind and body alike seemed creeping over him, only let him gain the light and warmth of the shanty again, and he felt that he would be content to lie down and sleep, sleep, though he never woke again to a world of broken strivings—of strivings in which the victory always fell to the lower promptings of his wayward heart.

Guided by the narrow bed of the creek, with many a fall and stumble over the stones now hidden by the deepening snow, at last he reached the opening on the hay meadows. The shanty and warmth and rest were only a few hundred yards away, but darkness was falling like a pall over the meadows, the spruce-clad hills were only marked by a deeper gloom, the air was thick with falling flakes of snow, the breeze that had heralded its coming was stilled. He dare not trust himself to find his way across the untracked meadows, and he was so weary. Surely Bert and Jim would come to look for him, at least for a little he would sit down and rest, so sweeping away the snow from a big boulder he sank down upon it, and buried his head in his hands.

Wearily his mind passed through again the perils and passions of the day. Already they seemed dimmed and uncertain, as though they belonged to a time long past, and that had no real part and share in his own life; the real Roland Vale was a boy again, and saying his prayer by his mother's knee, his mother's hand resting lovingly upon his bended head, "Forgive us our trespasses, as we forgive them that trespass against us, and lead us not into temptation, but deliver us from evil." A crash as if of thunder from the gloom of the ravine—a flash of lurid light—Roland Vale fell forward with outstretched arms, shot through the heart.

CHAPTER XXVI

When Bert Enderby and Jim Hardie started off with the horse and stone boat, to bring in the moose which they had shot in the morning, they fully expected to be back at the shanty before dark. The distance to the spot where the dead deer had been left was not great, and for a good part of the way they were able to follow the fairly open course of the surveyor's line, but when they had to turn into the bush, they made very slow progress. The trees were closer together, and the undergrowth thicker than they had realized in the heat of their excitement in the morning, and it was a slow and laborious task to make even the rough and narrow path necessary for the passage of the horse and the stone boat.

At last the spot was reached, and then it did not take very long to skin the moose, and to load the four quarters and the head with its wide branching antlers upon the boat, and they started again for the shanty. Jim, with his wider knowledge of the dangers of the bush, was urgent that not a minute should be lost; the snow was falling heavily from the leaden sky, and though he had no fear of losing his own way back, he was full of apprehension lest Roland should have left the shanty, and should be still in the bush when the storm came on. Just as they emerged from the thick wood on the surveyor's line, Jim stopped the horse with a jerk.

"Hark to that, Bert," he exclaimed, as a dull rumbling came to them through the snow-laden air. "Hark to that; it was a rifle, and not far from the shanty. I hope to God the lad is safe."

"Oh, it might not be him," said Bert; "there would be a lot of people out in the woods to-day—I guess Roland would be too tired to leave the shanty and the stove after his tramp this morning."

"Maybe, maybe," replied Jim doubtfully; "but those young fellows are venturesome when they first get out in the bush with a gun in their hands, but we must push on as well as we can." And they resumed their journey.

Full as they both were of anxiety, their progress was slow, for the snow was deepening on the trail, and there were many snags and half-rotted stumps, and now and again the horse would be stopped suddenly, as the stone boat struck against them, and then perhaps scarcely would one stump be cut away and a few yards more be traversed, when exactly the same thing would happen again.

Both men had the dogged endurance begotten of their western life, and after many such delays, they turned into the wider trail that led down to the shanty, and the horse quickened its step with a new confidence; though the darkness of night was deepening, the gloom of the storm and the path before them was little more than a blackness less pall-like than the massive gloom of the forest on either hand. They had ceased to use the reins for guidance, trusting rather to the instinct of the beast to find its way to its shelter and its mate, and tying them to the bunk of the stone boat, they plodded along in silence behind the load. More by feeling a gradual dip in the road and by a freshening of the air, they guessed they were out of the bush, and crossing the opening at the end of the hay meadows, another sloping rise and the horse stopped dead. Making his way round to its head, Bert thrust his hands into the darkness; they struck sharply against a flat surface.

"Say, Jim," he shouted, "we're home; the old horse has brought us to the stable door," and a loud whinnying welcome from the other horse within confirmed the good news. "Shall we make our way to the shanty, and see if Roland's safe, and then come back and put the horse away?" continued Bert.

"No, no; you get the lantern from the stable, and I'll unhitch the horse, and we'll get Jerry into his stall, and the harness off, and give him some hay," decided Jim, with the Canadian's habitual placing the care of his horse first. "If the boy's in the shanty, he's safe anyway; and if he's in the bush, God help him, for we cannot"; and Jim was already undoing strap and buckle, and by the time the lantern was lighted, Jerry was in his stall, and his wringing coat being vigorously rubbed down with a wisp of hay.

In a few minutes both horses were fed, and the two men were outside the stable door, Jim pausing to make sure that the rough bolt that fastened it was securely home. The stable lantern shone with a dull gloom, barely shedding a dim light through the falling snow, for a few feet; beyond that narrow circle all was impenetrable darkness. Bert was stepping off into the black night with the lantern, and had gone a few hasty steps when he was called back sharply by Jim:

"Back to me, Bert, back right to the door; you and me will be lost the first thing we know, if we leave the stable before we take our bearings, and we would be worse off with the lantern than in the dark."

"By Jove, you're right, Jim," said Bert. "I never realized how dark it could be; you take the lantern, and I'll walk right behind you," and he handed the lantern to Jim, who paused for a few minutes before stepping off, counting each step as he took it. "Thirty yards west from the stable door, and then ten yards right north, as straight as we can make it, should fetch the shanty."

So near was Jim's calculation, that they came to within a few feet of the shanty door, and then for a moment, his hand on the latch, Jim paused. His heart was sick at the quick flash through his mind: "If the poor lad were not there"; then throwing the door wide, he stepped into the shanty, raising his voice, harsh with anxiety.

"Vale, I say, Vale, are you here?"

No answering voice replied; Jim turned up the lantern, and held it above his head till its light embraced every corner of the little room. No Roland was there; the blankets of his bunk were folded neatly at its head, as Jim had left them himself in the morning. By the stove was the old easy chair, with the bundle of English papers lying on the floor beside it. On the table were Roland's pipe and pouch, and the pen and ink which he had used in writing to his mother.

Jim laid his hand on the stove, it was still warm, and when he raised the lid a few spent ashes glowed red within it; it must be two or three hours since it had been replenished with fuel.

"Poor lad, poor lad," said Jim softly, as he placed the lantern on the table, and unslung his rifle from his shoulders; "I'm doubting we should not have left him here by himself, and him know no more than a child what the dangers of the bush are."

"What are the chances, Jim, of his living through the night and finding his way back in the morning when the storm is over?" asked Bert.

"Chances," replied Jim slowly, "he had no chances. An Indian could not find his way through that snow. Unless before the darkness and the storm came, he had fallen in with some old hunter, who had taken him to shelter, he will have laid down to sleep—and to die before to-morrow's sun rises."

"But the rifle shot we heard when we were back north," urged Bert, trying to hope against hope; "if it were his, might he not be near by it, and fired it to warn us of his danger? Is there nothing we can do?"

"Well, we can fire a few shots from the shanty door, but the sound will travel but badly in this smother of snow, and I'm afraid if it reached where the poor lad is, he'll be past answering back." And Jim picked up his rifle and the two men stepped to the door, Bert holding the lantern. The air outside was mild and still, but full of heavy flakes of slow-falling snow, the very footprints of their tracks without the door were already filled, leaving no trace of their existence.

Slowly Jim raised his rifle to his shoulder and fired, and then both listened intently for a few minutes, and then he fired again. For a full half-hour they stood without the shanty door, Jim firing his rifle at intervals; but no answering sound came from the darkness. Both felt the hopeless futility of their efforts; both dreaded the admission of its futility.

"It's no good," said Jim at last, stamping his feet clear of the snow, and slapping his hunter's coat, as he turned and reopened the door. "It's no good we can do to-night; if it clears by morning, we can try and find his tracks near the new snow, if only the wind will keep down."

Sadly, and for the most part in silence, they made up the fire and set about preparing a meal—some bread and cheese, and some cold pork left over from breakfast. They had no heart to cook any of the moose-steak they had brought home at noon, and then they sat by the stove and smoked.

At midnight it was still snowing, though the blackness of the night was changing to a heavy sombre grey, for somewhere in the east, beyond the snow-laden clouds, was the rising of the last quarter of the moon. For a minute or two they stood and looked out of the door, and then, as they came back to the light, Jim noticed that his friend was almost staggering, from weariness of body and want of sleep.

"Do lie down, Bert," he said kindly, "lie down and get some sleep; we can only trust in God, and wait for the morning. I'll keep the fire on, and have a nod or two in the old chair. I'll call you by daybreak."

Throwing off his hunter's coat, Bert lay down in his bunk, and was soon in a heavy slumber, while Jim dozed and woke and woke and dozed in the old chair, always seeming to wake up in time to renew the fire before it was quite out.

At six Jim roused himself for the day, made up the fire, and put on the kettle and the water for the porridge, and had a refreshing wash before going to the door. The snow had ceased falling, the sky was clear, and to the south-west the waning moon was shining in a sharp and frosty air.

"If the wind keeps down we may find the poor lad yet," said Jim to himself, and there was a fresh hope in his heart as he roused up Bert, and then set about the cooking of the breakfast, which was ready by the time Bert was fairly awake and had washed the drowsiness of slumber from his heavy eyes.

"We must eat hearty, Bert, for we've some heavy tramping to do, if we can only hit the lad's trail," said Jim, as he put a smoking steak of moose meat on his companion's plate, and proceeded to help himself to its mate from the frying-pan. "The white man isn't a patch on the Indian, if it comes to going without grub," he continued reflectively; "but I couldn't eat last night when we were cooped in by the storm and the darkness."

Breakfast over, they took the lantern to go to the stable and feed and "fix up" the team. The fresh-fallen snow was up to their knees, but light and crisped by the frostiness of the air, and they made their way to the stable with little trouble, and Bert shovelled a rough path back to the shanty while Jim fed and groomed his team.

The first shining of the moon was dimming before the promise of the dawn in the east, where the advent of the sun was already heralded by a rosy glow of light. Their work done, the two men stood and watched the

116

swift-changing glories of the sky from the shanty door; the heavens indeed "declared the glory of God," but the very wealth of their vivid and glorious clouds filled Jim's heart with apprehension.

"It's splendid, Bert, just splendid; but it means wind, and a lot of it soon, and this loose snow will fly like feathers."

Almost as he spoke a curt puff of wind struck the tops of the spruce bluff behind the shanty, and died away as swiftly as it came, leaving a myriad of glittering crystals from the snow-laden branches floating in the air. Then came a stillness, a calm so absolute that the very atmosphere seemed to be holding its breath; a second volley of wind, and ere it had died away down the hay meadows, a third and fourth, a very battery from the army of the storm king of the north; the glories of the morn were drilled to a heavy crimson haze, centred by the now risen sun as by a bloody disc. The path to the stable was filled again with snow, and drifts were forming against the sheltered side of the shanty where the two men stood, numbed to helplessness by the suddenness and violence of the storm.

Then, as one startled from a heavy sleep, Jim shook Bert roughly by the shoulder and shouted in his ear: "For God's sake, rouse up, or you and I will never leave the bush alive," and opening the door he dragged Bert into the shanty and forced to the door.

Re-lighting the lantern, Jim placed it on the table, and throwing himself into the old easy chair by the stove, buried his head in his hands; but only for a few moments, and when he spoke again his voice had recovered its old quiet tone of confidence and resolution—of confidence in the Providence of God, and in a man's duty to his own manliness, coupled with an apology for his own weakness.

"You'll be thinking you're camping with 'a green horn,' Bert, instead of an old hunter. I've seen some pretty sudden storms, but this is a regular 'old timer,' and my mind was so set on doing something for the poor lad. God help him, but it's you and me we've got to figure on now, and the folk at home," and for a moment Jim's voice wavered. "The shanty is rough, but it's pretty solid, and I guess the roof is heavy enough to stand the racket."

"And the team?" asked Bert doubtfully.

"Oh, the stable will stand all right; the bluff will break the storm, but we shall have our own time in getting across to it, and will have to melt snow to water the team. We'd best get busy with it now, for it will be a slow job with only the kettle and the old iron pot." And Bert brightened up, with the prospect of something to be done.

By noon they had the stable buckets, the pot, the kettle, and an old boiler, in which they had brought down some of their supplies, filled with snow water, and they decided to have dinner before making an attempt to take it out to the team in the stable, and then, if the storm showed no sign of breaking, to give them hay enough to last till the following morning. What they knew would be a hard and perilous task proved to be impossible. On Jim's opening the shanty door, the snow was found to be drifted nearly to its top, and a curling eddy of wind swept a mass of the light snow into his face and past him in the room.

"It's no good, Bert; here we must stay till the gale does down," said Jim, forcing the door shut; and taking off again his fur cap and mitts, he came back to his chair by the stove. There the two men sat through the weary afternoon, speaking but little, and then of trivialities, for their deeper thoughts would not bear expression, and the free-masonry of the pipe and the tobacco plug robbed their silence of any feeling of unsociability. The dim light that struggled through the little window of the shanty was becoming still fainter through the gathering dusk of approaching night, when, after an unusually prolonged silence, Jim exclaimed suddenly:

"Bert, I believe it's letting up; it seems to me that there is a break in the force of the wind. Listen to that," as a furious blast struck the back of the shanty, followed by a sudden lull.

So it was, with the same startling suddenness with which it had arisen, the blizzard ceased. In the course of a few minutes there was only an occasional gust of wind; then followed an absolute calm. Opening again the door, they found the snow banked to its top, but they soon shovelled it back for a few feet, and then clambered through the drift to where the fierce wind had blown the ground clear. Everywhere, where it had been exposed to the force of the storm, the slope on which the shanty stood was swept bare. A mound of snow near the stable marked where they had left the stone boat and its load the night before; another mound in front of the shanty was the bob sleighs, in which they had come up to the bush; a third and larger mound, showing a rough log wall, where the wind had caught it, was the stable.

Bert and Jim set to work with a will to make the most of the twilight, before darkness fell or the storm returned. With hard shovelling they soon cut a way to the stable door, and watered the horses and fed them. The poor creatures whinnied with eager delight when they heard their voices, for they had been terrified by the roar of the storm. Then they dug out the sleighs, and dragged them as near as they could to the shanty door. One quarter of the moose they carried across to the sleighs, the rest they put in a corner of the stable on some clean hay; it would be safe there till they came back again later in the winter, if they came back. Then, tired out, they returned to the shanty and cooked their supper, after which they packed up such things as they absolutely needed, and put them in the sleigh—including poor Roland's bag. The night was still calm and clear when they lay down to sleep and to wait for the morning, a morning that came with a bitter and keener frost, but a clear and steely sky. With brave but heavy hearts they hitched up the team at the first glimmer of dawn, and started to fight their way back to civilization and home, and the anxious hearts that awaited them.

CHAPTER XXVII

The news of the catastrophe at Jim Hardie's hunting shanty spread very slowly through the settlement, for the day's calm after the big blizzard was followed for several days by a succession of lighter falls of snow, during which the settlers mostly stayed at home, waiting for some one else to break out the roads which were badly drifted.

Jim Hardie kept a close look-out on the town line, and questioned every returning party of the hunters who were making their way out of the bush, where the deep snow had made any further prospect of successful hunting out of the question; but, though he heard of many hardships suffered in the big blizzard, there was no word of Roland Vale.

For two weeks the mail carrier failed to make his way up from Minnedosa, but at the end of that time a fine mild spell came, and the mail day found several of the settlers gathered at the post-office, partly in hopes of receiving letters, for even a "dunner" is a break in the monotony of life in the west, still more for the chance of hearing a little news of their neighbours.

It was not the custom for those who came for their letters to receive a very hearty welcome from old Mrs. Dawson and Mary Ann, for although it was a public office, for the keeping of which "old Dawson" received a few dollars yearly and a percentage on stamps sold from the Dominion Government, they always had the air of distributing the mail under protest, and as a matter of favour. It is to be feared that old Mrs. Dawson harboured a spirit of deep-seated ill-will against some of the English settlers, purely on account of the large quantity of papers and letters which they received from the "old country," as she often said they "would track up her clean floor with their dirty boots, and they were that secretive, they wouldn't even open their letters till they left the office."

To-day, however, the Dawson family were in high feather, even to "Old" Dawson himself, who usually, like Agag, went delicately on mail days, for they had what, as far as most of the settlement was concerned, was "a corner" on a highly sensational piece of news—ill news too. Even Tom Dennis, a prime offender in the matters of dirty boots and a big budget of mail, was welcomed and given a warm corner by the stove. Old Mrs. Dawson had great powers of self-control, and Mary Ann and the "old man" were under excellent discipline, so no word betrayed their knowledge of anything of unusual interest till she judged the most effective moment had come, when, in a lull in the conversation of the group of men round the stove, she remarked casually:

"Jim Hardie was up the day before yesterday."

"Did he get a deer?" interrupted Tom Dennis.

"Jim Hardie would do better to stay at home, and look after that delicate wife of his, than to go after his deer-hunting like a wild Indian," retorted the old woman, tempted off the main track of her narrative for a moment. "I think he might be old enough," she added, with some acerbity, "to leave such foolishness to them as is not likely to get a wife, and are too lazy to help one if they had."

"But, mother, tell the folk what he said," broke in Mary Ann.

"He said as how—if my darter here will give me time to speak; when I was a young woman, children weren't so ready to snap the words out of their elders' mouths."

"Shall I tell the folk, mother?" and old Dawson laid his pipe down on the back of the stove and pushed back his chair. "You see, Jim said as how ——"

"When I want yez to talk for me, Samuel Dawson, I won't be skeered to ask yez," said his wife with great contempt; but she took up her story forthwith, before daughter or husband could recover from their discomfiture.

"Jim Hardie said as him and young Enderby had pretty nigh left themselves in the bush under the snow till spring came. They were two nights and a day in the shanty in the storm, and they had the terriblest time to get back home. They started before daybreak, and it was near midnight when they got back to Rosebank, more dead than alive, and his wife near crazy thinking he'd be lost."

"Well, I don't see what there is to fuss about," said Tom Dennis, with disgust at the tameness of the apparent climax. "They got out anyway."

"They got out," went on the old woman, with great deliberation; "but there was one as didn't."

"By Gad, young Vale!" ejaculated Tom Dennis. "Of course, he told me he was going up with Bert and Jim Hardie. What happened to him, Mrs. Dawson?"

"That's what I'm after telling yez, Mr. Dennis," went on the old woman more amiably, for the attention which she was now receiving was quite satisfactory, and she proceeded to recount Jim's story with much circumstance, and far more detail than Jim himself had supplied her with.

"Poor beggar, I guess he's under the snow," said Tom Dennis, "and he seemed to be a very decent chap too. I wonder whether he would go far in the storm or just lie down and go to sleep. I've heard people say that freezing to death is just the easiest finish a fellow can make."

121

"He was a real nice young man, as affable as could be," said Mary Ann sympathetically. "He was down at Mr. Hardie's at the threshing, and helped me and that young woman from Sweden with the dishes, just as friendly as never was, and it was always 'Miss Dawson,' just as respectful as could be, and his poor ma never knowing at this minute but what he's real well."

"I mind," began old Dawson, who had been slowly recovering from his previous rebuff, "I mind when I was a lad down in Onteerio there was a mort of snow early one winter, and Jake Macguire's nigh ox got lost in the bush"; but the fate of the nigh ox was left in mystery, for at that moment the house door was opened with a burst, and Dave, the Rosebank chore boy, entered with a rush.

"Sakes, boy, what do you mean by skeering folk like that?" asked old Mrs. Dawson shrilly, as soon as she could find her voice; "the likes of yez might knock at the door and behave."

"It's found. Jim found it." Dave gasped, as soon as he caught his breath.

"What's found, you young idiot?" asked Tom Dennis, giving him a shake; "what the devil are you talking about?"

"The corpse," gasped Dave, "the white and frozen corpse."

"Whose corpse?" demanded Tom Dennis quickly.

"Why, the young man from the Dingle, as went with Jim and Bert Enderby to the hunting—all white and stiff and weltering in its gore—and a bullet in its heart."

"Good God!" ejaculated Tom. "Had he shot himself?"

"Stop, Tom, and give the lad a chance," said Neil Grant, one of the older men in the group. "Now sit down and tell us all about it."

"Well, you see," said Dave more collectedly, as soon as he was seated, "Jim wasn't easy as soon as the rough weather was over, not to go back and see if he couldn't find any trace of young Mr. Vale, or if any of the Swedes out hunting might have seen him the day of the storm. So him— that's Jim—and Bert Enderby struck off yesterday morning with a team and the 'jumper' to try and break a trail out to Jim's shanty. They got there nigh on noon, and put the team in the stable, and had their dinner themselves in the shanty, and then started out on snow-shoes for the ravine at the end of the meadows, where Jim had told Mr. Vale he might find a deer. Well, sure enough, half-way down the meadows, where the new snow was blown away, they found tracks a-leading right along the hillside, up to the ravine as Jim spoke of. Well, when they got there, the old creek bottom was filled pretty nigh a-full with drifted snow, and they was just nigh turning back, when Jim, he saw something sticking up out of the snow some twenty yards up the ravine.

122

" 'What's that?' says he to Bert, pointing at it"; and Dave's Stepney Causeway bringing-up gave dramatic realism to his recital.

" 'What's that?'

" 'It might be the end of a rifle,' said Bert, and they looked at one another scared like, and then they took off their snow-shoes, and started to tramp through the snow up to it, and it was a rifle, and none of the cartridges in it had been fired off," and Dave looked round to see if he was producing the proper effect on the eager faces round him.

"There was no empty cartridges in it," he added impressively.

" 'Poor lad,' says Jim, 'poor lad,' and they neither of them liked to move their feet, for fear of what they might be a stepping on, you see. At last Jim, he began moving the snow gently away with his foot, and then he stopped for he felt something under the snow, kind of stiff, and he put his hand down through the snow and felt it, and it was him. So Jim and Bert set to to shovel away the snow with their snow-shoes till they got a clear space round it, feeling very sad-like, for they never thought but what he'd just got lost in the storm, and sat down and been smothered by the snow; and then they lifted him up and there, right under where he had been lying, was a patch of snow all bloody and red and frozen. Bert Enderby, he went faint-like, and sat right down, but Jim he picked up the rifle again and opened it, and took out the cartridges, three of them there was, and just stared at them, for not a one of them had been fired off. At last Bert, he spoke in a whisper, 'He has been murdered, Jim; whoever——'

" 'Don't say murder, Bert,' said Jim. 'He's been shot, poor lad, sure enough; but God only knows how, and we must take him home.'

"So they laid him down and brushed away the snow from his face, and Jim says he looked as peaceful and happy as a child asleep, Jim says; and then they went back for the 'jumper' and team, and started right back for home. They came straight to Jim's, and they put 'it' in the new granary, and Bert, he went home and tell his ma, before any one else could tell her sudden-like, and then Jim, he came in and lay down on the lounge till this morning, for we were all asleep, and never heard nothing. He called me at daylight, and when I got down, he took me outside and told me, and then sent me to go and feed the other team and harness them before I came in to my breakfast, and he went back to tell Mrs. Hardie. I stayed out in the stable a goodish while, for I was afraid to go in, for Mrs. Hardie is terribly easy scared, and she thought there was nobody like Mr. Vale."

"Well, never mind yourself," said Tom Dennis. "What's Jim sent you here for?"

"Why, Jim, he's gone to town to tell the police and the crowner, and he wants to know, Miss Dawson, if you will go down and stay with Mrs. Hardie, for she's in a regular taking."

"Of course you will, Mary Ann," said her mother. "Me and your father can sort the mail for once, and maybe Mr. Grant here will drive you down?"

"Sure, Miss Dawson, my team's tied up outside," said Mr. Grant.

"I'll just put a few things together, and I'll be ready," and in a few minutes Mary Ann reappeared, with a large bundle, and wearing her brother's fur coat, and a warm hood tied over her head with a large muffler, and was soon seated by Mr. Grant's side in his 'jumper,' and on her way to Rosebank. It was all very sad indeed, and very dreadful, and doubtless much neighbourly kindliness and sympathy were mingled with less admirable feelings in Mary Ann's heart; but she could not but be conscious that there were great romantic possibilities hidden in the tragedy, which had broken the usual tenor of the uneventful life of the settlement.

CHAPTER XXVIII

The coroner's inquest, which was held at the Dingle on the third day after the discovery of Roland Vale's body, threw very little light on the mystery of the manner of his death. In fact, as a judicial inquiry, it was rather perfunctory in its character, as the coroner, after talking the matter over with Mr. Hardie before the formal inquest, had formed his own theory on the matter.

Though it had not previously happened in his own district, it was a matter of common knowledge, that two or three hunters were shot, or at least fired at, every year, by too eager sportsmen, who, seeing a moving object in the bush, did not wait to make certain whether it were man or deer at which they shot.

"There's no doubt about it, no doubt at all," said the coroner, when Jim had finished his story. "Some fool of a 'green horn' had 'potted' him, in mistake for a deer, and then cleared off so as not to have to own up to it. I would give him a lesson to be more careful, if I could catch him, but, bless you, there were a dozen hunting camps within a few miles, and the storm has not left the shadow of a track in the bush."

"Well, doctor, I feel real bad about it. The poor lad was kind of in my charge, and I should not have left him alone," said Jim regretfully. "You see, 'doc' (for the coroner was an old friend), folk might blame me, him being so fresh and innocent-like of the ways of the bush."

"Not at all, Jim, not at all; you couldn't help it. You just get half a dozen of the neighbours to come into the big room, where they have the body," for Jim and the coroner were in the Dingle kitchen, "and I'll swear in a jury, and you and Bert can give your evidence, and any one else that may know anything about it, though it's quite plain to me how it happened, and then I'll come down to your place for a 'bite,' and get off back to town before dark."

There was no difficulty in getting the necessary number for a jury, as there were at least a dozen teams gathered round the house, and those of their owners, who were not fortunate enough to be sworn on the jury, crowded into the room till it was packed.

The coroner opened the proceedings by reading a few sections of the Act under which the inquest was held, and then called on Jim Hardie and Bert to give their evidence of the finding of the body, and of the events of the day on which Roland was lost.

This was listened to in breathless silence, and then the coroner in his capacity of doctor explained to the jury the nature of the fatal wound, and how it was impossible that it could have been a personal accident or self-inflicted. He was proceeding to give his own views of how it happened, and of the criminal carelessness of firing at ill-defined objects in the bush, when a little stir or whispering among a group of men standing just within the door caused him to pause.

"Is there any one there who has anything to say?" he asked sharply. "If not, I'd like order while I address the jury."

"Please, doctor, there's a young Swede man just up from 'Sweden,' and he says——"

"Never mind what he says," interrupted the coroner; "let him step to the front, and I will hear what he has to say," and Amanda's cousin Carl was pushed through the throng to the table where the coroner was seated.

"Now, young man, what do you know about this accident?" he asked.

"There was another man lost on the day of the storm, and I thought the Herr doctor might like to know."

"Another man lost? Who was that, and what has it to do with this inquest?" asked the doctor rather impatiently.

"It was the son of 'old man' Nielson, by the Otter Lake; he was out in the bush hunting, and never came back."

"Well, that's very unfortunate, but I don't see what that has to do with this inquest. You know that country, Mr. Hardie, where does this Nielson live from your shanty?"

"It's a matter of three miles or so south, through the bush, doctor; I know father and son well, and they're fine folks. It'll be a terrible blow, terrible, to the old man, if anything has happened to his boy; and him to get lost that's lived there since he was a child."

"Well, would there be any chance of the young men coming across one another in the bush?" asked the coroner, turning again to Carl.

" 'Old man' Nielson told me that Ludwig, that's his son, did not go out till the middle of the afternoon, and that he struck south along by the lake shore. When he did not come back by dark, and the storm came on, the old man let his big Dane dog loose, and it went off on Ludwig's trail, but they never came back, man or dog."

"Well, I'm afraid that's a bad business, too, but if he went south, I don't see what it has to do with Mr. Vale's death; and I think, gentlemen," and the coroner turned to the jury, "the only thing you can do is to bring in an open verdict: 'Found shot; nothing to show how, or by whom.' I'll write it out, and your foreman can sign it. I'll make out a certificate for burial, Mr. Enderby. Terrible shock for your wife and daughters; scandalous the way people use fire arms in this country. If you'll get my horse, Jim, I'll drive

126

you home." And the coroner kept up a running conversation while he wrote, and by the time Jim was at the door with his horse all the formalities of the inquest were over, the jury dismissed, and the crowd had dwindled down to one or two young Englishmen, who were talking over with Bert Enderby the arrangements for poor Roland's funeral.

Mr. Enderby followed the doctor out to his cutter, and the latter had already taken his seat, and was wrapping the fur robe round his knees, when a sudden thought struck him.

"I suppose, Mr. Enderby, there was no possibility of there being any suspicion of 'bad blood' between Mr. Vale and this young man who was lost?"

"Oh, not at all, not in the least," said Mr. Enderby emphatically. "Poor Vale did not know a soul in the colony, never been there before; the poor boy had nothing but friends here, had he, Jim?"

"Of course, of course; well, good-bye," and the doctor gave a jerk to the reins, and they started before Jim had time to give the answer which Mr. Enderby and the doctor took for granted.

Two weeks before Jim would have been ready with as emphatic and convinced an answer as that which Mr. Enderby had given to the doctor's question, nay, even to the day of the inquest, no suggestion of connection between the tragedy at the shanty and Ludwig Christian had for one moment entered his mind. Nor did Carl Swanson's recital of the disappearance of Ludwig at once strike him as a solution of the mystery of Roland's death, his deeply sympathetic nature being too quickly touched by a realization of how terrible the blow would be to the brave old sailor by Otter Lake, if indeed Ludwig had perished in the blizzard. Now in a flash the doctor's chance words, "bad blood," seemed to crystallize into definite and correlative form a variety of vague but disagreeable impressions, which hitherto he had charged to Mary Ann Dawson's gossiping tongue, and to the perversity with which she would turn the conversation at meal times from the daily routine of the farm life, in which for his wife's and the children's sakes, he sought to keep it, either to the mystery of Roland's death, or to his ill-fated intimacy at Rosebank, and to the night of the dance.

He hated the deductive methods of old Mrs. Dawson and Mary Ann sorting the mail to be applied to the intimate privacy of his own home, and of those who had sat at his own board. He tolerated it as a necessary but very distasteful evil, for the sake of having his wife freed from the burden of the work of the house, and from the care of the children, and usually sought refuge by going to the stables or the granary as soon as a meal was over—the horses and cattle did not gossip, and there was no scope for dispute in his relations with the "chore boy" or the "hired man." But now "bad blood" and the host of unpleasant suggestions, which he had brushed aside

127

individually, as he would brush off a mosquito, returned in a body, and seemed each to seek to fall into its inevitable place, like the fragments of glass in a kaleidoscope.

"Good God! If that's the truth," he groaned to himself, and then came the solid justice of his nature to his relief: "Go slow, Jim Hardie, go slow," and by a supreme effort he put the crowding thoughts from him, and turned to the present, to the necessity of keeping this dreadful thought within his own breast, till he should be free to think it out slowly to the bottom, and to see which way the path of duty lay. He was slow, and he judged himself very poorly in the matter of education and smartness, and he was "up against it," but he had an abiding conviction that God was behind the man that was "straight," and please God he'd be straight.

So the conversation turned to the state of the roads and the price of grain till they turned into the Rosebank Lane, where the deep snow and little beaten track brought the horse's trot down to a slow drag through the drifts.

"Make it as easy as you can, doc, on 'the little woman,' about the inquest," urged Jim earnestly, as they drew into the yard. "She's terrible shook about it all; she was fine before this happened, but she seems slipping back to what she was when you saw her before harvest, kind of downhearted and nervous-like."

"To be sure, Jim, to be sure," said the doctor, as he prepared to get out of the cutter.

"And you might drop a word, doctor, to Miss Dawson; she can't let things drop, and she's always reminding the wife about the poor lad being so much to our place and keeping it all so fresh in her mind."

"Just leave it to me, Jim," said the doctor briskly. "I often meet Mary Ann, nursing and so forth among the neighbours; I'll fix her so that she won't open her mouth about it for a week. Just throw the robe over the mare, Jim, and tie her up in the shed. I mustn't stop more than half an hour," and the doctor entered the house.

When Jim came back from the shed the doctor was already at the table, having the "bite" of which he had spoken, and talking cheerfully to Mrs. Hardie of the healthy looks of the children, and of how the baby had grown; of anything and everything except the reason for his visit to the Dingle.

For some time Mary Ann watched in vain for an opening in the conversation, through which she could drag in the question at the tip of her tongue; but the doctor had finished his "bite," and Jim had gone to bring the horse from the shed before it came. The doctor stopped talking for a minute while he struggled into his big fur coat, and Mary Ann was standing by to hand him his fur cap and gauntlets; now was her chance.

"My, doctor, wasn't it dreadful about poor Mr. Vale? Was he murdered?" Mrs. Hardie gave a little nervous scream at the word, but the doctor's answer was sharp and stern.

"See here, Miss Dawson, it was dreadful enough, without a lot of silly fools making it worse by talking nonsense about it; it was just a careless accident that might happen to me or any one else, with the bush full of inexperienced men with rifles. Now, good-bye, Mrs. Hardie; you must take the tonic I'm going to send up by the mail-man; don't work too hard. Now, Miss Dawson, if you'll bring my bag to the cutter."

As soon as they were outside the door, the doctor added a parting warning for Mary Ann's personal benefit. "You do a good bit of nursing among my patients, Miss Dawson, and you are very useful, but if Mrs. Hardie cannot be kept quiet and cheerful without a word about this accident," the doctor was very angry, "I'll move her down to the Minnedosa Hospital, where the nurses have some sense, and don't talk damned foolishness to nervous, critical patients"; and the doctor took his bag and strode off to his rig before Mary Ann recovered from the shock of his plain speaking.

The doctor had fulfilled his promise to Jim Hardie, and Mary Ann effectually "fixed," not a word more was said about the inquest that night. Jim was busy out at the granary, cleaning a load of grain to take to Minnedosa the next day, and it was long after dark when he came in, with a bundle of bags which needed patching, and threw them on the floor.

"Now, little woman," he said, kissing his wife, "do you go to bed, and get a good night's rest. I'll be off to town in the morning before you are up. If Mary Ann here will get me a bit of breakfast ready in the morning, while I bag the grain, I'd like to get away by daylight, for the roads are heavy."

"Can't I help you mend the bags, Mr. Hardie? I'm sure I'd be glad to," struck in Mary Ann, who saw her last opportunity of hearing the mystery of the inquest slipping away. "I often do it at home."

"Not at all, not at all," said Jim decidedly. "I always do my own patching, don't I, little woman? and you'll need all the sleep you can get, Mary Ann, for I shall be calling you bright and early," and Jim busied himself in getting out his bundle of patches and needles and thread, till the two women had got their lamps and retired to bed, when he sat down to his work.

All Jim's cheerfulness seemed to slip off him like a cloak as soon as he was alone. Mechanically he took up one of the bags, and turned it inside out to see what repairs it needed; mechanically he threaded his needle, and cut out the necessary patch, and started sewing it in its place, while his mind was slowly reconstructing their life at Rosebank since the day when Roland Vale first came there with Bert Enderby, reconstructing it by the searchlight of Mary Ann's suggestions, of Ludwig's disappearance, and of the coroner's afterthought, "bad blood."

Instinctively following the natural trend of his own character, he laid great blame on himself for allowing Amanda and Roland to be thrown so much together, and it was evident that they had been far more together than he knew of at the time. He knew of Ludwig's love, and of the hope of Ludwig's father for his son; he knew, or at least he thought he knew, that Ludwig's love was returned, and while there was little difference of age between Ludwig and Roland, the two men had been on entirely different planes in Jim's own mind. Ludwig was a man; Roland was a mere lad, well to look at, and pleasant mannered. Jim Hardie had had no thought but to teach him the ways of the country, and to make him feel at home in his new surroundings.

"How blind he had been, and his 'little woman' had encouraged it all. Why hadn't he warned her and told her about Ludwig? Here was Mary Ann saying that Roland worshipped the ground Amanda walked on. Mary Ann knew of the letter from Ludwig, which Ronald brought from the mail. Mary Ann had treasured up every incident of the threshing at Rosebank, of the decorating for the dance. Mary Ann had overheard the whispered conversation between Amanda and her cousin. Mary Ann had guessed why Amanda was so restless and excited as the night sped on and on. Ludwig came; Mary Ann had heard the sleigh-bells in the lane, and seen Amanda's flight from the house. Mary Ann had heard the broken-hearted girl's weeping, as she listened at the door of the little room at Rosebank, when all the excitement of the dance was over, and every one else had gone to bed."

Jim was a patient and not a profane man, but he swore this time.

"Damn Mary Ann," he said softly to himself. "Good God! the woman is all eyes and ears and tongue," and Jim laid down the bag which by this time was mended and picked up another. "I thought it was all her infernal gossiping," Jim went on to himself, "and here now is the doctor with his 'bad blood,' "—"bad blood" enough with Ludwig's passionate temper, if he only dreamt Amanda was false to him, and the two of them there in the bush with rifles and their hot young passions. Jim's mind ran over that fatal day of the hunting, how white and fagged Roland had been, so ready to stay behind in the shanty.

Ludwig went south from his father's house; but how if he struck the track of a deer and turned? Four or five miles would be nothing to him. But Roland was shot from behind; never would Ludwig do so dastardly a deed, and Ludwig was lost, or had fled. Far into the night Jim sat by the stove, long after the last bag was mended. Slowly his mind came to a settled purpose; if Ludwig never returned, or if his body was found in the bush, he, Jim, would keep all his dark fears locked in his own bosom. What profit to the dead, to darken Amanda's young life, or to add the shame of suspicion to the grief of the lonely old man by Otter Lake? If Ludwig should miraculously, as it seemed to be, have escaped the storm, then would be time enough for him to seek for the dispelling of the mystery which hung heavily on his soul that night.

"God forgive you, Jim Hardie, if any share of this lies to your door," and so praying Jim, first removing his shoes that he might walk the more silently, went slowly up the stairs to his chamber.

CHAPTER XXIX

We must now turn back to follow the fortunes of Amanda from the time when we left her, sobbing herself to sleep, in her little room at Rosebank.

When Jim Hardie went north to his hunting, it had been with a perfectly easy mind as to the care of his stock, and as to his wife not being lonely while he was away. He had hired for the winter a middle-aged man, who for years had done odd jobs in the settlement, one of those slow unprogressive mortals, of whom a specimen is to be found in every western settlement, devoid of ambition to advance his own fortunes, but perfectly trustworthy in working for any one else, and he and the "chore boy" between them would take the best of care of horses and stock; and for the rest, Amanda was to stay till after Jim's return, when she was to go home before Christmas.

"You'll be just fine without me," were Jim's last words to his "little woman," as he gave her a parting kiss before he started for the bush; but it was not destined to be so "fine" for his "little woman" as he anticipated.

On the afternoon of the very day he left, while Mrs. Hardie and Amanda were busily engaged in washing up dishes and pans, and trying to reduce the house to somewhat of its usual order—Amanda indeed heavy-eyed and pale and with but little of her usual energy—sleigh-bells were heard in the lane, followed by a hasty knock at the lean-to door.

"Run and see who it is," said Mrs. Hardie. "It'll likely be one of the neighbours," and Amanda went quickly to the door and opened it.

"Oh, August, whatever has brought you here? Come in, it's my brother, Mrs. Hardie," and Amanda ushered into the "living-room" a tall boy of fourteen or so. "It's my brother August," repeated Amanda. "There's nothing wrong at home, is there, August?"

"Please, Mrs. Hardie," replied the boy, ignoring his sister, and delivering an evidently carefully remembered message, "please, Mrs. Hardie, my father sends his respects, and would you let Amanda come home with me, right away, because mother is sick?"

"Mother ill—oh! what's the matter, August?" broke in Amanda anxiously.

"Mother is sick," went on August stolidly, "and there's nobody to 'do' for him and the children while she's in bed, and we are milking six cows, and there's the milk and the butter to mind, and, if Mrs. Hardie pleases, I'm to take Amanda right back in the jumper."

"But, August, is mother very ill? Do tell me what is the matter," urged Amanda.

"Mother is pretty bad," went on August, still addressing Mrs. Hardie. "She took sick with a chill two days ago, and father says it's settled on her lungs, and he's got old 'mother' Berg to nurse her, and will you let Amanda come home?"

"Of course, Amanda must go," said Mrs. Hardie. "It's too bad of Jim to go off and leave me in a fix like this," she added rather unreasonably.

"But how can you stay alone, Mrs. Hardie, with the children and all the work?" asked Amanda.

"Oh, I must manage as well as I can," said Mrs. Hardie resignedly; "Dave must help round the house, and Ted can look after the baby. It's always the way with me, when I want help worst I'm sure to lose it; but get your things ready, Amanda, while I get your brother a 'piece' and a cup of tea."

Mrs. Hardie quite recognized the necessity for Amanda going, though not very graciously, and after all with the "hired man" in the house, she did not really feel uneasy at being left alone for a few days.

Amanda ran up to her little room, and hastily made into a bundle such things as she thought she would need most at home, putting the rest back in the little home-made box, which had served her for a dressing-table. She turned to take a last look at the little room, where she had dreamt such happy dreams—how dull and forlorn it looked—the winter light struggling through the frost-covered panes of the window. There was hanging the little sailor hat she wore on the day she came; there, the tennis racquet Roland had lent her—here, dangling by their laces, the little pair of Indian moccasins, which Ludwig sent her on Christmas Day. "Why, why had she ever left her own home, and her own people, where every one was kind, and every one was true?" And Amanda took down the little moccasins, and thrust them into her bundle; they at least should not be left behind.

Even in her sadness there was a gleam of hope; she was going home. "Ludwig was angry, oh, so angry, but perhaps—— Ah! who could tell? And mother was ill, mother who had been so glad for her to come among English folk; but surely mother would soon be well again. God was kind, home would be home, and home would be a safe refuge." And wiping away the traces of tears from her face, Amanda hurried with her bundle downstairs again, where she found Mrs. Hardie warming an old "coon coat" of her husband's by the stove.

"Here, child, put on this, or you'll freeze before you get home. Some of your folk can leave it here again, as they go down to town. Now, good-bye, dear," and Mrs. Hardie kissed her kindly. "Jim shall come down to see how you all are when he gets from the bush, and you must come up again in the spring to see us all. Give my kind wishes to your mother, and I hope she'll soon be well," and Mrs. Hardie, whose heart was better than her usual manner, followed Amanda out to the "jumper," and tucked the wraps warmly round her as she took her place by August's side, and they started off.

Amanda always thought of it afterwards as the slowest and dreariest drive of her life. On account of his youth and his inexperience with horses, August could only be entrusted with the pony which was used for bringing home the cows from the meadows, or for taking the children to school when the roads were too heavy from rain for them to walk, and "old Jack" added to the slowness of years a personal dislike of being hurried, which neither August's voice nor whip could overcome for more than little sporadic canters, from which he would relapse into the slowest of walks, and there is no animal living, which is supposed to be locomotive, that can walk quite so slowly as an old native pony.

In his way, too, August was almost as trying to Amanda's overwrought nerves as "old Jack," for he possessed a full measure of his father's stolid and non-committal disposition, and all Amanda's questions about her mother's illness—when it began, how long it had already lasted, what "mother" Berg said, and the like—failed to elicit aught but most undefined and general answers. He admitted that "mother" had been a "kind of sick for two or three weeks past"—no, she did not stay in bed, but father had been lighting the fires in a morning; he and father had been doing the milking mostly since the cold weather came, till last Saturday, when father was at the store. Yes, mother helped that night, and she struck a chill when she came in, and went to bed early. She hadn't been up since, and father fetched "mother" Berg on Sunday night. He did not think mother was "real sick," because she would not let them send to town for the doctor. No, father was not working; he stayed right in mother's room most of the time, and had put up a little stove there. He, August, did not like the way "mother" Berg spoke to his two little sisters, so quiet and said like they weren't sick and it made him feel lonesome.

Putting all of which together, as best she might, Amanda stopped her questioning, and relapsed into a very sad and "lonesome" silence herself. The sense of her own causes for unhappiness, which had been so deep and real to her that morning when she awoke at Rosebank, seemed to be already a thing dim and far away, and vague but very dread forebodings of what might be awaiting her at home took its place.

Her Norse nature paid to the full the penalty of its sensitiveness to the moods and seasons of nature; the gathering gloom of twilight, and the deepening shadows of the pine and the spruce through which they were slowly passing, seemed by imperceptible but sure gradations to shut out every ray of hope from her heart. There came too, as an avenging angel from the dark recesses of the forest, the spirit of self-reproach, bearing in her hand, darts, cruel, but wholesome in their wounds, wounds which, while they revealed her thoughtless forgetfulness in her last weeks at Rosebank of aught but her own vanity and pleasure, yet set free deep springs of passionate love and longing for home, for her own people, and most of all for that mother who had loved her so unselfishly and without stint of sacrifice.

At last the clearing round the old home was reached, a light was shining dimly in her mother's window. As she stepped on to the veranda, the door opened, and her father stood in the dim flickering light of a lantern hanging within.

"So—you come, Amanda," and he kissed her gravely. "Your poor mother is very sick, and we're needing you home; she'll rest easier maybe when she knows her work is not getting behind."

"Oh, father, I never thought I should have been here to help her—but, father," and Amanda clung to him as she whispered the question, "mother is going to get better—mother is not going to die?"

"God knows, my girl, but she is very sick; 'mother' Berg says it will be a week before there is a 'turn,' and all we can do is to wait and hope for the best. Come, take off your wraps, and then you may see her; poor soul, she's been asking for you, though she hardly knows any one half the time."

It was with a sinking heart and trembling limbs that Amanda followed her father up the creaking steps that led to her mother's room. For a moment she paused without the door to gain some control over herself—she must be brave—and then she entered the room. "Mother" Berg, old mother Berg, who had nursed them all through their childish ailments, sat by the bed, knitting—Amanda never remembered seeing "mother" Berg without her knitting. With a warning "hush" she beckoned to Amanda to draw near, and Amanda stooped and kissed the wrinkled but kindly faced old nurse.

"Hush, my dearie, she's sleeping," and Amanda bent over and lightly with her lips touched her mother's flushed and fevered cheek, and then sank on her knees, her face in her old nurse's lap, and wept.

CHAPTER XXX

The "turn," of which "mother" Berg had spoken, came during the ninth night after Amanda's return home. The fires of the pneumonia fever had slowly burnt themselves out, the broken fitful sleep, which alternated with half-waking delirium, gave place at last to a long, deep slumber, during which the hectic flush passed from the sufferer's cheeks, and the quick gasping for breath fell to a breathing as gentle, and almost as imperceptible, as that of a sleeping infant.

"Mother" Berg watched alone during the hours of that night, for she knew how frail would be the grasp on life, when that slumber passed away, how narrow and perilous to be crossed the bridge that should lead over the gulf of eternity to the shore of recovery, when the fever strength of the heart died away. An emotion, even of joy, to the waking mind might tax too much the well-nigh exhausted reserves of vitality. Downstairs Amanda and her father kept vigil as the leaden-footed hours dragged their weary length to the late coming of the winter dawn. Obedient to her father's word, Amanda lay down on the old lounge that stood behind the kitchen stove, and closed her eyes, even if obedience could not command the sleep she so sorely needed.

Broken and fitful dozing did indeed bring short intervals of forgetfulness, but the least sound, the click of the stove door as her father replenished the fire, was sufficient to startle her into complete and alert wakefulness. Once indeed she awoke, not from any consciousness of a disturbing sound, but from a forlorn sense of being alone. The room was in darkness, save for a faint flickering ray of light from the half-closed front of the stove. She threw off the heavy quilt with which she had been covered, and started to her feet, with a sudden dread that her father had been summoned to her mother's room; and all that such a summons might mean flashed across her mind.

She listened intently; no lightest footfall or creak of a board betrayed any movement upstairs, and then she noticed a glimmer of light beneath the door of the little room, partitioned off from the end of the living-room in which she stood. It had been "the teacher's room" in the days when Evelyn Raye was with them, and since then had been set apart as her mother's sewing-room. "Mother" Berg had made up a bed on the floor for the two younger girls, Louise and Olga, that they should not disturb their mother; perhaps they had awakened and been frightened at finding themselves alone; and Amanda stole softly to the door, and pushed it gently open for a few inches and looked within.

The lantern, by whose light her father had made some pretence of reading in the earlier part of the night, stood on the sewing-machine, its light carefully screened by a book from falling on the faces of the sleeping children, by whose side knelt her father with head bowed low upon his breast in prayer. Even more silently than she had come, Amanda crept back to her lounge and lay down; she felt as if, with thoughtless and unsuspecting feet, she had stepped on holy ground, the holy ground of a husband and father's love in its hour of deepest supplication, that the healing power of the divine Saviour of man might give back the wife and the mother to the home. But there was a new sense of peace and hope in Amanda's heart, and in a little time she passed into a deep sleep, from which she awakened to find that daylight had come. Olga and Louise were seated at the table with their bowls of porridge, and "mother" Berg was softly crooning an old Norse folk song to herself as she stirred some beef-tea on the stove. Amanda was by her side in a moment.

"Mother?"

"Yes, dearie, mother is better this morning; the 'turn' came in the night, and she's had a fine sleep, and now we must nurse back her strength. Your father is with her, but she must be kept very quiet; to-morrow perhaps you may see her." And Amanda was content, for there was a cheerful confidence in "mother" Berg, that made waiting easy now the cruel suspense of the past night was gone.

For the next few days Amanda had but little time for thought. Her heart was filled with a deep sense of happiness in her mother's now assured recovery, and the pressing duties of moment left leisure, neither for retrospection nor anticipation. The blizzard, though its fierce force had been greatly broken by the heavy timber growing behind the house, had made much work to be done around the farm buildings, and Ole Swanson and August were busy from morning to night, breaking out roads to the strawstacks, and to the little lake where the cattle were watered.

There was much to do within the house, for during the weary time of waiting for the "turn" in her mother's sickness, Amanda had not had the heart to work; it had all seemed so forlorn and useless when perhaps——Now that hope had returned there were floors to be scrubbed and washing to be done, butter to be made and calves to be fed, and baking of bread and pies. For August and his father came in keen and hungry from their work in the sharp, frosty air. Louise and Olga were ever at her side, full of eagerness to help—happy in her return, and in their recovered liberty to laugh and play without a rebuking hush.

"Mother" Berg still spent most of her time in her patient's room, but when she was sleeping "mother" Berg would bring her knitting to the stove side, and keep the children quiet with weird old Norse fairy tales, while Amanda went on with her work. But, as anxiety for her mother wore away, and the pressure of the work about the house relaxed, other thoughts came stealing back to Amanda's mind—thoughts of Ludwig and his love, deep repentings of her wilfulness, of her trifling with his love; and of her half-jealous mockings of the place he had ever given to his father, when he tried to tell her of his passion for herself. Would he forgive her? How was he to be brought to know of how innocent she was of any thought of unfaithfulness to him in that moment, when he had seen her almost in Roland's arms on the unhappy night of the dance at Rosebank?

She could not for maiden shame seek him out and tell him; and it was more than two weeks since he went home to his father, and still there was no sign or token from him. The blizzard had indeed cut them off from their neighbours: no one had even made their way over from her Uncle Carl's, half a mile away. But Ludwig—the drifts were hard, and with his snow-shoes he would think nothing of the deep snow, if—ah, if—he wanted to come.

With such thoughts Amanda stood one afternoon at the window, there was a little space on the pane where there was no frost, watching her father and August, as with a team and scraper they were cutting out a road through the snow, to the opening in the bush road that led to Otter Lake, and thence to the main road of the settlement. They were resting the oxen after a hard pull, and she could see her father lighting his pipe.

"What is August pointing to? Now they are both watching, and August waves his hand; there must be some one coming through the bush. Can it, ah, can it be Ludwig?" and Amanda blushed to the roots of her hair.

Her colour faded as quickly as it came. There was no mistaking the short sturdy figure that emerged from the bush road for the tall lithe form of Ludwig Nielson; it was her cousin Carl, a dear, good-hearted, laughter-loving boy, her favourite among all her cousins; but he was not Ludwig, and Amanda was conscious of a very grievous disappointment, but perhaps he would bring some word from Otter Lake.

Amanda watched the group of three as they stood together, it was evident that Carl had news of some kind to tell, for even at that distance she could see that he was doing most of the talking, and that her father and August were keenly interested. Curiosity began to give way to anxiety; why did they not come up to the house? Now they are coming, but no, Carl is turning back to the road, by which he came, and her father is unhitching the team from the scraper, and giving the lines to August to take the oxen to the stable. How slowly and heavily her father walks! There is ill news in the very droop of his shoulders as he comes up the path to the house. Amanda meets him at the threshold.

"Why did not Carl come with you, father? Is anything wrong at Uncle Carl's?"

"All is well at your uncle's, but——"

"But what, father? Tell me."

"There is ill news from Otter Lake, my girl; come and I will tell you"; and he led her gently to the old lounge, and drew her to his side as he sat down.

"Be brave, my poor girl; remember your mother, how weak she is"; and slowly, and with many pauses, as if seeking for words to soften the heavy burden of his story, he told her of the disappearance of Ludwig, and of the inquest at the Dingle. Only once did she interrupt the dreary recital, and that was when her father repeated the suggestion made at the inquest, that there might be some connection between the death of Roland Vale and the disappearance of Ludwig.

"Why, father," she asked quickly, "did you not say Roland, the young Englishman, was shot from behind?"

"Yes, so Carl says; he was shot in the back as he was sitting on a stump in the ravine."

"Why then, how could it be Ludwig?" and quick as a flash, for one moment a flush mounted to her forehead, and an angry light came to her eyes. "Dare any coward of them all dream that Ludwig could kill his bitterest foe in that coward's way? Didn't Carl tell them that they lied?"

"Hush, hush, my girl. God only knows how it happened; and now I must warn 'mother' Berg that no whisper of this trouble reaches your mother till she is stronger to bear it."

Out of all the tears and despair of the night that followed, one firm purpose came to Amanda; she would go and see Ludwig's father, the poor old man in his loneliness by the Otter Lake. No pride or shame should keep her from telling him of all her foolishness, and of all her love; he at least should know that there was one whose heart was as full as his own of love and faith in his lost son. He would forgive her, even if Ludwig had passed for ever beyond the knowledge of the love that she had never confessed.

CHAPTER XXXI

On the afternoon of the next day Amanda carried out her purpose to visit Ludwig's father. As soon as the noonday meal was over, and the dishes and pans washed and put away, she brought down from her own room her snow-shoes, and the Hudson Bay blanket coat and toque which she had not worn since the previous winter. How full they were of memories of sleigh rides through the bush, and of toboggan parties on moonlight nights on the hill behind the old schoolhouse, when it was always Ludwig's strong arm and skilful foot that guided them down the steep and dizzy "chute"! How far away those happy times seemed to-day!

As she drew the toque warmly over her ears, and tied the scarlet sash of her coat about her waist, she turned for a moment to the little square mirror that hung by the window. The joyous times of last winter seemed no further away than the pale cheeks and heavy eyes reflected there seemed from the wilful, teasing, laughing Amanda of only a year ago. Would happiness ever come again?

"Tell 'mother' Berg I have gone for a walk, and shall be back by supper-time; good-bye, dear," and she kissed little Olga, who had followed her to the door with wondering question, "Why yesterday she was so happy, and to-day so sad?"

As soon as the snow-shoes were securely fastened to her moccasined feet, she stepped quickly along the road, cleared the day before, to the trail through the bush. She was conscious that her father was watching her from where he was working in the stable-yard, and waved her hand; she could not bear to tell him of the purpose of her walk, but he would guess where that trail was leading her, and she knew his sympathy would follow her on her mission to the Otter Lake, to his old neighbour.

When she reached the shelter of the spruce, she must needs go slowly, for here the unblown snow lay soft and deep, and even her light weight pressed down its feathery surface. The physical exercise and keen air gradually brought some glow of colour to her cheeks, the glorious winter sun overhead touched every snow-laden bough of spruce into a spray of diamonds, and two chickadees, the most cheery and optimistic of birds, fluttering from tree to tree a few yards ahead, seemed to be wooing her back, if not to happiness, to at least a less-forlorn abandonment to her sorrow. By degrees the ministering instinct of her sex drew her thoughts from herself to the childless loneliness of the old man whom she was going to see. The full measure of that loneliness came home to her heart, as at last she emerged from the road through the woods, and the little log house by the lake came in view.

The wind-swept ice of the lake glittered in the sun, long rolling billows of hard drifted snow marked the line of the hidden roads along the shore. The little garden, where she had so often as a child listened to the old sailor's stories of the sea and its wonders, as he worked among his flowers, was scarce marked here and there by the top of a picket showing for a few inches above the snow. Narrow paths had been neatly cut through the drifts to the stable doors, and to the little milk-house. A thin column of smoke mounted high from the chimney of the house, till it faded imperceptibly in the upper air. No lightest sound broke the stillness, not even the barking of a dog, and with a fresh pang Amanda realized that Trofast was lost, lost and perhaps even then lying frozen by his master's side in the pathless wilderness of the forest—Trofast, who had been wont to herald her approach with deep bayings ere she came in sight.

Slowly and more slowly she traversed the few acres of the opening till she reached the little wicket-gate, when loosing the snow-shoes from her feet, she stole gently to the door and paused, afraid to break the silence even by tapping with her hand, afraid to enter unannounced. Even now that she was at the very threshold, how gladly would she have retraced her steps, and made her way homeward again, without sign or word to him who was alone within, but the price of her love for Ludwig must be paid to the uttermost.

Softly she raised the latch, and entered the little room. The old sailor was sitting by the stove, his well-worn Bible lay open on his knee. For one moment Amanda stood in hesitation, holding out her hands, the next she was gathered closely to his breast.

"I have come, Herr Nielson, to tell you, to tell Ludwig's father, what a wicked and foolish girl I have been, and to ask you, now my heart is broken, if you can forgive me."

"Hush, hush, my child," Christian answered gently, "I knew the little Amanda was true, and that she would come to the old sailor in his sorrow."

With many a sob and many a word of self-condemnation she unburdened her heart of its anguish, unto ears so sympathetic that, even in telling, the bitterness of her self-reproach seemed to pass away.

Gently, very gently, he told her of Ludwig's last day at home, and of how sure he was that there was nothing but love for herself in Ludwig's heart when he left his home with his rifle; bitterness and anger indeed for the young Englishman, but not for Amanda—nothing but love.

"Do you think, Herr Nielson," Amanda whispered, as he spoke of Ludwig's anger, "do you think they could have met? Do you know what they

141

dared to suggest, those people down there in the English settlement?"

"Aye, aye, I know. Carl told me this morning, but let not that trouble you. I know, yes, I know that my boy is innocent of that poor lad's death."

"You know?"

"I will tell you. Ludwig's bitter resentment against the young Englishman lay heavy on my heart as I watched him take his way down by the lake shore; I too feared the consequences of his hot passion, if by ill chance they should meet. The sense of dread and impending evil increased upon me, heavily and more heavily, till it was well-nigh impossible of bearing, and then in my helplessness I called upon my God. The boy's mother and I," and Christian pointed to the old faded picture above the cross, "the boy's mother and I interceded for the soul of our child, and whether he be beneath the winter's snow or, by God's goodness, he still lives, our prayer is answered, and all is well."

Amanda gazed in awe and wonder on the old man's face; no sign of sorrow or anxiety was there, nothing but quiet confidence and peace.

"Is it possible that Ludwig still lives? Oh, Herr Nielson, do you think it is possible?" and Amanda hid her face on Christian's breast, afraid to look in his eyes for the answer.

"With God it is possible, but I dare not bid you yet, living here or with his mother there," and he raised his hand to heaven. "I have the assurance of One, who has never failed me, that all is well with the child God gave to our love, in the cottage by the far-sounding sea in the old homeland."

The sun was slipping behind the spruce-clad hills to the west of the Otter Lake, when Amanda and Christian left the little log house, for the old sailor would not hear of her going alone through the gathering darkness of the woods; and when they parted it was with mutual promises that every week through the winter, either Christian should come and spend the day with his old friend Ole, or else Amanda should go and visit him in his own house.

CHAPTER XXXII

The tragedy of Roland's death and of Ludwig's disappearance was a sensation for a month; by the New Year it was an old story to all, save the few whose lives it had nearly touched, ready to take its place in the limbo of reminiscences from which the "old timers" of the future would point a moral or adorn a tale by camp fire or in threshing caboose.

Tragedies lie thick in the record of the development of that vast new land of the west, where men of all classes of society and of every nationality are engaged in a battle for life, and its rewards in unfamiliar surroundings, and in a vigorous and treacherous climate. The perils to life, and the vicissitudes of fortune to which all are exposed, while they arouse a spirit of mutual helpfulness and hospitality, breed also a swift forgetfulness when the calls of the necessity of the moment have been met.

With the New Year a fresh interest came into the life of the English settlement, the Dominion Parliament was dissolved and the whole country-side was thrown into the whirl of a contested election. For nearly four years, from a month after the last election, all political interest had been lulled, for party feeling in the west has little of the steady continued zeal with which the course of public affairs is followed in the "old country."

Apart from the brief midsummer madness preceding and following an election, the average settler is far more concerned with the doings of the council of his own municipality and the amount of public money that is to be spent on the road past his own farm, than he is with a Canadian Navy or a transcontinental railway. But, if his public spirit is very intermittent in its action, it is very vigorous while it lasts, and by the middle of February, the time to which our story has now come, the fever was at its height. Men were no longer English or Canadians, or even British or foreigners, they were "Grits" or "Tories," and as such to be taken to the bosom, or the "bar"; or to be spoken of with pity for their ignorance, or contempt for their depravity.

It was a great time for old Mrs. Dawson and Mary Ann, who willingly endured the "tracking up" of their clean floor, in return for the enjoyment of the scandalous rumour with which the air is filled at such seasons. "Old" Dawson himself, as having a vote, assumed an importance in his own house, denied him at other times, and alternated between a mysterious reticence in the presence of a mixed company, and a rancorous self-assertion, when he felt quite sure of his auditors. His office of postmaster, with its paltry pay, had been given to him in the old days of Sir John A. Macdonald, and he firmly believed that if he were openly to take sides in an election, Sir Wilfrid Laurier himself would assist at his dismissal. He always got the credit with his own party for voting "straight," though as a matter of fact he had voted "Grit" ever since the Liberal party came to power, his wife having an abiding distrust of the secrecy of the ballot, and being quite determined, as she told him very frankly in wifely confidence, not to risk losing the office "for the sake of humouring an old fule who was of no account to nobody."

It was the last mail-day before the polling, and a motley crowd were gathered in the office, waiting till Mrs. Dawson and Mary Ann completed the sorting of the letters and the weekly papers.

Most of the settlers who got their mail at "Old" Dawson's were Tory in their leanings, and the "Grit" minority as they got their letters drifted outside, where they could talk over the prospects of their candidate in a more sympathetic atmosphere. Relieved of their presence "Old" Dawson, who had hitherto been strictly non-committal in his attitude, allowed himself to become reminiscent of the rash ardour of his youth, and told of the daring way in which he and sundry other "Orange" heroes, "down to our town," had invaded a meeting of "Black" Irish, and shouted "to hell with the pope."

This amiable recital, which was familiar to most of his hearers from previous elections, failed to arouse the interest which "Old" Dawson thought was its due, but it served incidentally to turn the conversation to the Galicians, who, as Roman Catholics, were regarded with great distrust by "Old" Dawson and his kind. "You can never tell how them 'furriners' vote," he asserted, with great contempt; "they just follows their priest like a lot of sheep, and has no sort of independent spirit."

"Speaking of foreigners," said Tom Dennis, who formed one of the party, "how do the 'Swedes' vote up north? They must count a lot if they all go one way. You know them pretty well, don't you, Mr. Hardie?"

"Yes, I know quite a few of them," replied Jim, "quite a few, and some of them voted 'right' last time."

"I guess you can do more with them than anybody else, Jim," said Bert Enderby; "you know their reeve, Ole Swanson, and his wife, and I've heard people say that if you have Mr. Swanson's good word, you have the best help you can get in the colony."

"I'll allow Ole counts quite a lot, and I know him pretty well," admitted Jim rather unwillingly; "but I did not figure on doing much electioneering this trip. I've got all my hay to get down from up north, and if this thaw lasts the roads will be breaking up."

"Say, Jim," said Tom Dennis, "I'll give you a hand with the hay-hauling, if you can let us have a couple of loads for the seeding; we're pretty near out."

"Well, I can let you have the hay all right," said Jim, "and I'll be glad of an extra team for two or three trips."

"That will suit me first rate," said Tom; "how will Monday be for a start?"

"And you can drop in at Swanson's on your way up," said Bert, "and have a talk with Ole; it'll be better than if you went up on purpose."

"Well, I'll see," replied Jim doubtfully; "I'll be ready for you at daybreak, Tom, anyway, and if I should drop across any of the folk I know up there, why I'll just have a word or two about the voting." He could not explain to Bert and the rest that it was his dread of running across Amanda or Christian Nielson which had made him put off going for his hay so long.

"Did you say you were going to Swanson's, Mr. Hardie?" broke in Mary Ann at this point. "There's a letter for him put in our bag by mistake, that should have gone to 'Sweden,' and you might take it along. The post-office folk at Neepawa sent it here with a note to say it had been left there by one of them 'Galation furriners' you were speaking of; he'd carried it round and forgot to post it, and the address was pretty near rubbed off, and they sent it here; you can just read 'Chris' something, care of Ole Swanson."

"Well, I'll see Ole gets it," said Jim, putting it in his pocket; "if I don't go to the house, we'll likely see some of his folk as we go by. So long, Tom; we must be bright and early on Monday, before the frost gets out of the trail," and Jim started for home.

He was very glad that he was going to have Tom Dennis's cheerful company for his trips back to the shanty, and to the scenes of his terrible experiences in the blizzard, and at the time of finding Roland's body. All the winter through he had fought against the suspicions born of Mary Ann's suggestions, and the chance question of the coroner, and still they lay heavy on his mind. He hated suspicion and mystery with all his honest mind, but how dread might be the dispelling of that mystery if it should come!

145

CHAPTER XXXIII

On the mornings of their two first trips to the shanty, Jim Hardie and Tom Dennis did meet a good many of the settlers in "Sweden," for the thaw still continued, and the Swedes were busy trying to get as much as possible of their fire-wood drawn to town before the trail quite broke up. With such as they met, Jim had also a good many words about the election, and of the desirability of their supporting the Tory candidate; but he did not go, he could not bring himself to go, the short distance necessary out of his way to call on Ole Swanson. On the second evening they met Carl Swanson returning from town, and to him Jim gave the letter to his uncle, which had been entrusted to him by Mary Ann Dawson, and sent messages of kindly greeting to Ole and Amanda.

By the time they reached the shanty on the third day, the snow was thawing so rapidly on the more open parts of the road, that it seemed doubtful if they would be able to draw their loads of hay over the bare spots on the trail. On the two previous trips, they had driven their sleighs to the side of the haystack on arriving at the hay meadows, and then put their teams in the stable, while they put on their loads, after doing which they made a fire in the shanty, and ate the dinner which they brought with them, and had a smoke, by which time the horses were sufficiently rested for the return journey to Rosebank, where they arrived soon after dark. To-day not only were there the bare spots on the trail, but the snow on the open stretch of meadow land had all gone, except a few wasting drifts by the margin of the sloughs and along the ridges of the hills, where it was sheltered by the spruce from the sun and the warm south breeze. With much splashing through the shallow pools of melted snow which lay in every hollow of the land, the horses dragged the sleighs with their wide-spreading hay racks to the side of the stack.

"By gad, Jim," said Tom Dennis, with an Irishman's appreciation of a "tight" place, "we may get our loads on, but I'm thinking we shall have a devil of a job to get them home."

"It's too bad, too bad," admitted Jim. "And you'll be getting your feet wet and all," he added, as Tom splashed over boot-tops in a hole, as he unhitched his team.

"Oh, never mind my feet; they'll dry again. But do you think the horses can pull a load through this slush?"

"Maybe if we put both teams on one load at a time, we could get them up to the bush trail," said Jim; "but there"—and he paused doubtfully.

"But what?" asked Tom.

"Why, the trail itself will be getting rotten by the time we are ready to start, and the horses will be breaking through, and we'll have trouble. We might——" and Jim stopped, as if unwilling to express the alternative he had in his mind, and then went on, "I'll guess we'll have to just wait till evening. There's sure to be a touch of frost when the sun goes down, enough to stiffen the trail, and there's a full moon. It'll be late when we get home; it's too bad." And with his usual acquiescence in the inevitable, Jim followed Tom to the stable.

They proceeded very leisurely in putting on their loads, for not only was the noon sun almost as warm as on a summer's day, but it was necessary that the loads should be firmly packed, and well balanced to escape being overturned between the Scylla of the bare spots, and the Charybdis of the "pitch holes" where there was more snow.

Tom, as the less experienced, threw down the hay from the stack, while Jim packed and trampled it solidly down on the racks. It was nearly three o'clock before the two loads were built to Jim's satisfaction, and the two men were sweating and breathless from pulling and hauling on the ropes with which the hay was bound to the racks.

"Well, Jim," said Tom, as he slid off his load after tying the last knot of the rope to the binding pole, "if anything goes, it will be the whole blooming load anyway. Say, but I'm hungry; if you are as sharp set as I am, we won't leave much grub behind us to-day."

"I guess there will be no trouble on that score," replied Jim. "My little woman generally puts enough for two in my bag, and, I never thought of it before, there's the best part of a moose frozen under some hay in the stable. I put it there after the blizzard, and I hated to put it on the load that time I came back with Bert Enderby. I guess we could chop some steaks off with the axe."

Tom went up to the shanty to put on a fire, and to melt snow for making tea, while Jim proceeded to the stable to feed the horses and to cut the steak.

There was little talking during the preparation and eating of their dinner, for both men were hungry, and on Jim's spirits there rested a sense of depression from his surroundings, and from the dread lest Tom Dennis should revive the subject of Roland's death.

Though they lingered over the meal, and over the washing up of their few dishes afterwards, there still remained a full hour's daylight before the drop in the temperature, which usually comes towards evening, would begin to harden the trail. Little by little the casual conversation about the

147

election and the prospects of an early spring died away, and the two men sat moodily by the stove; but Tom's mercurial temperament could not remain inactive for long.

"Hang it, Jim," he exclaimed at last, "it will give me the 'blues' if we sit mouching here any longer; let's take a turn outside, and see if it is getting any colder," and he got up, and putting on his cap, went and stood at the door, where he was followed a minute later by Jim.

The sun was dipping behind the ridge of spruce to the west, and already a good part of the hay meadows was in shadow. The wind had dropped and there was a sharpness in the air which promised well for a frosty night. Jim walked round to the end of the shanty, and wetting his finger, held it up in the air.

"I guess we'll not have to wait long, Tom," he said, as he dried his finger on the flap of his jacket; "what little air there is stirring is coming from the north, and the frost will come with it."

"Say, Jim," and Jim knew that what he dreaded was coming, "say, Jim, where was it you found young Vale's body?"

"Away down there, at the end of the meadow," replied Jim, pointing with his hand; "there where you can see the opening of a ravine."

"Have you ever been there since?" pursued Tom.

"No, and I've not wanted to," replied Jim reluctantly. "I guess I'll go and have a look at the horses."

"Oh, the horses are all right," said Tom; "but there might be something to show how it happened, now the snow is going. See, Jim, there are a couple of wolves stealing along the top of the ridge by the ravine; wait till I get my rifle, I may get a shot," and Tom ran back into the shanty.

"They'll be far enough away before we get within reach of them," said Jim as Tom reappeared; "it's just wasting your trouble."

"Hang the trouble! Come along, Jim," and Tom started off, followed very unwillingly by his companion.

Stooping low Tom ran quickly up the western slope to gain the shelter of the spruce, followed closely by Jim Hardie. One wolf disappeared up the ravine, while the other was watching them from the top of a drift at the end of the meadow.

"That chap's wide awake," whispered Tom; "but I may get a chance at the other if he stays in the ravine. Come along, Jim."

As they neared the opening of the bed of the creek, Tom slacked his speed, and with a warning gesture to Jim for caution, crept silently to the bend of the hillside, while Jim crouched down in the shadow of a spruce. The place to Jim was full of horror, but the suspense of waiting was only for a moment, and the crack of Tom's rifle was followed by a joyful shout.

"I've got him, Jim, I've got him; quick, for fear the beggar gets away."

Jim ran quickly along the side of the ravine, where most of the snow was already thawed. A second shot and a second shout greeted him as he ploughed his way through the snow, which deepened as the ravine narrowed.

"He's dead this time, but, bedad, he's had a great time first, Jim," said Tom, as his companion made his way to him in the bed of the creek. "Look at that, Jim," and Tom pointed a few yards off to where, in deep and bloody snow, lay the torn and mangled body of an elk.

Jim sickened at the horrid sight.

"Good God!" he exclaimed involuntarily; "which of them shot it?" and he stopped as suddenly as he had begun.

"Which of who?" asked Tom quickly.

"I mean," and Jim, slowly recovered his grip of himself, "I wonder if young Vale shot that deer; it was down there, only a few rods, that we found him."

"Well, that was a running go, poor beggar, and I guess we'll never know." Tom was too elated with his success to notice Jim's agitation.

"Say, Jim, here's my knife. Will you take the hide off the brute?" and he dragged the dead wolf out of the snow. "You know how to do it better than me."

Very unwillingly Jim took the proffered knife, he had done such a job dozens of times without a qualm, but to-day his whole soul and body revolted at the sight and smell of the still hot flesh and blood of the wolf. It was done at last, and he threw the reeking hide at Tom's feet.

"There's your pelt, Tom," he said.

"Now we'd best be going, and keep along the ridge, it's easier walking. I'll catch you up in a minute when I've washed my hands."

Tom started up the side of the ravine, and Jim stepped a few feet off to get some clean snow with which to wash off the traces of his bloody task. With much rubbing and scrubbing with the sharp gritty snow, he succeeded in removing the last trace and vestige of blood, and was just starting to follow his companion, when his eye was caught by a glitter in the snow a few yards below where the deer lay. The eye of the hunter and the woodman misses nothing, but so slight was the impression created by that momentary gleam of light on the snow, that Jim had already gone a few steps up the ravine side before he wondered what it might be. "I guess I'll see, anyway," he said to himself, and retraced his steps. Twice he let his glance fall on the spot, and perceived nothing but the white snow, with here and there an odd spray of scrub showing through.

"Ah, there it is again!" Keeping his eye upon the point of light he tramped through the intervening snow, and stooped to pick up whatever it might be: it was the haft of a hunting-knife! How well he knew that knife;

149

many a time he had seen it hanging on the wall of the little log house by Otter Lake. It was no ordinary hunter's knife, such as might be found in every hunting-camp in the bush. It had been made by Christian himself, as a present to his son, from the broken blade of an old sword-bayonet, which the old sailor had kept as a reminder of his youth, when he was a sailor in King Christian's Navy. The blade had been fitted in a strong oaken haft, and the haft itself decorated with a sailor's skill, on the one side by a Danish cross, and on the other by a small anchor outlined by copper nails.

It was the glitter of a ray of light falling on the burnished copper which had caught Jim's eye. His outstretched hand was almost upon it before he realized the truth and withdrew his hand, as one who had unwillingly touched a deadly snake.

"Good God!" he ejaculated, "that settles it. What's to do now, Jim Hardie? Poor old man, it'll kill him if he ever knows, but there's the poor lad that was shot!"

Jim groaned within himself, as he realized the hard choice between compassion for the living and justice to the dead, which the providence of God seemed to have laid upon his conscience. In an agony of indecision he gazed still on the hateful witness of Ludwig's guilt, his whole nature shrank from being forced to become the instrument of retribution, where the punishment should fall on the innocent, lonely old man. But to bear the burden of such a secret? He would feel as if a portion of the guilt of the dastardly deed rested on his own manhood, were he to tamper with the evidence which the hand of God was inditing before his eyes.

"Jim, Jim Hardie, are you coming?" called back the voice of Tom Dennis from the mouth of the ravine.

"Ay, ay, I'm coming right along," and his answering voice sounded hollow and unreal to his own ears, and with half-averted glance, Jim plucked the knife from the snow, and hid it quickly beneath his tunic. He must have time, he must have time; and he must have solitude, in which to work his way to the path of duty. It would never do to put this tangled skein of the tragedy of the living and of the dead into the impulsive hands of Tom Dennis. "It's a hard road to hoe, Jim Hardie," he said to himself, as he slowly made his way along the track, which Tom Dennis had left in the snow, down the ravine, "it's a mighty hard road to hoe, but you've got to hoe it alone for a while longer. Poor old man, and the lad gone to his reckoning with never a minute's warning."

CHAPTER XXXIV

The drawing of the two heavily laden sleighs from the stack side to the beginning of the bush trail was a slow and laborious task, and to Jim's relief left little time for thought or speech about anything else. At last it was safely accomplished and, each mounted on his own load, the two men started on their homeward journey.

Jim, as the more familiar with the bush road and the better teamster, went first, and though the trail was rapidly hardening under the increasing frost, it required all his skill to negotiate this load safely over the rough and uneven trail. Of necessity they went slowly, and for the most part in silence, save for an occasional shout back of warning to Tom, when Jim had safely passed an especially deep "pitch hole." Of necessity they went slowly, yet Jim was possessed with a sickening anxiety to get clear of the bush and its horrors; above all to get past Christian Nielson's house. His shanty trail crossed the corner of the Nielson homestead, and for a hundred yards or so was in full view of the little house by the Otter Lake. In the old days he was always on the look-out for Christian, that he might wave a hand and shout a word of greeting to the old man, if he were in sight as he went by. To-night he was glad of the lateness of the hour, and of the scant light of the moon not yet above the tops of the spruce; once past the opening, there would be little chance of an encounter, which he felt would be intolerable.

As he drew clear of the bush he gazed eagerly across to where the house and its outbuildings were dimly outlined by a deeper shadow against the snow. The little square curtained windows showed faintly from the light within the house, and, as Jim looked, the door opened, and two figures, one bearing a lantern, stepped outside, and the door was closed. With a subdued "whoa" and a jerk on the lines, Jim stopped his team, afraid lest the jingle of the sleigh-bells should reveal his presence. For a few minutes the men stood talking by the door, and then the one with the lantern moved towards the stable, and the other struck down the path which led into Jim's trail at the further end of the opening.

"That's the old man sure enough," said Jim to himself, as the figure bearing the lantern disappeared within the stable. "Poor old man, I guess he may sleep in peace to-night anyway."

"What's up, Jim?" shouted Tom Dennis, who by this time had drawn up his team close behind; "anything wrong?"

"Just resting the horses a bit, Tom; we're all right," and with a "click" and a shake of the reins Jim started again. "I guess that's one of the Swanson boys," continued Jim to himself; "maybe he won't stop at the crossing of the trail; he won't matter anyway."

But the figure did stop, and was evidently waiting for them to come up. It was young Carl Swanson, and as Jim was for continuing his way with a "Good-night, Carl," he stepped up to the horses, and laid his hand on the rein nearest him.

"Say, Herr Hardie, say," and he spoke eagerly, with evident excitement, "say, have you heard the news?"

"News, why, what news?" and Jim's heart sank. There could be nothing but ill news come from the house back by the lake. "Why, what news would I be hearing back here in the bush!"

"Why, Ludwig Nielson's saved; he's alive; he never was frozen," and Carl's voice rose to a higher pitch; "he'll be there, here with the 'old man' maybe in a week. Isn't it great, isn't it just great, Herr Hardie?"

Jim's throat and lips had gone suddenly dry at Carl's first eager words. "Ludwig saved!" He struggled hard to regain his composure, and to find an answer.

"It's too, it's too——" and his old formula almost escaped him, but just at that moment Tom Dennis's voice broke in.

"Say, what is that fellow saying, Jim? Who's saved and all?"

"Why," shouted back Carl, taking the answer, "why, Ludwig Nielson, that was lost in the big blizzard at the deer-hunting."

"The devil he is," ejaculated Tom, slipping down from his load, and making his way to where Carl was standing.

"What do you make of that, Jim?" added Tom meaningly.

"It's too hard for me, Tom," replied Jim slowly. "But how did it come about, Carl? Where's he been all this long while?"

"Why, I'll just tell you, Herr Hardie, just as the old man told me there back in the house an hour ago; but it's a long story, and in some ways kind of mixed, you see."

"All right; we'll listen," broke in Tom eagerly; "you just go right ahead."

"Well, you see, it is this way," and Carl settled down to his tale. "First, that letter you sent up to uncle's yesterday was from Ludwig; it was written more than two months ago, and given to a Galician on the other side of the mountain to post at Neepawa, and the fellow forgot it till the other day, and then took it into the office at Neepawa, and the only part of the address that was plain was my uncle Ole's name, and Minnedosa, and the Minnedosa people sent it to Old Dawson's office to see if he knew where it should go."

"Yes, yes, that's plain enough," interrupted Tom, who was getting impatient of Carl's preliminaries, "but what did he say?"

"I'm coming to that," went on Carl. "On the day of the blizzard Ludwig went south from his father's, and passed old Black Hawk's teepee—you know the old Indian, Herr Hardie?—and then round the south end of the lake. He intended to cross the ice by their own place, and there he ran into a deer, a big elk. Ludwig wounded it badly, and followed its track, and just when he was coming up to it, some one else fired ahead of him and brought it down."

"Who was it fired?" broke in Tom eagerly.

"The old man did not say. I don't know if Ludwig knew," went on Carl; "anyway, by that time it was getting dark and the storm was coming on, and Ludwig struck into the bush and got lost. I cannot understand his getting lost, he knows every turn and twist in the bush; can you, Herr Hardie?"

"It was a terrible storm, terrible," said Jim; "but where did he get to?"

"Well, he seems to have wandered on and on, and he says in his letter he cannot remember what happened that night. He must have lain down in the snow, for the next thing was he woke up and found himself lying in a bunk in a little shanty, and Trofast—you remember the big dog, Herr Hardie?—licking his hand."

"But where was he, Carl? Why didn't he come home?" Jim could not keep back the question, though he dreaded the answer.

"He was ten miles south-east from here, at 'Little Philip's.' You've heard of 'Little Philip,' Herr Hardie, that lives alone, just over the mountain? He does a bit of blacksmithing for his neighbours, and trapping and hunting in the winter."

"Yes, I know him all right," admitted Jim. "He's a fine little chap, and would use any one real well. He's a man, that's what 'Little Philip' is, but ——"

"It seems Little Philip's own dog was restless after the storm lulled, or a bit towards morning, and Philip, he got up to let it out, and when he stood at the door he thought he heard a howl away in the bush. He listened and he heard it again, too deep for a coyote, and Philip, he struck off into the bush, his own dog running ahead, and there, not very far in the wood, he found Ludwig, nearly buried in the snow, and good old Trofast calling for help. Philip went back to his shanty, and got a big hand sleigh and somehow got Ludwig down to the shanty. Ludwig had some pretty bad frostbites on his hand and one foot, and for nearly a week, Philip told him afterwards, he lay in a kind of fever, before he came to."

"I guess he came pretty near to handing in his checks all right," said Tom Dennis; "but why the dickens didn't he come home when he got bet-

153

ter? Ten miles is not such a deuce of a way, even in this frozen-up, no-road, God-forsaken country."

"Well," admitted Carl, "that's the part the old man Nielson did not read to me of the letter. He said Ludwig was well again when he wrote, and was going into one of the lumber camps, Shaw's, I think, and would not be back before spring. That's what I don't understand, when he's just got a team here, and all last winter's cord-wood to draw out, why didn't he come home? Anyway, I'm taking a letter to our office from the old man to Ludwig to tell him to come right home."

Jim had been very silent during Carl's recital and glad that, lying on the top of his load, he was screened from the sight of the two young men on the ground. Every point in the narrative seemed but an additional link in the chain of evidence that pointed to Ludwig's guilt, and upon him seemed to be laid the burden of taking the first step to bring that guilt home. He could, hard as it might be, bear the thought of bringing the guilt home to the son, but the thought of the dreadfulness of the blow to Christian, the brave old man whom he had respected for years, whose kindly hospitality he had received, was intolerable.

"What do you make of it all, Jim?" asked Tom meaningly, when Carl's story was finished. "You know what we saw."

"We must be getting home, Tom," Jim spoke hastily and almost harshly; "it'll be all hours before we reach Rosebank. Good-night, Carl, good-night. It'll take us three hours yet, and the wife will be thinking we've had a breakdown, and be getting uneasy. Keep your team moving as lively as the trail will let you, Tom."

It was indeed late when they reached Rosebank, and every one had gone to bed. After putting away and feeding the horses, the two men stole quietly into the house, and his anxiety not to disturb Mrs. Hardie while getting their supper was a very welcome excuse to Jim to avoid any discussion of the event of the day and of the startling news of Carl Swanson. Tom had been sleeping at Rosebank for the past two nights, and when he had had a silent pipe, stole in socked feet upstairs to share the bed of the "hired man." When he had gone, Jim carefully closed the door, and unlocking his writing-desk, hid away the hunting-knife which he had kept concealed all the way home. He then resumed his place by the stove, and relit his pipe. It was long after midnight before he, in his turn, sought his bed. His course of action still lay dark and uncertain before him, but he had at least decided on the first step to be taken. From all his anxious thoughts it emerged as the right thing to be done, the step must be taken, and the after consequences left where in the last resource all consequences lie, in the guidance and providence of God.

154

CHAPTER XXXV

"Why in the name of all that's reasonable, Jim Hardie, did you let me land myself in such a confounded mess as this?" and Thomas Casey, doctor of medicine and coroner, leaned back in his old easy chair in his little office, and regarded Jim Hardie with a mingled glance of sympathy and vexation. "You let me go blundering along on the wrong track, like a hasty old fool, till I'm in up to the neck, and then you come along with that," and he pointed to a hunting-knife lying on his open desk, "and a whole string of evidence you've had up your sleeve till I've made all kinds of a 'giddy goat' of myself all over the country."

"It's too bad, doc, it's too bad, and I'm sorry; but I thought——" Poor Jim submitted without resentment to the old doctor's onslaught.

"Yes, you thought," went on the doctor relentlessly, "you thought till I'd ranted all over town about hunters' carelessness, and written a long letter to the *Free Press* showing how it all happened, and sent in a report to the Attorney-General, suggesting all sorts of restrictions on the issuing of 'big game' licences; and then you come along with your dime sensational of love and jealousy and hunters' knives, and evidence enough to hang a man, and every damned fool, from 'Old' Dawson down, will say Tom Casey is in his dotage, and ought to be sent to the scrap heap."

"It's too bad, doc, and I'm real sorry; but you see, doc, till I found 'that,'" and Jim indicated the knife by a turn of his thumb, without looking at it, "and till Carl told us his news last night, I thought that there might be some other way out of it. You see, doc, if both men had been *dead*, I'm not so sure as it mightn't have been allowable to let it rest at that."

"Well, maybe there's something to be said for your way of thinking, Jim," replied the doctor, cooling down after his outburst, "but you see you've put me in a deuce of a 'fix.' What did Tom Dennis say about it when he heard young Swanson's story? Does he suspect anything?"

"Well," admitted Jim, "I think he has figured it out pretty well for himself; but I kind of put him off last night, till I could come and tell you, and see what you might be thinking I ought to do."

"It's a nasty slap for me, Jim, there's no denying; but let that go. It's going to be pretty rough on you," and Jim steadied himself as one preparing to receive an inevitable blow, for there was no mistaking the sternness that came into the old doctor's face, and the decision of his voice; "it's going to be pretty rough on you; but justice must be done, and those that commit crime must suffer for that crime, even if the innocent suffer with them. This country, with all sorts of good and bad from half Europe, would soon be a hell, if men like you and I, Jim Hardie, began to tamper with all of law and order that the 'old flag' stands for."

"I know, doc, I know; I'll stand for it. You know how these things have to be done." Jim's face was haggard and worn from his loss of sleep and mental distress, but the hard path was becoming plainer before him, and there was the courage born of the old battles of his past life, behind his steady purpose, to do the thing that was "straight."

By this time the old doctor's professional training, and the decision of character won by having to act on his own judgment in many critical cases, reasserted their supremacy over his natural Irish impulsiveness. Patients with trifling ailments often thought he gave them less sympathy and attention than was their due, and his careless dress and brusque fashion of speech, full of the rough-and-ready colloquialisms of the west, gave great offence to "old country" people, accustomed to the prim preciseness of a "family" medical man; but there was no lack of clear-cut thought, and of prompt, decisive action when the necessity for their exercise arose.

By the change in the doctor's tone of voice and manner of speech, Jim knew instinctively that the control of the future course of events had passed from his hands into those of one who would not falter till the last claim of justice and right had been satisfied. The burden of responsibility and the decision between the conflicting claims of the living and the dead were removed from his shoulders. The mystery and suspicions of the past few weeks had been well-nigh intolerable. Would the full light of the revelations which he felt were at hand be more easy to bear? Jim watched the old doctor in silence, as he turned round to his desk and read carefully once more the depositions of the witnesses at the inquest, pausing now and again to make a note on a piece of paper by his side.

"Now, Mr. Hardie, I think we are ready," the doctor said, as he carefully folded his papers and put them in his pocket. "First of all we will step down to the office of the Crown Attorney, and he will tell us what is the next step to take."

Jim rose from his seat, and waited while the doctor put on his overcoat and gloves.

"What about that?" asked Jim, when they were ready to start, pointing to the hunting-knife.

"Ah, yes, we'll need that; perhaps I had better take it," and the doctor dropped it into the little handbag which stood on the desk.

The two men walked in silence down the street to the office of the lawyer who acted as Crown Attorney, and Public Prosecutor for the judicial district of which Minnedosa was the centre. Here Jim was left in an outer room for a full hour, while the doctor was closeted with the Crown Attorney in his private office.

At last a summons came for him, and Jim followed the clerk into the private office, where the doctor and the Crown Attorney were seated at a table on which lay the record of the inquest, and the ill-fated knife.

"Good morning, Mr. Hardie; take a seat," and the Crown Attorney pointed to a third chair by the table. "This is a bad business the doctor has put before me, and I'm afraid it places you in a very painful position."

"It's too bad, sir, too bad—but I seem to be a kind of drove," replied Jim, speaking slowly and in a low voice. "I wouldn't hurt Oldman Nielson for a farm; but I couldn't take it on me to hide what—what the Almighty, so to speak, brought out in the open."

"I'm sure, Mr. Hardie, everybody will appreciate your high sense of duty," said the Crown Attorney kindly. "The doctor here has told me how very trying your position is from your past relations to the young man Vale, and to the father of the young man who seems to be very seriously implicated in Mr. Vale's death."

"I suppose, doctor, he does not see any other way out of it?" and Jim suggested the Crown Attorney by a slight motion of his hand.

"I'm afraid not, Mr. Hardie, I'm afraid not," said the doctor. "The Crown Attorney thinks the evidence you have laid before me makes it necessary to act—to act at once—in the interest of Justice."

"Well, if it must be, it must be, and what's to do next?" and Jim turned to the Crown Attorney.

"I will make it as easy for you as I can, Mr. Hardie," replied the Crown Attorney, "and for the present I do not think you need appear publicly in the case, though, eventually you will have to give your evidence in open court. I will take down your statement of the events of yesterday, including your discovery of the knife, and your conversation with the young man Carlson, and you must make a declaration of its truth. Then you had better furnish me with the full names and addresses of any whom you think likely to have any information of value bearing on the case. The doctor here has his notes of the evidence taken at the inquest, and these, with your declaration, will be sufficient to justify the police magistrate in issuing a warrant for the arrest of Ludwig Nielson. You will be notified, if the arrest is effected, of the date of the preliminary enquiry, and I expect the accused will be sent down to the Assizes, which are held here next month."

"Thank you kindly, sir, for your thought for me," said Jim gratefully, "and you may depend on me, sir, to be on hand when the time comes. I hope it won't be necessary for my 'little woman'—my wife, I mean—to be brought into this—this muss—so to speak?"

"Oh, I don't think so," said the Crown Attorney, "though I cannot promise at this stage—but I'll spare you as far as my duty will let me. If you will repeat to me the statement you made to the doctor, I will take it down."

At last with many pauses and corrections, for he was sensitively anxious to be exact, Jim's story of the events of the previous day was finished and duly sworn to and signed.

"Now," said the Crown Attorney, as he folded up the declaration, "you had better go to some quiet place for an hour or two while the doctor and I 'fix' this up with the magistrate, and then if he does not require to see you, you will be free to return home."

"Yes, yes, that will be best," said the doctor. "Just go to my place, and I'll 'phone to my housekeeper to get you something to eat, and make yourself as easy as you can till I come back."

"Thank you, doctor, you're very good; it seems to me I'm giving everybody a deal of trouble—it's too bad," and with a sympathetic shake of the hand from the Crown Attorney, and a short "so long" from the doctor, Jim left the office and made his way back to the doctor's house.

Though he had but a scant breakfast before he left home soon after daybreak, Jim did but little justice to the good things set before him by the doctor's housekeeper soon after his return to the office, and that worthy soul herself was much exercised by his lack of appetite and evident depression. Not to seem unappreciative of the doctor's hospitality, Jim made such an attempt as he could to respond to her invitations to try this or that, but he was glad to escape again to the little office and the solitude of his own thoughts. The time dragged slowly along, and it was a full two hours before the doctor returned, and it was evident that he was in no very enviable humour, for he threw his bag down on the desk with a bang and something very like an oath. He had done his duty, but it had been excessively unpleasant in the doing.

The police magistrate, who was also a leading merchant in the town, had been down at the sample room with a commercial traveller, and the doctor and Crown Attorney had had to await his return to his place of business—and the doctor's temperament was very impatient of waiting inactive when there was anything unpleasant to be done—he liked, as he often said, whether in politics or medicine "to get at it and get through."

The delay had made him irritable—some joking remarks of the police magistrate that he would have "to take back water" with the town hunters had made him furious.

"Well, it's done at last, Jim Hardie, and I guess you may as well get home. The warrant is out and a couple of constables leave for Franklin tonight and will strike for Shaw's camp early in the morning. It's a devil of a bad business, and talking about it won't make it any better—we had both of us best keep our mouths shut about it till we have to speak in court. Now, good-bye,"—and he added, as he saw the utter dejection of Jim's face: "Keep a stiff upper lip, Jim; you've done what you thought right, and don't mind if I've been a bit rough in my manner—that police magistrate touched me on the raw—confound him. Will you have a drop of rye to keep you warm on the way home? Well, if you won't, good-bye," and with a second hearty shake of the hand, a final "good-bye," he followed Jim to the door and watched him, as with hanging head and heavy steps he took his way down the street to the livery stable, where he had left his team.

CHAPTER XXXVI

Shaw's lumber camp on the east side of the Riding Mountain was not at all the wild and godless place of the lumber camp of fiction. There might be one or two reckless characters who watched any newcomer driving up to the "boss's" shanty, dreading lest beneath his winter's wraps there should be pinned the metal badge of the provincial constable, but for the most part, they were quiet and law-abiding settlers. A good many of them were farmers' sons from the Neepawa country, who were glad in the slack winter season to find work for themselves and their horses in drawing logs from the bush to the saw mill, or in taking the cut lumber to town. They were roughly divided into English-speaking and "foreigner"—the "foreigner" being some dozen or so of Galicians. The two elements agreed well enough, eating together and working together, but having separate shanties for sleeping. Ludwig Nielson had naturally taken his place with the English-speaking, among whom were two or three other Scandinavians, though none, to his relief, from "Sweden." Testimonials of character are not at all *de rigueur* in the bush, and the only questions Bob Shaw, the boss, asked were, "Can you chop?" and "What do you want a day?"

Satisfied on these two points Bob Shaw's curiosity ceased and Ludwig was left to settle down into his place with the crowd. Though he talked but little and showed no disposition to exchange confidences with any of his mates his reticence provoked no resentment—he was always quietly courteous when spoken to and very ready to give a helping hand at any odd work that might turn up in the camp. He was, too, an exceedingly expert axeman, and physical strength and skill count for much among such men. Trofast had accompanied his master to camp, and Ludwig was a little afraid that there might be some objection to him.

"I hope you do not mind the dog staying with me?" he asked Bob Shaw, "he is quiet and good-natured."

The "boss" looked at Trofast rather doubtfully.

"I will gladly pay for his food," went on Ludwig.

"Oh, it's not that," replied the other with a good-natured laugh, "there's enough 'grub' wasted round here, I guess, to feed a pack of hounds—but he's a big brute and, if he turned 'ugly,' he'd do for any one."

"Oh, but he shall be good," and Ludwig's hand rested on the big Dane's head. "Give the Herr Boss your paw, Trofast," and Trofast solemnly raised his paw and placed it in Bob Shaw's hand, as if he fully understood and confirmed his master's promise.

Henceforth Trofast's position was assured, and he became from his grave friendliness a general favourite in the camp, though he could never be coaxed out of his master's sight—he followed him to the cutting in the bush, he stood behind him at meal times, and lay by his bunk in the shanty at night.

It was early in December when Ludwig came to the camp, and till the end of January all went on monotonously enough. There was a little break in the steady work of the camp at Christmas time, when several of the "English" went to their homes for two or three days' holiday, and a less pleasant experience at the Russian Christmas shortly after, when most of the "foreign" element visited their homes in the neighbouring Galician settlement, and returned to the camp in a rather battered and quarrelsome condition, bringing with them sundry bottles of a deleterious and fiery spirit, that could only by extreme compliment be called whisky. For two nights after their return there was a "rough house" in their sleeping shanty, by which time the "whisky" was all consumed, and with the last of their "booze" went their valour and love of fighting.

Bob Shaw extremely disliked anything that interfered with the work of his camp and the steady running of the saw mill; still, he was quite prepared to make allowances for the "boys" at Christmas; but he had a deep sense of personal injury when he heard that there was to be an election the latter part of February. So deeply was he stirred that he visited the men, when they were all gathered together at supper-time, on the night the news came, and was nearer making a speech than he had ever been before.

"See here, boys," he began, "there's going to be some darned foolishness of an election, three weeks come Friday, and I suppose most of you chaps have a vote somewhere or other, and you'll find you have a whole kit of friends who never care 'a continental' whether you're dead or alive at any other time. Now see, boys, as far as I'm concerned you can give your vote, or sell your vote, or do what the blazes you like with it, but till voting day we're all going to saw wood, and I'm not going to have the camp all broke up with 'heelers' and their 'dope.' Any man that wants to can have the day off to vote, if that's not good enough he can 'get his time' and strike the 'trail' now."

On the whole Bob's speech was effectual, and there was little interruption in the work of the camp. Early in the morning of the Sunday before voting day the Galicians' priest came up accompanied by a very prosperous-looking fellow-countryman from Winnipeg, who had evidently risen above or fallen beneath the necessity of manual labour. This gentleman had a prolonged "pow-wow" with the "foreign" voters in their own shanty after their spiritual exercises were concluded, and later in the day they had other visitors whom it would only be permissible to call "heelers" in the heat of a contested election—and as Bob Shaw said, it was none of his time, and none of his "funeral" whence came the crisp new five-dollar bills with which the Galicians bought lavish supplies of tobacco and cigarette-paper at the camp store, after the last of their visitors had departed.

When Friday came the "free and independent" voters among the Galicians went off in a body to their home settlement, and no doubt averaged up among themselves the value of the guidance they had received at their Sunday meetings.

Any insinuation there may seem to be in the preceding paragraph is diffused, so that any suggestion of political corruption that it might be taken to imply, may be placed by the discriminating western reader in its right place—on the shoulders of the party with whom his sympathies do *not* lie.

Such of the "English" portion of the men as were not too far from their homes took the day off, and by noon the camp was deserted except for the "boss" himself, two or three stray young Englishmen, and Ludwig Nielson.

The little party had just had dinner together and Bob Shaw was walking across to the mill to have a look at the engine, when he saw a team driving up from the south with a double sleigh and two men.

"If that's me they're coming for," said Bob to himself, "they can save themselves the trouble; I'm not going to leave this camp to-day to vote for the Emperor of Russia, that's sure," and he waited till they drove up to where he was standing.

"Say, mister," said the driver as the horses stopped, "is this Shaw's camp?"

"I guess it is," answered Bob in a non-committal tone of voice.

"Well, then," continued the first speaker, "is the 'boss' around?"

"He might be," said Bob; "what would you be wanting him for? If it's anything to do with the voting, you needn't worry to see him."

"If he's here, I've got to see him," replied the other sharply, "and I'll thank you to let me know where he is pretty quick."

"Well, if it's as important as all that," and Bob drawled a little, for he resented the other's tone of authority, "if you're at all rushed, I don't mind admitting that I'm the 'boss' myself."

"Oh, I beg your pardon, Mr. Shaw, for speaking so short, you see this is a serious business; my mate here and myself are Provincial Police," and the speaker turned back his coat to show the badge on his vest, "and we think you have a man in your camp that's wanted."

"What's his name, and what's it for?" asked Bob Shaw. "Of course I will give you any information I can."

"Well, I don't know what name he may have here, Mr. Shaw, but his real name is Ludwig Nielson, and he's wanted for murder."

"Ludwig Nielson—and for murder!" ejaculated Bob Shaw. "Good God! who would have thought it possible? Why, he's the quietest, civilest chap in camp, and for chopping there's not a man can come near him in a day's work."

"Well, that may be," replied the constable, speaking in a low voice, "that's who it is, and that's what it's for. If you will tell us where we can lay our hands on him, why, the sooner, the surer, and then if you will give us a 'bite' and a feed for the team, we'll be on our road back; we've got to have him safe in Minnedosa gaol to-night."

"Well, well, I am real sorry," and Bob Shaw spoke with deep regret. "How did it happen?"

"Shot a man in the bush up in 'Sweden' last deer-hunting; I've the warrant here and that is all I know," said the constable.

"Maybe it was an accident," suggested Bob Shaw.

"Maybe it was, but that's no truck of mine. I'm sent for the man and I'd like to take him as quietly as we can, but he's got to go," and the constable threw back the robes and stepped out of the sleigh. "You watch the team, Jack, and I'll go with Mr. Shaw."

"Wait a bit, constable, wait a bit," urged Bob Shaw, "this is not as easy as it looks—he's a great strapping chap, and if he got 'ugly' there would be the devil to pay if he got his hand on an axe or anything."

"Oh, I've got what will quiet him," said the constable, slapping his pocket meaningly.

"Yes, but he has got a great big dog with him that will go for you, dead sure, if you lay a hand on his master. See here, Nielson is in the big shanty with two or three English chaps that will not have gone to the voting; you go to my office over there by the mill, and I will call him out and bring him over to you without the dog. Don't take him 'on the rough' if you can help it."

"All right, just as you like," and the constable strolled across to the office and, entering, closed the door.

Mr. Shaw had little taste for the task that lay before him. He had not "run" a lumber camp for ten or fifteen years without coming in contact with some rough characters, nor was it the first visit he had had from the police in search of men that were "wanted" by the law; nor, though a quiet man and usually of few words, was he lacking in personal courage, but he could not think that this silent, sad-eyed young fellow, with his courteous manner and helpful ways, could be guilty of a crime of violence, still he could not interfere, and the sooner it was over the better.

When he entered the shanty he found the young Englishmen sitting round the stove smoking and reading the last batch of papers that had come to camp, and Ludwig was helping the cook to wash up the dinner dishes, while Trofast was busy with a large pan of scraps from the table.

"Oh, there's a team up from Minnedosa," said Mr. Shaw, speaking as carelessly as he could, "and there's a man in the office that would like to see you for a minute, Nielson."

"To see me, Herr Shaw?" and the start Ludwig gave was not lost to Bob Shaw's observant eyes; "it cannot be——" and Ludwig stopped suddenly.

"Well, step across with me—leave the dog to finish his dinner."

With a word of command to Trofast, Ludwig took his cap from a nail on the wall and left the shanty, closely followed by Shaw, who closed the door after him.

The two men walked across to the office without speaking, for both were busy with their own thoughts, Bob Shaw wondering if, after all, he had been mistaken in his estimate of the young fellow by his side, while a whole whirl of possibilities, circling round Amanda and the little house by the Otter Lake came swiftly to Ludwig's mind—how many, and how dreadful things could have happened in the two months' silence that lay between his awaking to consciousness in Little Philip's shanty and now!

Bob Shaw stopped for a moment as they reached the office.

"Say, Nielson, I've an idea there's bad news ahead of you; just pull yourself together a bit."

"Bad news, Herr Shaw, bad news? Ah, then, I must know," and with a quick hand Ludwig opened the door and passed its threshold with a hasty step.

"Stand, hands up," and he was confronted by the gleaming barrel of a revolver within three feet of his head. "Hands up," and the constable's voice was harsh and compelling.

Ludwig's face went white, and mechanically he raised his two open palms to the level of his face, while he turned to Bob Shaw by his side with appealing voice: "Tell me, Herr Shaw, what means this?"

"It means," and the constable spoke slowly, still keeping Ludwig covered with his revolver, "it means that you, Ludwig Nielson, are my prisoner, and that you are wanted for the murder of Roland Vale, a young Englishman, in the bush in 'Sweden' on the day of the big blizzard."

"The young Englishman murdered! My God! and by me?" and Ludwig sank into the office chair, and buried his face in his hands.

"See here, my man, you had better say nothing and go quietly; stand up and hold out your hands—now, Mr. Shaw, if you'll fix these," and the constable drew a pair of handcuffs from his pocket with his left hand and gave them to Bob Shaw. As one stupefied, Ludwig staggered to his feet and submitted to the placing of the handcuffs on his wrists and then sank back again in his seat.

"Now that's what I call being sensible," said the constable, as he put his revolver back in his hip pocket. "I'm much obliged to you, Mr. Shaw, and if you'll tell my mate to take half an hour for his dinner, and then come and relieve me while I get mine, why the team will be ready and we'll be out of your way."

"He's a cold-blooded brute, but I guess he has to be," said Bob Shaw to himself, as he went to deliver his message to the other constable and to give orders to the cook to make up a meal for the two men.

"What's up, Boss?" asked one of the Englishmen as he entered the shanty. "Nielson got to go and vote?"

"No, no, I guess it's some kind of trouble—some police writ or other—and these men are to take him down to Minnedosa; see, cook, you get them something to eat, and one of you boys give the team a feed. Jack Ross, the dog is kind of a pet of yours, see if you can get him down to the tool-house and shut him up; we'll have trouble if he gets it into his wise head that there's something wrong. Now, boys, don't you worry these men with a lot of questions, and it would be just decent if you'd keep out of sight when they start; the poor chap is pretty well broke up, and whatever he's done he's acted 'white' while he's been here," after which long speech for him, Bob Shaw went off to the engine house, and did not reappear till the constables and their prisoner were in the sleigh ready to start.

The chief constable was anxious to pay for their meal, but Bob Shaw would take no money from such men. They were necessary, no doubt, but his sympathies were with Ludwig, and he found the chance for a few words at parting:

"See here, Nielson, you let me know if there's anything fifty dollars can do for you down there. Keep a good heart, and remember Bob Shaw is ready if you want him, and I'll look after the dog. Good-bye."

Under pretence of sending him for his mate, Jack Ross had cajoled Trofast into the tool-house and turned the key. For a time the dog remained quiet, but when the bells of the constable's sleigh rang out as they started on their return journey, he began to bark loudly and furiously and to throw himself against the locked door.

It needed nothing to tell him his master was being taken away, and it was in vain that Jack Ross tried to quiet and comfort him. When Jack woke up in the middle of the night, that howling, grown deeper and hoarser, still penetrated to the sleeping shanty where Jack lay in his bunk. Jack rolled and tossed and buried his head under the blankets, but it was no use. "Hang the boss's orders," he said at last to himself, and, turning out of bed, he pulled on his moccasins, and, putting on his overalls, he stole out of the shanty and made his way to the tool-house. The barking ceased as he drew near and was followed by a pitiful whine as Jack gently called to the hound by name:

"Trofast, old boy, good Trofast," and Jack turned the key and opened the door. With a bound the dog was past him, running first to the living shanty and then to the office, and back to where the constable's sleigh had stood.

For a few minutes he ran round the beaten snow with his nose to the ground, and then with a loud and joyous bark he started down the trail by which his master's captor's had gone.

When the janitor of the gaol at Minnedosa opened the outer door of the court-house early the next morning, to sweep away some fresh snow that had fallen during the night, the first object upon which his eyes fell was Trofast, white with the hoar frost of frozen sweat and stiffened with the cold, but with open and steadfast eye, waiting patiently till his dog's providence should restore to him his master.

CHAPTER XXXVII

By eleven o'clock on a winter's night the quiet streets of Minnedosa are usually deserted, even the curling rink is in darkness, and the most enthusiastic of curlers has retired to his rest to make in his dreams those marvellous "combination shots" which are so rarely achieved in his waking hours. "Voting day," however, is outside all rules for ordinary times, and though it was past midnight when the constables with their prisoner drove up Main Street and turned down to the court-house and gaol, the little town was full of life and stir. Long lines of sleighs and cutters were drawn up on the street in front of the livery stables, and groups of eager politicians were on every street corner. The centre, however, of all the excitement was in Pearson's Hall, for here the election returns, not for their own constituency only, but for the whole Dominion, were posted up as they were 'phoned over from the office of the C.P.R.

Hither, also, the tired constables made their way, after safely delivering over their prisoner to the governor of the gaol, to make their report to the Crown Attorney. The hall was densely crowded, and it was with some difficulty that the two men made their way to the platform where the Crown Attorney and a few of the more prominent officials of the town were seated at a long table, keeping a record of the various contests as they were received.

The figure and office of the chief constable were familiar to most there, and there was a little hush of anticipation and curiosity, as, stepping on to the platform, he leaned over the table and engaged in a whispered conversation with the Crown Attorney. In a minute or two afterwards the Crown Attorney rose from his seat, and beckoning to Doctor Casey, who was also at the table, to follow, he retired with him and the chief constable into one of the little rooms at the side of the platform, used as a dressing-room when the hall was utilized as a theatre.

By this time the whole room was on the *qui vive*. A crowd is always hasty in its deductions and apt to rush to precipitate conclusions on insufficient evidence—a western political crowd is far from being an exception to this rule. The larger number of those present were ardent Tories; the rest, those cautious souls who do not say which way they have voted till the returns show where the victory lies; then they are solid on the winning side.

Though the returns for the constituency of Minnedosa were not in from the farther outlying districts, it was evident, early in the evening, that the

Tory candidate was the chosen of the people; consequently the Grit element had faded quietly away and gone to its bed.

The second constable, who had remained in the body of the hall, was at once the centre of an eager, questioning throng, who were fully satisfied that "the Grits" had been guilty of some outrageous political crime. The constable, however, stolidly refused to make any admission beyond that they had been sent to fetch in a man who was "wanted," and that the "wanted" individual was now safe in the gaol. That information, though slight, was sufficient for the crowd to build upon. Of course, he was a d——d Grit—he had impersonated an absent vote—he was caught taking whisky to "Sweden"—he had been giving a five-dollar bill to a Galician—he had tried to burn a ballot-box! The constable remained obdurate to all suggestions. He had never been so entirely on "the inside track" in the matter of exclusive information, and he was not going to sink into insignificance by a premature revelation.

At last the door of the little room opened, the doctor appeared on the platform, and an expectant hush fell on the whole crowd. It was evident that he was excited, and he spoke quickly.

"Is there any one here that lives up in 'Sweden' near Ole Swanson's?"

A low murmur passed through the hall. It was the "Swedes," then, who were guilty of this "unknown crime," and each man began to tell his neighbour that he had always known they were not to be trusted. Yes, there are several here from "Sweden"—here's "Andy Johnson" and "Little Pete" and "Big John" and young "Carl Swanson."

"That will do," called out the doctor, "send Swanson up here," and Carl was pushed and hustled through the crowd and on to the platform. The doctor took him into the little room, and the hall became a Bedlam of loud and angry discussion, which could not be lulled into silence by the chairman's bell, even to listen to fresh returns from other constituencies.

When at the end of a quarter of an hour the door of the dressing-room opened, and the Crown Attorney and its other occupants filed on to the platform, there was a perfect roar of angry demands for the name of the sinner against "the party" and electoral purity, a roar that lulled slowly into silence in response to the uplifted hand of the chairman. The Crown Attorney spoke sharply and clearly:

"You are all labouring under a mistake, gentlemen. The chief constable was merely reporting to me an arrest which had nothing whatever to do with the election. A young man has been taken up on suspicion of being connected with the shooting of a young Englishman last deer-hunting."

The information was a distinct disappointment, and the constable in the crowd was roughly rebuked by more than one for making such a mystery out of nothing. "What did one Englishman more or less matter on election night?" And the crowd returned to its politics.

Carl Swanson had stepped off the platform while the Crown Attorney was speaking and now quietly made his way from the hall into the sharp, frosty air. He turned the collar of his fur coat high around his ears, and taking the middle of the road that he might not be stopped and questioned by any casual passer-by, he took his way across the river to the livery stable, where he had left his team and jumper.

His mind was in a whirl of conflicting emotions. He had come down to town earlier in the evening, bringing the ballot-box and returns from the polling at the schoolhouse near his father's house, and also to post a letter from Christian Nielson to Ludwig. Now he had to return and bear the heavy tidings to the old man, and to Amanda, that Ludwig, his old friend and playmate, was lying in Minnedosa gaol on a charge of murder!

The eastern sky was rosy with the promise of sunrise when Carl turned his tired horses into the stable-yard at his father's homestead. After putting them in their stall and covering them with their blankets, he walked slowly up to the house, where he found his father lighting the fire in the big box stove, to warm the house before the rest of the family should arise.

"Well, Carl, my boy, so you're safely back, and how did the election go?" he asked, without looking up from his task of cutting the kindling with his draw-knife.

"Yes, father, I'm back, and, father, I've bad news."

"Why, Carl! why, Carl, my son!" for Carl had sunk into a chair and buried his face in his hands.

"What is it that is wrong?" and his father stepped quickly to him and laid his hand on his son's shoulder. With a strong effort Carl checked his sobs.

"Father, they have taken Ludwig on a charge of murder," and Carl's voice broke again, "and he's in the gaol in Minnedosa."

"Ludwig and murder. Why, who?" asked his father hastily.

"They say," and Carl's voice was steadier, "they say he shot the young Englishman back at Herr Hardie's shanty, and the police people say I am to tell the 'old man'; and there's Amanda—and her father. I cannot do it; it will break their hearts."

Slowly, and with many pauses, Carl told the whole sad story of Ludwig's arrest.

"Well, it is just too hard," said his father when he had finished, "it is too hard for you. You are worn out and wearied. Do you go to your bed before your mother and the rest come down, and I—yes, I will see your uncle Ole, and between us—God help us—we will do the telling as best we can," and, helping Carl off with his wraps and coat, he half led and half supported the poor lad up the narrow stairs to his own room.

CHAPTER XXXVIII

"Old" Carl, as he was commonly called to distinguish him from his son, "Young Carl," felt a growing distaste for his task, as, breakfast over, he took his way through the half-mile of bush that lay between his own homestead and his brother Ole's.

The more he thought over the details of the supposed crime (for the Crown Attorney had read over Jim Hardie's information to young Carl), the less certain did he feel of Ludwig's innocence.

The idea of connecting Ludwig with such a deed, which seemed so impossible to young Carl, was far less wildly improbable to the older man. In his younger days, Old Carl had "followed the sea," before the mast in timber ships, trading between his own country and Hull, and he knew full well what bloody doings may follow the encounter of young hot blood, inflamed by drink or jealousy. Ludwig's quick, passionate temper, moreover, had always been a thing to be reckoned with from his boyhood, and though his love for Amanda had had no more formal acknowledgment than is given by good-natured teasing and sly innuendo, yet it was taken for granted that it existed and would in due season end in marriage. "Sweden" lacked the niceties of etiquette which mark Winnipeg "Society" in such matters, but in its simple and bucolic way it understood itself, which, perhaps after all, was all that mattered.

Though his sea-faring experience led old Carl to doubt Ludwig's innocence, and perhaps dulled his horror of what seemed a treacherous crime, it doubled the difficulty of his task that morning in another way. By some strange moulding influence of calling upon character, those who go down to the sea in ships are the tenderest of men in the presence of a woman's sorrow and a woman's tears; and when youth and beauty are added to sex, there never was the sailor who would not rather face a nor'wester on a lee shore. Among the "Swedes," even outside her own relatives, from her beauty and unconscious refinement, Amanda stood a little apart—they occasionally perhaps criticized, but it was a matter of national pride, and to her uncle Carl she was especially dear. "A sailor's lass, every inch of her, trim and taut, a neat ankle and a laughing eye. Why, what more would you have?" Ole Carl often asked his wife when that good woman would express the thought that Amanda should be settling down to the ways and work of the farm, and should dress and work like other girls.

Her uncle had been over to his brother's only the day before, and had rallied Amanda greatly on the change in her looks and spirits since the letter came to Otter Lake, and Amanda had defended herself as well as she could, with much blushing and embarrassment, against his jovial, if rather broad humour. When Old Carl left to go home he congratulated himself with much complacency on the way in which he had "livened the folk up"; now he felt that he had to undo his good work, and that he would leave nothing but sorrow behind when his mission was fulfilled.

As he went to the door of his brother's house he swore an old-time sailor-man's oath to himself, as a last support to his courage, in case Amanda should "cut up rough" when he told his news. If there were to be any tears he felt he would be entirely unmanned. Old Carl knew the ways of the sea better than he knew the ways of the fair sex, and had yet to learn that a girl cries more often for joy than for sorrow, and more often to get her own way than for either. When brute force was given to the man, nature adjusted the balance in other subtle ways of her own.

He was greeted with a chorus of welcomes as he opened the door and entered the living-room, for Uncle Carl was a great favourite with his brother's children; but the welcomes died away almost ere they were uttered, for he had no gift of deception, and ill news was written on every line of his rugged face.

"What is it, Uncle Carl?" cried Amanda quickly. "Is aunt or any of the children sick?"

"No, no, they are all well enough, but——" and he looked appealingly at his Brother Ole.

"Is it—I mean, did Cousin Carl see——" and Amanda blushed and dropped her voice. "Is it news of Ludwig?"

"It's your father I am speaking to, Amanda," and Old Carl kept his eyes resolutely fixed on his brother. "You see, Ole, Carl did hear down to town as there was some sort of trouble between Ludwig and the young man that was shot at the deer-hunting, and the folk are saying——"

"Yes—folk are saying," and Amanda stepped before her uncle with blazing eyes, "folk are saying, and I suppose Uncle Carl is saying too, that Ludwig Nielson shot a helpless man in the back, and then ran away to hide."

"Hush, hush, my child," and her mother laid a rebuking hand on Amanda's arm; "you should not speak to your uncle so. Let him tell us what has happened."

"Let the girl be, sister-in-law, let the girl be," said Old Carl soothingly. "It's a bad job, and I'm not minding. You see, Ole, things do look pretty bad," and slowly he told the whole story of the finding of the knife and of Ludwig's arrest.

Each of his auditors was affected by the gloomy recital in his own way. The little girls, Olga and Louise, were filled with a wondering fear of some ill beyond their understanding, and sought refuge at their mother's knee. August stole away out of doors to the stable, and Ole sucked hard at his pipe and kept silence. Amanda's eyes, clear and undaunted, never moved from her uncle's face till the last word of his tale was told.

"And does his father know?" and Amanda spoke quietly.

"No," replied her uncle. "Carl had a message for the old man to go down to Minnedosa. There is to be a kind of trial on Tuesday, and I thought, maybe, your father would take him the word; and if it's a team and the like, why Carl would take him down to-morrow. It's a Sunday, but I'm sure the boy would go quite willingly."

"Thank you, uncle, you are very good, and I know Cousin Carl will stand by his old schoolfellow. Father, let me go across to Herr Nielson's— yes, father," as Ole shook his head doubtfully, "I must go," and Amanda's voice was quietly determined. "The good old man shall never hear of such trouble but from one whose faith in Ludwig's innocence is as staunch and true as his own," and again the colour mantled in her cheek, and high courage lightened the dark depths of her clear grey eyes.

"Well, my girl," and Ole spoke slowly, having first by a questioning glance won his wife's consent, "you shall go and bear to him his old friend's sympathy. All that I have is at his service. He has but to tell me how I may help him."

Ole's mind worked slowly. As yet he was far from seeing his way to the truth in this tangled skein of mystery, but certain principles were deep-seated and sure in his nature, let the facts be what time should show them to be, his present course was clear—a man stands by his friend and Norse by Norse. There might be more to be done, there was no more to be said.

In a few minutes, Amanda, who had run upstairs to change her print frock for something warmer, reappeared in her blanket coat and toque. To her uncle's immense relief and admiration, there was not only no trace of tears on her face, but she was quite composed and cheerful.

"So long, mother," she said, as she stooped over the back of her mother's chair and gave her a kiss. "So long, uncle; perhaps I'll call in at auntie's on my way home, if Herr Nielson has a message for Cousin Carl; and, uncle, don't fancy foolish, foolish things about Ludwig, or your little Amanda will be really, really angry with you, and not——" and with a light kiss on the small spot on his cheek which was not covered by his whiskers, she opened the door and was gone, leaving the old sailor bewildered by this new revelation of the intricacy of the female character.

Yet the swift change in Amanda's humour was neither strange nor inexplicable in itself. Her belief in Ludwig's innocence was absolute and entire.

To her the manner of Roland's death was final. To her the supposition that Ludwig could have done such a deed, in such a way, was not only disloyal, it was ridiculous. At her uncle's first telling of his story, his hesitancy and his unexpressed fears aroused in her a momentary feeling of resentment; but then, who knew Ludwig as she knew him?—she, and the brave old man by the Otter Lake? There would be no doubts and fears there. What did any one else matter? Uncle Carl was kind and he meant well, but he did not know!

Amanda walked quickly across the opening and down the familiar trail through the spruce. A certain sense of exhilaration in her own spirits seemed to respond to the keen and frosty sharpness of the morning air. The last few days had been a time of suspense, and suspense was very trying to her impulsive temperament. For the first day or two after the news came that Ludwig was still alive, her heart had no room for any other emotion than a deep gladness that he still lived; but by degrees she was conscious of other and more embarrassing sensations. Ludwig still lived—but why had he not sooner returned home? Ludwig still lived—but had his love survived her waywardness and the cruel shocks of doubt and jealousy to which she had exposed it? And if his love were still all her own, how was she to cover her capitulation with any form or show of maidenly reserve? While Ludwig was lost and hope of his return was well-nigh dead, she had unveiled every tender emotion of her bosom to the dear old man, his father, only so had she kept her heart from breaking. Ludwig to be living and to be claiming her confessed love—with what blushes must she meet him!

Now, as she hastened along her way, all her mingled doubts and fears and shamefaced modesty were gone. Ludwig was the object of doubt and suspicion, he was accused of a hideous crime, he was even now lying alone, with no friend by him, in prison; and Amanda's courage rose high and unfaltering to the call of love. By what as yet unthought-of means his innocence was to be made plain and open to the light of day, she did not pause to think, but that the way would be opened to her own and his father's love she never doubted.

Without pausing for a response she tapped at the door of the little log house and entered. Within, all was in confusion, the walls were stripped bare of their usual simple adornments, and the few articles of furniture were gathered in the middle of the room, while Christian himself was busy by the stove mixing a pail of whitewash.

"Why, my little Amanda, you have caught me finely this morning," he said, laying down his brush and greeting her with a kiss on either cheek. "Here I am cleaning up our little cabin, and making it shipshape before our boy comes home. But why so early? and you are breathless with your quick coming."

174

"Oh, Herr Nielson," and Amanda gave a little sob, for the confident happiness of his anticipation went to her heart. "Oh, Father Nielson, I'm afraid Ludwig will not be home for a long time yet, but we must be brave ____"

"Why, my girl, what is it that you have to tell me? Have you heard from Ludwig?"

"Yes, I have heard, but not from him—those people to the south know him so little that they believe he shot the poor young Englishman, and now —now, while I am telling it to you—they have Ludwig in their cruel prison."

The colour faded from the old sailor's face, and for a moment he leaned heavily against the table; but it was only for a moment, and when he spoke his voice was full of quiet confidence.

"I know that such a thought was in their minds when the body of the young man was found and Ludwig was lost in the storm, and Ludwig himself, in his letter to me, spoke of a great temptation that he had encountered that day ere the storm fell. But, my little Amanda, I have the word of my boy that the temptation was overcome, and the Spirit of my God sealed to my heart the assurance of his innocence."

"Indeed, Father Nielson, you and I need nothing else to make our hearts sure of Ludwig's innocence, but how are we to make it plain to those who know him not? for it was a cruel story Cousin Carl brought back from Minnedosa last night," and Amanda told him of Jim Hardie's discovery, and of the bringing of Ludwig to the gaol.

Even then, when he had heard all that Amanda had to tell, Christian had little apprehension of real danger to his son. There would be delay in his boy's return, and his heart had been very eager to welcome him back—for these young people the delay would be hard to bear—but for himself, he had long been schooled to patience. He must hasten to his son's side as soon as might be, and he had no doubt that Ludwig's innocence would be established in others' minds as clearly as it was in his own. His own life had long been lived on such simple lines of trust in God and of truthfulness with his fellowmen, that he never doubted that innocence should be its own sufficient protection.

When Amanda left to return home, his preparations for his journey were all made. He would be ready for Young Carl at daybreak on the Sunday morning, and Amanda promised that her father or August should come every day while he was away, to care for the horses and cattle at Otter Lake. To Ludwig he was to bear a tender message of love and trust from Amanda herself.

CHAPTER XXXIX

Ludwig's preliminary trial before the police magistrate was little more than a matter of form. It only lasted for a couple of hours, and at the end of that time he was committed for trial on the charge of murder at the Spring Assizes, which were to be held in Minnedosa in three weeks.

In his simplicity and ignorance of the world's ways, Christian Nielson had thought that all that would be necessary for Ludwig to do to clear himself would be to tell truly all that happened on that fateful afternoon in the bush. He never dreamt that Ludwig's explanation of losing his hunting-knife, and of his going to Shaw's camp would only add to the probability of his guilt in the eyes of the law. He never even thought that it would be necessary for him to entrust Ludwig's defence to a lawyer. In his simple mind lawyers were only a rather undesirable class of men, whose function it was to enable dishonest people to avoid paying their just debts, or to keep the guilty from suffering the due punishment of their misdeeds. Surely, innocence could stand alone!

Fortunately for father and son they had friends of their own people in Minnedosa, who were more versed in the ways of the world. Under their persuasion Christian was induced to entrust his son's defence to a clever young lawyer, Hubert Darcy, who already had a considerable practice among the settlers in "Sweden," and who was glad of the opening which his conduct of such a serious case would be for bringing himself into public notice. Very unwillingly Ludwig consented, on his advice, to meet the charge with a bare plea of "not guilty," Mr. Darcy stating on his behalf that no evidence would be offered till the time of trial at the Assizes.

The greater part of the day following the committal were spent by Mr. Darcy and Christian in Ludwig's cell. Mr. Darcy took notes of every minute detail of the day of the tragedy, and also made a list of all their neighbours by the Otter Lake, who were in the least likely to be out in the bush deer-hunting. While he himself was prepared to accept Ludwig's statement as true, he would not hear of Ludwig's being put into the witness-box to tell it to the jury, except as a last resource. When his enquiry was at last over and Christian had taken farewell of his son, Mr. Darcy's last words to Christian were:

"Now, Mr. Nielson, we have done all that we can for to-day. We must hope for the best, and leave no stone unturned that may throw light on this terrible affair. But, humanly speaking, our case rests on two things; we must either discredit the circumstantial evidence of the Crown, or we must produce the man who, either by accident or design, did the shooting. When you get back home and discuss the matter with your friends, keep your mind fixed on these two points, and it is possible, just possible, I say, that some chance suggestion may put us in the track that will ultimately lead us to the truth and to a clear verdict."

If Ludwig's arrest had aroused little general interest on the night of the election, it was far otherwise as the time of the trial drew near. A public, jaded by their keen if short-lived excitement in politics, turned gladly to this new promise of sensation to tide it over the dull season of the "break-up" of the winter. The people of the Canadian West are nothing if not practical, and the horror of the good people of Minnedosa at the crime was sensibly moderated by the consideration that a sensational trial would bring many people to the Assizes, the hotels and boarding-houses would be filled with guests, money would be spent, and for a few days at least the town would be brought before a larger public than usual by the "write ups" of the trial in the Winnipeg papers.

Up in the English settlement the interest was naturally far more personal in its character from the connection with the case of the Enderbys and of Jim Hardie. Equally naturally all there was of rumour and surmise in the settlement came to a focus at Old Man Dawson's. On the mail-day before the trial, the post-office was filled with a crowd who had gathered, less in the expectation of receiving letters, than of hearing something new about the murder in Sweden. Public opinion would have nothing less than murder, and a cautious Scotch suggestion of Dugald McLeod's, that it would be better to wait for the evidence before calling it by such an ugly name, was received with distinct disfavour by most of those there. As one of those present expressed it to one of his neighbours:

"If you want a mean-spirited 'cuss,' give me a Scotch Grit every time."

Though the crowd was very talkative and sure of itself, the Dawson family was unusually reticent, not from any native diffidence, but Old Man Dawson and Mary Ann had been subpœnaed as witnesses for the Crown. It is true Old Man Dawson was only required in his capacity of postmaster and on the off-chance that his evidence might throw a little light on the communications between Ludwig and his father. Still, he was to be a witness, and the few words which he let drop from time to time were calculated to give the impression that the whole case would hinge on his testimony. He hinted darkly that, by the time the trial was over, the Pope o' Rome would be seriously compromised; the Swedes were "furriners"; "furriners," in default of evidence to the contrary, were clearly "Romans," and every "Roman" is the accredited agent of the Pope and the devil.

This line of thought, though very conclusive and logical to Old Dawson himself, did not appeal at all strongly to most of the company. What counted far more with the older settlers was the fact that the information had been laid by Jim Hardie, a man who knew more of the "Swedes" and had more influence with them than any man in the English settlement; and Charles Grant, one of Jim's neighbours, summed up the general sentiment correctly enough when he remarked: "If Jim Hardie laid a charge against me, I should want to have a pretty straight answer before I went into court."

Many attempts were made to get Mary Ann to discuss Roland Vale's relations with the Hardies and with Amanda, but while she felt the strain of secrecy very severely, she could not be induced to anticipate her evidence at the approaching trial, by a single word about what she had seen or heard at Rosebank.

"Them as goes to the trial will hear what I have to say, and they'll know what I know, and maybe one or two coroners and such-like will wish they had listened to me afore they were so sure of themselves. Maybe there are other 'fules' in the world beside 'wimmen folk.' Anyway, them as listens hardest will hear most."

Beyond this Mary Ann could not be persuaded to go, though, when the mail was sorted and the crowd began to disperse, she did vouchsafe one piece of information to Tom Dennis, whom, as a fellow witness, she regarded as a privileged person.

"You and me, Mr. Dennis, knows a deal more than most, but there's one thing I only heard from the mail-man to-day."

"Why, what's that?" asked Tom curiously.

"Why, just this. When he came up last trip he passed Old Nielson, the young man's father, on the road, and he had Amanda with him; and he heard in town last night that they took the train east, and have not come back. I'm not saying the young woman has gone away, and I wouldn't tell those other folk, but you and me can think for ourselves," and with a look of much meaning she handed Tom his mail, leaving him in a state of great doubt and mystery as to what she would imply.

CHAPTER XL

It was half-past nine on the morning of the second day of the Assizes, and although Ludwig's trial did not begin till ten o'clock the court-house at Minnedosa was packed to the doors. Outside, it was one of those damp, muggy days which often herald in the "break-up" of the Manitoba winter, and a fog, born of the rapid evaporation of the snow's wasting under a south wind, lay heavily over the little town in the valley. Within the court-house itself the atmosphere was already stifling. The caretaker of the building, with the perversity of his kind, had fired up his furnace to a point which would have been sufficient to counteract an outside temperature of forty degrees below zero. He was a man of methodical habits, and regulated his fires by the almanac rather than by the vagaries of the climate, and as he said: "He did not 'figger' to let up any till the first of April."

To add to the physical discomfort of the crowd the greater part of them were still wearing their heavy winter fur coats, and as most of them had come from the care of their horses and stock before driving to town, the hot and heavy atmosphere was more than reminiscent of the stable and the farmyard.

Nowhere are appearances more deceptive than in the west, and a new-comer from the "old land," finding himself for the first time in such a crowd, would most probably form very erroneous impressions of the means and manners of those around him. The Canadian of the west rarely grooms himself as carefully as he does his horse, and varies between an ill-kept beard and a shave at uncertain intervals. His clothes are adapted to stand the cold and hard work, and he thinks less of their style and fit than of the fact that they are paid for. In his manner of speaking he is rough and ready, free and easy, he neither gives to others nor expects for himself a "handle" to his name. His language is full of careless but expressive collo-quialisms, and if his "folk" down east were "old country" born, there is usually a survival now and again in his conversation of old words and ex-pressions, which were learnt in his days of childhood. His slovenly dress and careless fashion of speech are no index to his standing in the commu-nity, and are both consistent with a name that is good for a large sum at the bank, and for a personal reputation which stands high on the roll of honour of church members.

His general intelligence and capacity for taking care of his own interest in a business way are altogether out of proportion to the formal education he has received at school, and his off-hand, casual way of buying and selling, with his fine indifference as to whether he does either, have many times betrayed the "cock-sure greenhorn," to his grievous undoing, in a deal for cattle or land. There is nothing which he is anxious to sell, and, excepting his wife and family, nothing which he will not sell, if there is money in it. He has little or none of the sentiment which binds an Englishman to the village where he was born, and to the home where he played as a child. His homestead, even when he has attained considerable prosperity, shows but a scant appreciation of natural beauty, and often little care for his own creature comforts. If his "woman" cares to "truck" with a simple flower garden in her rare moments of leisure, or seeks to coax some wild hops or Virginia creeper to rob his porch of some of its bareness, he submits with good-humoured tolerance, but his machinery for his farm work is the latest production of an inventive age, and the first evidences of his increasing prosperity are to be found in his large stables and handsome barns, rather than under the roof which shelters his wife and children. Yet, with all his materialism, the western Canadian has often a most emotional temperament, and a western lawyer, who has but a poor case for his client on matters of fact, knows that his best chances of securing a verdict rest on his being able to convince the jury that the prisoner has not had "a fair show," or that his condemnation will involve his innocent wife and children in want and misery.

Such, broadly speaking, were the majority of those who had gathered at the court-room for Ludwig's trial. There was a sprinkling of young Englishmen, either farming "on their own" or farm pupils, in the surrounding settlements, and, seated by themselves, at the back of the court-room were most of the "Swedes" who lived round Otter Lake, including "Old" and "Young" Carl, and Ole Swanson.

Outside those who, as near-by neighbours or as witnesses, had a personal interest in the trial, most of those present had come in very much the same frame of mind as to a circus or other travelling show, with this additional advantage that there was no fee for admission. It was rumoured, too, that a "Cracker Jack" of a criminal lawyer, from Winnipeg, had been brought up to assist in Ludwig's defence, and there were lively differences of opinion as to whether he would be able or not "to down" the Crown Attorney.

Mingled among the crowd, chiefly distinguishable by their unusual smartness of dress and by the wearing of "boiled shirts," were those who had been summoned to serve on the petty jury and from whom the "twelve good men and true" would be selected to try the case. These maintained a certain aloofness of manner and speech, due partly to a lively appreciation of the dignity of their office, and partly to a sense of physical discomfort;

to a stiff and starchy discomfort appropriate to the Sabbath, but rather embarrassing on a weekday.

Seated at a long table in front of the dais, on which was the judge's seat, were the Crown Attorney, Mr. Hubert Darcy, and the other lawyers of the town who had cases down for trial. There, too, was the "Cracker Jack" from Winnipeg, Matthew O'Leary, K.C., a big, jovial Irishman, who wore his shabby barrister's gown and ill-tied tippets with a careless ease and disregard of appearances, greatly in contrast to the prim neatness and spick-and-spanness which marked his provincial brethren of the law. At the present moment he was retailing with infinite humour the evidence given in a breach of promise case, in which he had taken part the week before at Brandon; the bursts of laughter from those around him were taken by the crowd as a good augury for their own entertainment when he came to cross-examine the witnesses for the Crown.

On the stroke of ten by the big court-house clock, one of the doors at the end of the hall opened, and the stentorian voice of the court crier demanding "silence" announced the entrance of the judge. The laughter of the bar and the buzz of conversation through the hall died suddenly away, and with much shuffling of feet and pushing back of chairs all rose and remained standing while the sheriff conducted the judge to the dais.

The judge was a fine, handsome old gentleman of some sixty-five years, with refined and kindly features and an easy and courteous manner, which, though very reassuring to nervous junior counsel and truthful though embarrassed witnesses, was capable of swift change to biting sarcasm and keen denunciation, if one or the other were led by its sympathetic kindliness into flippancy of speech or trifling with the truth. His dress had none of the gorgeous paraphernalia of scarlet robes and wig which mark his English brother. His simple morning suit under his gown was even less formal than that of most of the lawyers present.

A bow and "Good morning, gentlemen," to the bar, a bow and "Thank you, sheriff," to the sheriff, and the judge took his seat. With a second demand for silence, rendered necessary by the sitting down of the crowd, the court crier, in time-honoured formula, in which there was much mention of "Our Sovereign Lord the King," declared the court open.

The general interest slackened a little during a short conference in low tones between the Crown Attorney and Mr. Hubert Darcy with the judge, but it reawakened to a breathless silence when the clerk of the pleas stood up from his seat below the dais and read from the report handed to him by the foreman of the grand jury.

"Our Sovereign Lord the King versus Ludwig Nielson; indictment for wilful murder. True bill." The sheriff quickly left the hall by the door leading from the court-house to the gaol, and again for a few minutes there was

181

a murmur of subdued voices through the court. Again the scandalized crier called for "silence," and in the hush which followed his voice the door re-opened, and, preceded by the sheriff, came Ludwig, in charge of the chief gaoler.

For a moment Ludwig hesitated, and a hot flush mounted to his fore-head as he faced the staring, eager eyes of the crowd, and then, with firm step and as if unconscious of the grasp of the chief gaoler upon his arm, he passed through the narrow opening between the counsel's table and the crowd, and took his place at the bar.

"Ludwig Nielson, prisoner at the bar," and the voice of the clerk of the pleas was clear and full of solemnity, "you stand indicted by our Sovereign Lord the King of the wilful murder of Roland Vale. Do you plead guilty or not guilty to the charge?"

For a moment Ludwig stood stifled by the intensity of his own emotions, and then his voice came clear and strong:

"Not guilty."

Ludwig Nielson was on trial for his life.

CHAPTER XLI

It would involve a wearisome repetition to follow in detail the evidence given on the first day of Ludwig's trial. It was plain to all from the opening address of the Crown Attorney that the latter intended to rest his case on two points; first, on proving that, within narrow limits of time and space, Ludwig, and Ludwig alone, could have encountered Roland Vale in the bush; and secondly, that Ludwig, and Ludwig alone, could be shown to be animated by motives of outraged love and jealousy, sufficient to allow of such a crime being committed in such a way. Though the Crown Attorney's case thus hinged on the evidence of Jim Hardie and of Mary Ann Dawson, he had not neglected a single subsidiary detail, which could support, corroborate, or increase the inevitability of the conclusions to which their testimony led. There were photographs of the Otter Lake and the little log house by its shore, of Jim Hardie's shanty and the hay meadow, and one, the most realistic of all, of the spot where Roland's body was found, with the wolf-torn body of the elk in the foreground. Every settler's homestead and every hunter's camp for miles round was shown on a carefully drawn map, and every hunter and settler who could conceivably be implicated in the remotest degree was subpœnaed to account for himself, if need be, for the whole of the day of the shooting.

The great lawyer from Winnipeg found the case more interesting than he had anticipated, and could not withhold his professional admiration of the skill with which the young Crown Attorney had marshalled his evidence. He had come up from the city to make an easy three or four hundred dollars "among the farmers." But it was not going to be so easy as he had expected; as he said in an undertone to Hubert Darcy, "If we cannot break down his main evidence he hasn't left us a hole big enough for a bush rabbit to crawl through." So Mr. Matthew O'Leary, K.C., went very warily.

The evidence of Jim Hardie was so evidently sincere, and marked by such an anxiety to say every kind thing that he could of Christian Nielson, of Amanda, and of Ludwig himself, that Mr. O'Leary accepted it without cross-examination as to the facts, and contented himself with drawing the attention of the jury to the high esteem in which the prisoner was held, even by one who was compelled by a strong sense of duty to give evidence against him. If, however, Mr. O'Leary dealt very sympathetically with Jim Hardie, it was far otherwise when he rose to cross-examine Miss Mary Ann Dawson.

It was a great day for Mary Ann; one of the many thrilling and tragical experiences of which she had read so often in the literary supplements was to be realized in her own person. This was to be the *dénouement* (literary supplement), and for the past three weeks she had been qualifying herself to play the leading part. Not only had she read and re-read every trial scene for murder in the big pile of literary supplements stored in her bedroom at home—and it was a poor supplement which did not yield at least one blood-curdling crime—but she had raked the rubbish heap of her memory for every trivial incident within her knowledge or power of imagination which could hurt the reputation of Amanda or glorify Roland Vale. As she stepped confidently and smilingly on the witness stand, she was, as Tom Dennis whispered to Bert Enderby, "loaded for a bear."

On the day before the trial the Crown Attorney had received a warning from old Doctor Casey, expressed in very drastic, if rather coarse terms, that if he were not careful he might find his witness knew far too much. Accordingly, the Crown Attorney in his examination did his best to confine his questions to simple matters of fact. But Mary Ann was not to be robbed of her opportunity. More than once the judge interposed with a warning to Mary Ann to limit her answers to matters within her own knowledge. More than once he suggested to Mr. O'Leary that, if "Brother" O'Leary objected, this or that answer should not be put down by the court stenographer; but "Brother" O'Leary was all smiles and affability, and said that he was charmed with the responsiveness of the "young lady," and that he should wish her to have the fullest latitude. Mary Ann positively beamed upon "Brother" O'Leary and looked to him, and not in vain, for an encouraging nod or smile every time the Crown Attorney endeavoured to check her volubility. The crowd was highly amused, the jury puzzled, the judge rather scandalized, and the Crown Attorney was rapidly losing his head when the judge came to his assistance.

"Do you think that is all, Mr. Attorney?"

"Thank you, my lord, that is all I wish to ask the witness"; and the Crown Attorney sat down hastily.

There was a little restless movement through the hall as the crowd for a moment relaxed its attention; a warning call of "silence" from the ever-vigilant court crier, and "Brother" O'Leary in easy, leisurely fashion, with a hitch of his gown, rose to cross-examine. Nothing could exceed the blandness with which he led Mary Ann over the various points in her evidence, the listening at doors, the peeping through windows, the overhauling of poor Amanda's little box, the reading of letters, the deductions of her mother and herself in sorting the mail, about some of which little ways Mary Ann had had a passing uneasiness before she came to court as to how they would strike the outsider, all seemed so natural and fitting to

"Brother" O'Leary that, as Tom Dennis expressed it in a second aside to Bert Enderby, she was "in it up to the neck" before she realized her danger.

Then in a flash, like a western hailstorm from a handful of cloud on a summer's day, the crash came. "Brother" O'Leary stooped over the table and laid down the sheaf of notes from which he had been quoting. The easy lounge of his figure and the kindly humour of his eyes were gone as swiftly as the light dies in the turn of the switch on an electric lamp. The luring softness of his Irish tongue vanished so utterly that it was hard to believe it had ever been. With a wide sweep back of his gown, he swung round squarely to face her, and even before he opened his lips.

"Now, Miss Dawson, if you please."

Mary Ann fairly gasped. Somewhere in her "supplements" she had come across the phrase *un mauvais quatre d'heure*, and she had been rather taken by it and had used it herself once or twice tentatively, and with some little doubt as to its exact force, when she wished to impress a friend with her literary culture. She never need doubt its meaning again. The "poor Mary Ann" of the old Welsh song, whatever her woes may have been, was surely never more worthy of compassion than our "poor Mary Ann" when "Brother" O'Leary, as a terrier tosses away a worried rat, flung the mangled remains of her facts and surmises, her spite and vindictiveness to the jury, and with a fine scorn and thundering voice demanded:

"Now, gentlemen, are you prepared to hang a fellow-man on the words of a woman, who, on her own confession, is a shame and a dishonour to her sex?"

Mr. O'Leary had allowed himself to go rather far in his denunciation of Mary Ann, and she was indeed a pitiable object, as on the curt command of the judge to "stand down," she turned to leave the witness stand, and, sobbing in hysterical anger, allowed her ashamed brother to lead her to the refuge of the room reserved for Crown witnesses.

With her departure the interest of the crowd seemed to die away, and many of them stole quietly from the court-house to the street corner outside, where, unawed by the court crier, they could discuss her "laying out" by Mr. O'Leary with complete freedom. The "Cracker Jack" from Winnipeg had more than fulfilled the public expectation.

With a quick turn in popular feeling very characteristic of the west, the guilt or innocence of the prisoner seemed to have dropped into quite a secondary place. The sporting instinct, which has "followed the flag" into every corner of the earth, was aroused, and bets were freely offered and taken as to whether "Cracker Jack" or the Crown Attorney would "win out" in the verdict. The Crown Attorney had the better case, but then the prisoner had the better lawyer. The last desideratum for the full enjoyment of all gambling was supplied by a "dark horse," in the person of the judge himself.

With the examining of two or three witnesses of little importance the court-room rose for the day. The judge retired to his room to disrobe, the jury filed out in charge of the sheriff, and Mr. O'Leary and Mr. Darcy followed their client to his cell, to consult on the course to be followed in his defence on the next morning. They found Ludwig worn and haggard from the conflicting emotions of the day, yet full of a quiet confidence that all would still be well. All the bandying to and fro of his own name and of those he loved best seemed only part of an unreal dream, in which he and they had no personal and living concern. Two things alone mattered after all. He was innocent and Amanda was true! For the rest "let Herr Darcy and the Herr Lawyer from Winnipeg do as they thought fit."

CHAPTER XLII

A brisk breeze from the north-west sprang up during the night, bringing with it a sharp return of frost, and when the sun rose bright and clear the next morning the rough ridges of mud and snow on the streets were frozen hard, and the plank sidewalks were white and slippery with the hoar frost. Within the court-house itself the air was fresh and even chilling though the sun was shining brightly through the eastern windows. The caretaker had been summoned before the judge the preceding morning and received a reprimand for the heated and stuffy condition of the atmosphere, a reprimand couched in such courteous but sarcastic terms that the unfortunate man went forthwith to the opposite extreme and let his fires out completely.

It still wanted half an hour to the opening of the court, and Hubert Darcy and Mr. O'Leary spent it in walking briskly to and fro in the sun on the broad granolithic side-walk along the east of the court-house, where they were sheltered from the sharpness of the breeze. Mr. O'Leary's Irish temperament responded to the change in the weather, and he was far more hopeful than the night before.

"Honestly, Darcy," he said as they walked along, "honestly, I believe your man is innocent, though they've got an uncommonly ugly lot of evidence against him, and it looks pretty bad that we've not got his father and the girl here after putting them down on our list of witnesses. They'll say we are keeping them out of the way. Still, I'll do my best for him with the jury, and the 'old man' (the judge) has a kind heart, if you don't rub him the wrong way."

"You don't think, after all, you'll put young Nielson himself in the box?" asked Darcy.

"No, no," replied Mr. O'Leary decidedly, "I'll win it or lose it without that. You see, on his own confession to us he came to so uncommonly near 'doing the trick' with the knife, that no jury would believe him. I'll trust to the unwillingness of the jury and of the 'old man' to running any risk of hanging the wrong man. I'll give the jury some cases of circumstantial evidence that have gone wrong that will make them shy at a straight verdict of 'wilful murder.' If the worst comes to the worst, Nielson can make a statement after the verdict, and it may be good for a petition afterwards. But don't look so glum about it, Darcy, in court; just look as if you had a straight 'cinch.' It's my rule, and you'll find it works out all right. Just

187

think you are going to win, and keep a stiff upper lip till you see the 'old man' feeling round in his coat-tail pocket for the 'black cap,' and then I guess it's all in; and there goes the 'old man' into court and we'd best be going in too."

The morning proceedings brought little that was new to light. Such hunters as were examined were able to show that they were too far to the north of Jim Hardie's shanty for them to be connected either by accident or design with the tragedy, and the settlers who were called as witnesses had been engaged in their usual work round their own homesteads. When the case for the Crown closed, Mr. O'Leary contented himself with calling Ole and Old Carl Swanson to speak to Ludwig's character and bringing up, and then he asked for an adjournment till the afternoon, when he would be prepared to address the jury for the defence.

Long before two o'clock every seat in the court-house was crowded, and as many as could press in were standing in the aisles between the seats and along the walls at the back. Ole Swanson and his brother had left their seats at the back of the hall and were seated in the chairs nearest to the prisoner's bar—Ole, prompted by a dogged resolution to stand by his own people, while in Old Carl's mind there was a wild idea if Ludwig were found guilty of rushing the gaolers and of rescuing the prisoner, somewhat after the fashion in which in the days of his sailoring he and his shipmates had rescued a brother seaman from the "land sharks" in a foreign port. Next to the two Swansons were Jim Hardie, Bert Enderby, and Tom Dennis. The three last, especially Jim Hardie, had been regarded with some resentment by the "Swedes" generally at the beginning of the trial, but that feeling had entirely disappeared after their evidence was given, and only that morning Ole Swanson had learnt from Mr. Hubert Darcy that it was Jim Hardie who had guaranteed the cost of bringing up Mr. O'Leary from Winnipeg. Far away at the back of the hall, Mary Ann Dawson, closely veiled, sat between her brother and father. Her brother had vainly endeavoured to persuade her to return home the night before, but in spite of her anger and shame she would not give up a forlorn hope that, by some turn in the evidence, she might be reinstated in the public estimation.

There was little need for the court crier's second demand for "silence," after the judge had taken his seat and the jurors had filed into their places, and Ludwig was again placed at the bar. The crowd settled quickly into an absolute and attentive silence, for it felt that the address of the "Cracker Jack" from Winnipeg to the jury would be the *bonne boa b* of the whole trial, and it did not wish to miss a word that fell from his lips.

"Now, Brother O'Leary, if you are ready. Gentlemen of the jury, you will please attend," and the judge sat forward to his desk and placed a pad of foolscap and a pencil ready to his hand.

Very slowly Mr. O'Leary rose to his feet, and with great deliberation arranged his notes in order on the table before him. Very quiet and very solemn were his opening words, yet audible to the last corner of the big hall.

"My lord and gentlemen of the jury, I rise to address you with a deep sense of my responsibility to yourselves and of the duty which I owe to my client, the prisoner at the bar. Gentlemen of the jury, upon you is laid by the oath which you have taken the terrible burden of deciding in the sight of God and by the light of your conscience and by your sober judgment, whether that young man shall be restored to his liberty and to his father's home, or shall leave this world, in which he has scarcely begun his career, by the shameful exodus of a felon's death upon the scaffold."

For a moment the counsel paused, and into the breathless quiet of that pause came the sharp sound of a door hastily opened, and an usher passed quickly to the back of Mr. Darcy's chair and, leaning over, whispered in his ear.

"My lord," and Mr. Darcy was on his feet. "My lord, witnesses of the utmost moment to our client's defence have arrived, and I have to ask that Mr. O'Leary and myself may be allowed to retire and confer for a few moments?"

"Certainly, Mr. Darcy, certainly, if Mr. Attorney has no objection," and the Crown Attorney bowed consent.

"The court is adjourned for half an hour," and the judge stepped from the dais and retired to his private chamber.

Almost before the door closed behind the retiring jury and the prisoner, the court was in an excited uproar. The little group round Jim Hardie and the Swansons alone had the least inkling as to whom these new witnesses might be, and they were afraid to put into words any new-born hope in their hearts, lest it should lead to only a more bitter disappointment. They could guess the names of the witnesses, but none of them could tell what tidings of success or failure they might bring. Through the general body of the crowd the wildest surmises passed from one to another, and no theory was too improbable to find eager supporters. The excitement grew in intensity when, at the end of a quarter of an hour or so, the Crown Attorney was summoned from the court by one of the ushers. Surely the whole case was not going to collapse! That would be too bad, when the "Cracker Jack" from Winnipeg was only just started, and there was no money to be returned at the door if the "show" did not come off!

It still lacked a few minutes of the half-hour when an usher passed through the court to the judge's chamber, and almost immediately afterwards the judge himself re-entered and took his seat as the jury filed into their box, and Ludwig was once more led to the bar.

From mere force of habit the court crier called for silence, though a pin could scarce have fallen to the floor unheard. Every eye was turned eagerly to the door leading to the witness-room. At last it opened, and the Crown Attorney and Mr. O'Leary passed quickly to their seats at the table; next came Mr. Hubert Darcy leading Amanda, and last Christian Nielson and a tall spare figure clad in the long cassock of a Roman priest. With a convulsive start the prisoner struggled to his feet and held out his fettered hands, "Amanda at last!"

"Ludwig, oh, Ludwig, my love, you are saved!" and Amanda fell half-fainting into Hubert Darcy's arms.

In vain for some moments the crier called for silence; the whole crowd was on its feet, and those at the back were standing on the chairs and benches. "Silence!" and the crier was well-nigh bursting a blood-vessel in his effort to quell the uproar. "Silence," and half the crowd itself is repeating the word, and at last some vestige of order was restored.

"Silence!" once more, and the court crier sat down and mopped his face with his handkerchief. Mr. O'Leary was on his feet and the last sound died away.

"My lord," and a tear on his cheek and a quaver in his voice showed that the hardened pleader in the courts was not unmoved by the pathos of the scene. "My Lord, I have to crave your indulgence for the disorder in the court of which I may have been unintentionally the cause. I have, with the full concurrence of my brother, the Crown Attorney, to put in certain sworn statements, which I am prepared, if necessary, to support by the evidence of witnesses now in court. I purpose, if your lordship approves, to preface the evidence of the witnesses and the reading of the depositions, by giving a general outline of their purport, so that the court may more readily follow the very remarkable, I may say, the very startling, and as regards my client, the very happy, conclusion to which they lead."

"The course you suggest. Brother O'Leary, is rather irregular, but if the Crown Attorney fully concurs" (the Crown Attorney rose and bowed); "as the Crown Attorney concurs," the judge proceeded, "I am willing for you to follow that course, and I am sure the jury will give their most careful attention to what you wish to lay before them; but I must insist that there be no manifestation of feeling by those present in the court, otherwise——" and the uncompleted sentence was most expressive and effectual.

There was a wonderful contrast between the Mr. O'Leary who rose to make his statement to the court, and the Mr. O'Leary of half an hour before. Then every word and gesture was full of a solemn deliberation, and the sense of responsibility under which he laboured seemed to communicate itself insensibly to every one in court. Now the advocate was gone and in his place was the sympathetic Irishman, with the Irishman's gift for telling a story of mingled dramatic surprise and feeling.

"Gentlemen of the jury, it's not long that I will be keeping you with my statement, and it is but right that I should at once relieve the young man at the bar from the terrible strain and suspicion under which he has suffered for three weeks in prison, and for the past two days in this court. Gentlemen, I hold here in my hand the full confession of the man who committed the crime; a confession in every way strictly according to Roy—I should say, meeting all the requirements of the law. The crime was committed, not by the prisoner at the bar, but by a person whose name so far has not been mentioned in this court, but who is probably known to many of those who have appeared as witnesses." Mr. O'Leary could not forgo the luxury of holding the crowd in a momentary suspense, "the doer of the deed, gentlemen, was an old Indian called 'Black Hawk.' But you will ask what prompted to such a deed? The motive is not far to seek. The old Indian was a Sioux, an outcast from his tribe, and for some years had pitched his teepee by the Otter Lake. His only human companion was his son, a sickly, half-grown lad. Father and son were well known to the Nielsons, and had often received from them little gifts of food and tobacco and the like; but last fall the younger Nielson came across the Indian lad in the bush as he was ill-using a dog, and he administered to him, it may have been deserved, but very ill-advised, chastisement. The parental instinct, gentlemen, is as strong in an Indian as in a white man, and he has a long memory. Twice, during the absence of the younger Nielson from home, incidents of much suspicion occurred; once a haystack of the Nielsons was burnt, and once during the night fire was set to an out-building. On hearing of these 'accidents' on his return home, the prisoner expressed his intention of calling the Indians to account, and as ill-luck would have it, as he tracked through the bush on the day of the hunting, he ran quite undesignedly into Black Hawk's camp. The interview that followed was not friendly. It confirmed young Nielson in his suspicions, and that hasty temper, of which you have heard, betrayed him into threats of reprisal. All this, gentlemen, was known to Brother Darcy from the first, but the Indians had disappeared and there seemed no conceivable means of connecting them with the crime, and we had nothing to justify us in suggesting suspicions which we were entirely unable to substantiate. But those missing links have been supplied by the unfaltering faith of the brave old man, the elder Nielson, in the innocence of his son, and by the devotion of—if it is permitted to me to say so—the exceedingly beautiful young woman, whose emotion on seeing the man of her choice at the prisoner's bar, has, I am sure, touched a responsive chord in the heart of each one of us."

"Three days after the committal of the younger Nielson for trial, his father and Miss Swanson, impelled by what seemed but a forlorn hope, set out on the long, and at this season of the year the perilous, journey to the Roman mission on the western shores of Lake Manitoba. They arrived there but little more than a week ago, but they found that the hand of Providence had guided them aright. Black Hawk was there on his death-bed.

"The following day he died, but ere he passed to his account he made a full confession of his crime to the priest in charge of the mission, and that confession I hold in my hand. It is a sad story of revenge, nursed to the moment of opportunity and then missing its mark. Till he lay there dying in the hospital of the mission, Black Hawk believed, and, God forgive him, found gratification in believing, that it was Ludwig Nielson whom he shot in the gathering gloom of the storm, after tracking him from his teepee to where the deer lay in the creek bed in the ravine by Hardie's shanty. Gentlemen of the jury, I have done. If ever it should fall to your lot to be again the arbiters of a fellow-man's life or death, beware of trusting to the evidence of circumstance alone, lest the revealing of the truth come too late."

The reading of Black Hawk's confession and the evidence of the Roman priest in charge of the mission occupied but a few minutes, and at its conclusion the Crown Attorney expressed his willingness to withdraw the indictment or to leave the case at once to the jury.

"Gentlemen of the jury, are you prepared to consider your verdict, and do you wish to retire for that purpose?" asked the judge.

There was a hurried whispering among the jury, the foreman stood up. "We are prepared to render our verdict, my lord; we find the prisoner 'not guilty.'"

The court crier was already on his feet and anticipated trouble by shouting "silence," but the crowd, though full of excitement, held itself well, and the judge hastened the concluding formalities as swiftly as might be and adjourned the court for the day. No sooner had he stepped from the dais than there was a scene of wild confusion. The "Swedes" led by Old Carl cheered wildly, and the English led by Tom Dennis broke into their national anthem upon all joyful occasions, of "He's a jolly good fellow," and Jim Hardie, as he kissed Amanda and clasped the hand of Ludwig, for once forgot his usual preface, "It's too bad—too bad."

Under cover of the excitement, Old Dawson and Mary Ann stole away to the livery barn and got their team, and started for home. The next day Old Dawson forwarded to Ottawa his resignation as postmaster. It was time for all "true blues" to assert their principles, when in open court a furriner was acquitted of a crime on the personal evidence of an emissary of the Pope o' Rome.

CHAPTER XLIII

Ludwig and Amanda were married early in July—within three months of his acquittal—long before the time which Ludwig had hoped for in the most optimistic of his dreams in the old days.

When once the spirit of self-confidence has come to a too diffident lover, the rapid growth of that spirit is little short of the marvellous. Even in her most intimate communings with her own heart, Amanda never more had room for wishing for a more ardent or masterful lover. She knew, ah, so well! that for her, life and love and Ludwig were all one, but there was a new timidity, a trembling, happy timidity, when she discovered that Ludwig knew it too. It is hard to defend a citadel with any resolution when the defender's heart has even secretly gone over to the attacker, but when the attacker knows, why, even the appearance of defence is hopeless—and Ludwig knew. Ludwig knew; no longer on the assurance at second-hand from his father, which seemed now too tame and matter-of-fact to satisfy his ardent spirit—Ludwig knew, not only on the steadfast loyalty and courage with which Amanda had dared the dangers of the journey to Lake Manitoba, and the more hateful dangers of slander and misconstructions of the tongues of such as Mary Ann Dawson. Ludwig knew—knew with a knowledge that came, complete, in a flash, deep, wide, and full, and never to be questioned in the years to come, in the cry of joy and love and victory with which she hailed him as her love in the presence of the world, even as he stood a manacled prisoner in the felon's dock.

When they left the court-house on the day of the trial, Amanda would have gladly stolen away to quietness and solitude, but it was not possible so to escape the congratulations of new and old friends alike. Ole Swanson was anxious to start at once for "Sweden," to bear home the good news to his wife; but "Brother" O'Leary insisted that they should all first be his guests at an early supper at his hotel, and Amanda, at least, was so far grateful to him that it enabled her to defer for a little time her interview with Ludwig alone. Her capacity for emotion had been tried to its uttermost for the last few days, and even happiness was almost past the bearing. At last they began their long journey. Christian and Ludwig, with Jim Hardie in his democrat, for they were to stay for the night at Rosebank, and Amanda and her father and Young Carl in Old Carl's waggon. Only once did Ludwig speak to her apart, as he stood on the hub of the wheel and wrapped the robes warmly around her—a whispered word that only Amanda heard:

"Good night, dear love, good night, till Sunday," and Ludwig leapt down from the wheel, and the team started.

Sunday afternoon at Ole Swanson's followed the type of Sunday afternoons at nine out of ten western homesteads, whether English, Canadian, or "foreign," with the same little time-honoured, innocent "make-believes," which enable every one to relax from the hard work of the week without too obvious an admission of pure idleness. The "chores" following the noontide meal have all been done. Amanda and her mother have washed the dishes and pans, and "tidied up" the living-room. The two little girls in their Sunday frocks, with hair splendidly released from the Saturday night "curly rags," and furnished with hymn-book and five cents for the collection, and a parting injunction to be good, have gone off to Sunday-school in the Lutheran Church near by the "Sweden" store.

Ole and August have fed the oxen and the pigs, and August, with a commendable conscientiousness, has gone to return a halter of Cousin Carl's, which he has been fortunate enough to discover in the stable. This should be sufficient to insure for him a long ramble in the bush, with the discovery maybe of an early hawk's nest, to be robbed when he is free from the dangers of climbing in his Sunday clothes, and then supper at Uncle Carl's, and auntie's cake. Amanda cannot help thinking that it is nice of August to be so thoughtful—for Carl!

Ole is a little slow of thought for any new rôle, but this one has the finish of many rehearsals.

"You had better lie down, mother, and have a good rest while the house is quiet."

"Well, I have my dress to change and a letter to write, but perhaps I may just lie down for a minute or two."

"Ay, ay, mother, I'm sure you need it, and I'll have my pipe and a look at the paper, and maybe take a nap myself on the lounge."

"And don't hurry, mother, I'll skim the milk and get supper ready," and Amanda had the grace to blush as she kissed her mother and added, "and if any of the neighbours come, why, I shall be here, or just around the place somewhere, and I'll get tidy right away," and she ran off to her room.

"Just round the place." An hour later on the old swing beneath the big spruce tree in the bluff at the back of the house, on the old swing that used to be so comfortably wide enough for two—and not too wide. "Just round the place," and there is an opening wide enough to command a view of the trail to Otter Lake, if any one should be coming that way, as some one often used to come on a Sunday afternoon. Amanda is not swinging—not to say swinging—though she keeps up a gentle swaying to and fro with an occasional jerk of her dainty foot on the ground, and Amanda is not reading—not to say reading—though there is a book of Anderson's *Fairy Tales* on her lap, and perhaps when she looks every now and then down the opening she may be wondering, just impersonally, whether it was through such a path from the deep shades of the forest that the prince came. "Ah! there is some one coming now," with strong, free step across the opening. It is too late to escape and to seek refuge in the house; perhaps he will go straight up to the door—perhaps he will remember the old swing and the little path through the bluff. Love needs no guide—nearer and nearer fall the footsteps; lower and lower sinks the rosy, blushing face of the "Rose of Sweden," over the blurred and misty page of the book open upon her lap. The prince is here—and seals his conquest with the conqueror's seal upon her lips!

The sun is sinking to his late setting beyond the spruce-clad hills of the Otter Lake, sinking as if regretful that he must leave such a scene of quiet loveliness and peace. He lingers to take a last farewell of the blue waters of the lake, of the springing, waving green of the few acres of corn in the opening, and rests for a parting benediction upon the red shingled roof and the white walls of the little log house—for a parting benediction upon the young man and maiden that stand hand in hand by the wicket-gate of the garden.

Trofast, who has been close by his master's side all day, and has been puzzled to the limit of his dog's wisdom by such a mingling of smiles and tears, wonders still more why they should stand there so long and so silently, and wonders most of all, when Amanda sinks down by his side and clasps him round the neck, and kisses him on the puzzled wrinkle between his grave eyes.

"They say you are only a dog, good Trofast, but you saved my love for me, and may my love and faith be as true as yours." Trofast was rather touched and a little scandalized, and for the sake of his dignity walked slowly to the flagstaff and laid down at its foot, and looked in solemn and absent-minded fashion across the waters of the lake.

Printed by Hazell, Watson & Viney, Ld., London and Aylesbury.